MOONLIT GENESIS

CHRIS ANDREWS

CREATIVE MANUSCRIPT SERVICES

This book has been a long time in coming, and couldn't have been produced without the help of some wonderful people. I would like to thank:

- The members of the Canberra Speculative Fiction Guild's Novel Critique Group
- My amazing beta readers Davida De La Harpe, Val Ackroyd, Megan Crossin, David Lockwood, Brian Kuhnle, Jane Thompson and Elizabeth Close
- My wife and kids, of course

PLEASE LEAVE A REVIEW

Thank you for purchasing Moonlit Genesis.

If you enjoy it, I would consider it a personal favour to me if you left a review wherever you buy good books.

Reviews are the best way to spread the word about stories you like.

Thank you.

CHAPTER 1

The uniformed woman looked at Kyle's passport, then at Kyle, then back down again with a frown. She had half a dozen silver rings on her fingers, the stink of them making him want to sneeze or at least hold his breath. Anything silver did it, and touching silver was worse. It could leave a red welt.

"Anything to declare?" she asked, meeting his eyes with the flat stare of someone who'd had arguments from too many people already today and wanted to be somewhere else. Her severely braided hair matched her expression.

"No," he said, trying not to let her see his discomfort from the scent of silver.

He hated the risks he was taking in coming here, silver being the least of them. His fake identity could cause a lot of trouble if it didn't pass, but at least the passport used his real name, which made lying easier.

Something felt wrong, though. He could smell it as well as he could smell the reek of her silver rings. After several hundred years, he'd developed an instinct for this sort of thing. If she flagged anything it could mean questions and deportation at best, or charges and a lot of trouble he'd struggle to escape otherwise.

He forced himself to return a pleasant smile. She was just a human doing her job. No threat, at least not physically. Just a human with authority. And silver rings. He hoped that meant nothing. Lots of humans wore silver, after all. He wanted to fidget, but held still and kept his pleasant smile in place.

She returned her eyes to his passport, lips pursed.

What was the issue? He'd paid a lot of money for that passport. Maybe the woman had a thing against short people, or at least hadn't seen a lot of men his size. He was a product of his age after all, but still built like the blacksmith he'd been in his first profession. Five foot nothing and about the same across the shoulders, or at least that was the joke.

She looked back at him again and handed over his passport. "Enjoy your holiday, Mister Smithson." As simple as that, the ordeal was over.

He almost breathed a sigh of relief. So much for his instincts. The money he'd spent on the passport was an excellent investment, now he'd proven its worth.

Trying not to look like he wanted to run and put as much distance between himself and Customs as possible, he casually slung his carry-on bag over his shoulder and made his way out of Sydney International Airport. A quick hop to the domestic terminal, one more flight to Canberra, and he'd be finished travelling after a good twenty hours. He needed a shower and a beer, and not necessarily in that order, although the locals may disagree.

Outside the terminal he sniffed the hot Australian air, crinkling his nose at the late afternoon reek of traffic. Despite that, the air was different to American air and other places he'd been to. Every country smelled different, but they were also much the same.

Right now he was in a city of millions, the human scents combining with salt from the ocean, mild pollution, and the distant but sharp smell of eucalypts. It was the heat he noticed most, though. It was winter in the States, but summer here. He broke out in a sweat the moment he left the international terminal.

After an uncomfortable bus ride to the domestic terminal where he sat next to a woman who reeked of curry, he found himself on a short flight to Canberra within two hours. If he'd had a car, he could have driven there in roughly the same time as flying, but flying was far easier, particularly in a foreign country.

As his last flight took off, he rested his head against the seat. The sun was setting and the hot summer evening settling across the country. The jet-powered tin can rose through the clouds to reveal a bright orange moon appearing on the horizon. At the sight of it, his body shuddered with unexpected need. He hadn't reacted so strongly to the moon in decades. He really was tired.

He took a deep, calming breath and reclined his seat, resisting an urge to grip the armrests. Some werewolves could ignore the full moon entirely, most transformed, and then there were those like Kyle. He could control himself most of the time, but occasionally it caught him out, and it was never fun. Tired, stressed and confined, he wanted to tear into someone.

He took another deep breath.

"I take it you don't enjoy flying?" said the man beside him in a well-travelled business suit. He had a big gut and smelled like junk food. The man would be tall and imposing when he stood, but he'd let himself go soft, reducing the impact. There was a spare seat between them which he'd used to dump his headphones, a computer and a magazine. What caught Kyle's attention was the accent. There wasn't an accent quite like the Australian accent. He wasn't sure if he loved it or hated it.

Kyle looked past the big man through the window. The clouds would be luminous when the moon fully transitioned from orange to a silvery yellow. "No. It's the full moon. Us werewolf types get antsy for a few nights each month."

The man grinned and drew a dog-eared paperback from the computer bag at his feet. It seemed to have done more travel than both the man and his suit combined. Although his hand hid the title, the castle, magical mist and battle-scene on the cover suggested an epic fantasy. "You saw my book, didn't you?"

Kyle smiled. He'd meant to put the guy off but had caught his attention instead. Time to change the subject. "You from Canberra?"

"Yeah. Heading home for a few days, then off to Perth. Where are you from? I can't tell if it's the US or England."

"Born in Wales. Lived most of my life in the States." At least the conversation was a pleasant distraction from the bloodthirsty urges his instincts were pushing him toward. When alone or in an open space they didn't bother him much, but cooped up in a tube with nothing but people and aviation fumes to breathe, the desire to lash out was getting to him. "Can you tell me where I can get a cold beer in Canberra?"

The man named several places, and taking pity on Kyle's overwhelmed look, he wrote them down on a notepad, tearing the sheet of paper free. "That one's probably quieter tonight," he said, pointing to the third name. "Irish pub just on the edge of the city, but still pretty close to the centre though."

Kyle took the offered paper. "Thanks. Been a long trip."

It wasn't the trip that was making him sweat, though. It was the moon. Better to head it off now than risk losing control in a contained space. He took a couple of garlic tablets from his coat pocket and threw them back, swallowing them without water. It felt like dowsing his tongue with chilli powder. He stiffened as he tried not to let the pain show on his face while they burned their way down his throat.

They'd take the edge off for an hour or two, long enough to get into the city and suck down a couple of beers. He'd seen garlic burn through the skin of a vampire once, and it didn't do him any favours either. It wasn't normally lethal, but if a vampire bathed in a tub of minced garlic, there wouldn't be much left in the morning.

He needed a beer. Alcohol would help dull the burn spreading like a hot poker through his stomach, though on a short flight like this he wasn't likely to get any.

"You sure you're alright?"

Heart pounding, Kyle blinked perspiration from his eyes. "Yeah. Give the tablets a few minutes to kick in." He didn't think of himself as being part vampire, but more a werewolf tainted by vampire blood. Whatever the truth, he'd never been entirely vampire or werewolf. His tainted genesis was the secret to his immortality and the reason he found garlic obnoxious, but he didn't have many other vampiric traits beyond a desire for a blood Slurpee every full moon.

The full moon seemed to be where the two sides of his nature met and melded.

It took about half an hour for the garlic's effects to settle down, although it still burned through his veins and his stomach was ready to void itself. Still, it was far better than tearing into someone, or everyone. He could breathe normally again by the time they landed, the moon fully up and illuminating the runway and surrounding hills, which were mostly covered in eucalypts.

After the plane taxied to the terminal, the businessman struck up the conversation again while they waited to disembark. "So, why'd you come to Canberra?"

Kyle hesitated, but figured it wouldn't hurt. "To see a friend. A very old friend. We have a lot of history."

Why did Kimbriel want to see him? The question had been burning at him for weeks now. She hadn't said, and he hadn't asked, but maybe he should have. He owed her his life and more, and so he didn't feel that it was his place to question her, but still... It was the first time she'd asked anything of him in three hundred years.

Whatever she needed had to be important, so he'd do it, no questions. As far as he could tell she could have appeared before him at any moment no matter where he was, yet she wanted him in Australia. Her home. Why?

As the crowd began moving off the plane, Kyle stood and opened the overhead locker to get his bag. He'd find out why tomorrow, he guessed.

"Nice meeting you," he said, holding up the slip of paper with the bar names. "Thanks."

Suzannah Ranger, Zannah to everyone, raised an eyebrow at the underage girl. "You're eighteen?" she asked as she tried to hide a smirk. The petite girl, her long dark hair braided artfully, barely looked sixteen despite the heavy makeup. Her skirt wasn't much longer than the width of a belt, either. First time doing this, probably.

Her three friends had gone to a table as far from the bar as possible, no doubt to avoid scrutiny. They didn't look any older than the girl ordering the drinks.

"Uh, yeah. The bouncer let me in, didn't he?"

Zannah glanced at Reg, who stood at the open doors, arms crossed. He caught her look and gave her a 'what' shrug. She narrowed her eyes, but he couldn't help himself and grinned. She had trouble not returning it. *The bastard*, she thought affectionately. Despite his size and tattoos, he was a teddy bear and had saved her hide a couple of times from oversized, angry drunks.

Still, he was risking a huge fine or getting sacked just so he could get some eye candy. *Idiot*. By his expression he knew exactly what he'd done, and he was relying on Zannah to sort it out for him. He was going to be buying her a drink or two if he knew what was good for him.

"ID?" Zannah asked the girl.

With her large gold hoop earrings jangling about, the girl fished through her small black clutch purse and pulled out a license. She flashed it before returning it to her purse. "There. Can I have my drinks now?"

Zannah held out her hand, already knowing where this was going. "Let me see it or you and your friends will have to leave."

The situation would be fun if the fines weren't so serious. Hell, she'd let the girls stay if it was up to her. Better for them to have a few quiet drinks here under Zannah's casual supervision than wherever they might end up next.

The girl rolled her eyes and handed the license over. "See?" She held out her hand immediately, impatient to get the license back.

Zannah held the license up to one of the half-powered down lights. "Says here you're... twenty-seven? Really?" The photo wasn't her, but it could have been her big sister or another close relative.

The girl lifted her chin, her heavy makeup failing to hide a massive zit on her jawline. "Yeah. Of course."

"Well, you see..." She read the name. "Megan. I can get into a lot of trouble for serving someone alcohol before they're eighteen, including a huge fine or being sent to prison for a year. So, unless you have some ID that actually looks like you, you and your underage friends over there need to walk out the door." She handed the license back.

The girl stuffed it in her purse. "How about I call the cops? If you don't get the drinks I ordered, I'll call them and sue you for discrimination. Or... or something."

Zannah pursed her lips at the threat. The girl was just trying to do what Zannah herself had tried many times at the same age, though she'd never threatened the bar staff. How she hadn't got into trouble she'd never know, but suspected it was due to the sympathy of people like herself.

"Wanna use my phone?" Zannah asked. "I have the local police station's number saved as a favourite. I'm sure someone there would be happy to come by and chat with us."

The girl hesitated, meeting Zannah's eyes to see if she was bluffing. It barely took a heartbeat before she realised she wasn't.

"Screw you." She turned and walked to her friends, thumb pointing over her shoulder at Zannah. They got up and left, giving Zannah glares as they went. She felt bad. They just wanted a bit of fun and excitement.

"Hey Zannah?" Tim walked over. "I need you to work a double shift tonight. Dizzy called in sick."

She couldn't hide her disappointment. "No way, Tim. I started before lunch and I'm already into overtime. Besides, I've got an assignment to finish by Monday and about six hours of reading to do. I haven't even started reviewing my course notes and I've got an exam on Friday." God, she hated uni, but it was the only way to get ahead.

His expression softened, but judging by his body language, she guessed she was his last hope. No doubt he'd already called everyone he could. "There's only you, me and Fitzy tonight. Just a few more hours and you can clear out by midnight. I promise."

A group of ten walked in, followed by a smaller group. She

sighed. It was going to be a busy night and tough on Tim and Fitzy if she didn't stay. "Fine, but I'm taking a fifteen minute break and you're paying me double time."

Tim gripped her shoulder as he met her eyes and nodded. "Done. How about you come in tomorrow at lunchtime and I'll give you the back room for study, with lunch and coffee on me? Dinner too if you're still here then."

She wanted to get mad at him, but he was a bloody good boss and he didn't have to be so nice. "Thanks, Tim."

He gave the shoulder a slight squeeze. "You look after me and I'll look after you." He nodded toward the door. "Looks like Mister Shining Armour has arrived. You better go announce the riches I've forced on you." From the tone in his voice it was clear he didn't particularly care for David, her boyfriend, though he'd never said anything to suggest it.

David caught her eye and smiled, raising his eyebrows with a nod toward the door to indicate it was time to leave. She returned the smile but beckoned him toward the bar entry. She took him through and out the service door at the back, and into the heat of the wide alley. The beer garden across the alley was vacant, the owners of the bar having gone bankrupt recently.

Cars were parked beside the buildings, and several massive trees grew down the centre. It was more a service area than an alley, though it was narrow at both ends and wide in the middle. A large, long rectangle.

"What's going on?" David asked, his posture stiff as if he already knew what she was going to say. "I thought you were finished?"

"Yeah, I was supposed to be. Tim's short staffed. Wants me to work back."

He glared at the back entry to the bar. "You need a real job. He's taking advantage of you."

"Hey, he looks after me. Said I could have the back room to study tomorrow. Food and coffee on him."

David shrugged. "You could study at home or the library. He's just sucking up."

It was true, but Tim didn't have to be nice about it. "I said I'd stay. Can you pick me up around eleven-thirty? Maybe twelve? I'm really sorry."

"Geez, Zannah. That late?" He pushed his fringe aside, a habit he hadn't lost since he'd had long hair.

"C'mon David. We need the money to get to Europe next year."

He rolled his eyes. "How about we skip Europe and go backpacking around Australia? Way cheaper."

Not this argument again. She forced annoyance down. "Tight-arse," she said, softening it with a smile as she gave him an overly friendly slap on the arm, letting it turn into a mollifying caress. "I need a break from uni, and the further away the better. I want to relax and see the sights, not crash in hostels full of drunks and drugged-up people speaking languages I wish I knew. Besides, I've seen half of Australia already."

"Going overseas is a huge waste of money. We've got everything we need here."

Her good mood disappeared, and she let her hand drop. "I've got to get back to work. Can you pick me up later or should I get a taxi?"

He grimaced. "It's drinks with Kelly and Sam and the rest. We'll be well into it by eleven."

It was the answer she expected and couldn't really blame him. "Fine. I'll get a cab."

He looked over her shoulder and paled, eyes going wide in fear. "Run!" he said, snatching for her arm, missing, but still turning and sprinting for the alley entrance, leaving her behind.

Zannah, heart suddenly pounding, spun to see what had frightened him and stumbled as someone shoved past her. By the time she turned full circle, a man had caught David and was holding him off the ground by the front of his shirt with one arm. He wasn't quite as tall as David, but definitely stronger. As David opened his mouth to yell, the guy threw him hard. He hit the brick wall, head cracking against it, and crumpled to the ground, unconscious.

"Oh shit," Zannah whispered, backing away. No one was that strong. The attacker turned his attention on her, his expression like a cat watching a mouse. His lips parted in a grin and it scared her more than if he'd pulled a knife.

"Shit, shit, shit," she whispered, her heart hammering. She glanced at David, but he was out cold. Even if she could get to him, she couldn't drag him to safety.

The guy wasn't broad and probably not even as tall as Zannah herself, but he clearly had a lot more muscle than she'd have guessed. He had long mousy-coloured hair pulled back in a ponytail, and a suit jacket over a business shirt without a tie. Classy for a mugger. Any other day she'd say he was just an average guy, but right now he looked like a predator.

She glanced at the bar's service door, but he was closer than she was, and she'd seen how fast he was. She backed another step, hoping she could circle around him and get David out through the alley entrance, assuming David woke by then. There'd be safety in the street at least.

The man's grin broadened as if he could read her thoughts. "How about we play a game, little girl? You run. I chase. If you can get out of the alley, I'll settle for your cowardly boyfriend. You lose and I get you both. Fair?" He had an accent. European. French, perhaps.

Zannah didn't give him a chance to taunt her further. She turned and sprinted for the opposite exit, desperately hoping there was a cop nearby.

CHAPTER 2

Kyle paid the taxi driver with the refreshingly colourful Australian money and got out, slinging his travel bag over his shoulder. "Keep it," he said as the man began looking for change. He forgot tips weren't the norm here. It felt wrong not to throw in a little extra, however.

The Irish bar he'd been directed to was across the street on the corner. There were tables on the sidewalk interspersed among trees standing sentinel against a slight breeze, which entirely failed to drop the temperature enough to matter.

Half a dozen young men and two girls stood at the entrance to the bar as if trying to decide whether to enter, while several tables out the front already had patrons. Music washed out into the street, but not the horrible dance crap that seemed so popular these days. It was still canned studio crap, but had actual instruments that made it closer to real music. Gone were the days of live music in pubs, it seemed. Bloody shame, that.

He waited for the taxi to drive off before crossing the road, careful to check both ways as Australians drove on the wrong side of the road. The last thing he needed was questions about why he'd been used as a speed hump and not killed. He was halfway across the road when a woman screamed from a service alley a little to his left, the sound a quick rush drowned out by the music and laughter. No one else seemed to notice, but it sent a thrill of unexpected fear through him.

He stood there for half a second, surprised, but then ran into the alley, the area barely lit by rear shop lights.

A young woman cried again as she skidded to a stop at the far end of the service alley, a man with a ponytail already there before her. She spun and ran toward Kyle where another man was slumped against a wall, unconscious. The pursuer gave chase, toying with her. She dodged toward one of the huge trees in the middle of the alley, the man moving impossibly fast as he cut her off again.

Kyle swore. Not a man. A Creature, and he was playing cat and mouse with her. She ran around the tree, but the Creature was there already, teasing her like he didn't want the game to finish. Kyle threw his bag against the wall and yelled, hoping to distract her attacker.

The girl, tall and athletic but certainly no match for a Creature, cried out in surprise and ran in Kyle's direction again, hope and fear on her face. Within two steps, she stumbled on a broken piece of road a tree root had lifted and crashed to the ground. Rather than cower, she got to her feet, palms bleeding, and ran again.

"Hey!" Kyle yelled, trying again to distract the Creature, but he ignored him. Kyle wasn't sure what it was, perhaps a vampire, but it could have been an incubus or ghoul or anything equally deadly at night. Vampires were fairly common in cities though, whereas ghouls and incubi tended to avoid notice.

The Creature got to the girl before she'd made three more steps and caught her from behind by the neck.

Kyle couldn't hope to hold his own against a vampire or incubus at any time but the full moon, so he was in luck tonight. If he changed form, he'd have the edge unless the vampire was really old, but he didn't have the time or dare risk the exposure. It'd cripple him for a good ten seconds at least.

"Stop," the Creature said with a warning glare at Kyle. He lifted the girl off the ground with one arm, though he wasn't any taller than her. She struggled, reaching behind to try to grasp his wrist to pull it away. She kicked back, catching the Creature on the leg, but he didn't even flinch. She was definitely a fighter, but dangerously outmatched.

Kyle held a hand out and showed the other to prove he was unarmed and not a threat. "Please put her down."

With one eye on Kyle, the Creature drew a sharp fingernail down the girl's right cheek, drawing blood. She cried out and tried to fight, but it did no good.

Kyle had failed to catch the scent of the blood from her fall, but the smell of the fresh cut hit him like a spray of acid. His adrenaline spiked and the hair thickened on his arms as bloodlust burned away the residual traces of garlic in his body, made worse by the sight of blood sliding down the girl's cheek. Kyle couldn't take his eyes off the blood.

"Please, help," the girl said, still trying to pry the Creature's fingers from her neck.

The Creature smiled as he tasted the blood on his fingernail. "Go get your own, stray."

The words brought Kyle back. He took a slow step forward, hand up and palms still open. "Please, just let her go. I'm not looking to move in on your turf. I'm just passing through."

The girl mouthed the word 'help' again, though she seemed to be losing consciousness. The Creature's fingers must have been cutting the blood in her arteries to her brain.

"Please," Kyle repeated, not sure if the urge to fight was his own or driven by the moon and bloodlust. "I don't want to fight you, but I will if you make me."

The Creature smiled as if Kyle had just made his night. "That sounds like a challenge I can't turn down." With a twist, the Creature broke the girl's neck and dropped her to the ground.

Rage shattered Kyle's composure. He yelled and ran in swinging, his fist connecting. The surprised Creature staggered back, but the return punch to Kyle's jaw knocked him to the ground. The Creature had to be old to hit that hard. A couple of centuries at least. Kyle rolled and knocked aside a kick at his head before coming to his feet and driving a fist into the Creature's ribs, hearing one crack.

The Creature grunted, but his next blow threw Kyle back against one of the trees in the middle of the courtyard area, knocking half the wind from him. Kyle dodged another blow and got in close, slamming his knee into the Creature's cracked rib.

He grunted again, an elbow catching Kyle's ear and knocking him to the ground with the force of a truck.

Staying down for a moment, Kyle swept a leg around. The Creature jumped, yet it gave Kyle time to get to his feet and face off again. The Creature was still favouring his ribs. No Creature healed broken bones in less than hours, giving Kyle a slight advantage.

A frown touched the Creature's face as he realised the same thing. "What are you?" the Creature asked. "A werewolf in human form couldn't match me, even on a full moon, yet all I can smell is dog."

"And I can see a vampire," Kyle said, hoping for a reaction to give him a hint of what he faced. He hadn't been able to catch the Creature's scent amid the reek of the alley, probably due to the garlic he'd eaten earlier. It dulled all his senses, not just his desire to kill.

Breathing hard, Kyle looked the Creature over. Even injured he wasn't sure he could drive him off, and every second they delayed the Creature recovered a little more.

"Smart doggy."

So he was a vampire then. Shit. Kyle might be harder to kill than most Creatures, but there weren't many he could take on in a fair fight, at least not in human form. "Come a little closer and say that," Kyle taunted, hoping to anger and distract the vampire. Anything to gain an advantage.

He clenched his fists, fighting the urge to transform. If he did, he'd be much stronger, but transforming brought its own problems, the main one being his inability to shift back until dawn. He'd lose his clothes and bag too, and the identification and money in the pockets.

The vampire smiled, clearly intrigued by Kyle. "Another night, pup. You can keep the dead girl. A gift."

Kyle risked a glance at the girl. Her body struggled with short, sharp gasps that were probably nothing more than an unconscious reaction and her body's efforts to stay alive. Even if her neck hadn't completely broken, she'd still be dead in minutes without medical help.

"Some advice, dog. Get out of town before my mistress discovers you. Ferals aren't tolerated in Canberra."

Ferals? What the heck was going on in this city? Werewolves often worked for vampires, but they were rarely troubled if they didn't cause problems. A coerced werewolf didn't make a good ally, and it was usually more trouble than it was worth to root out a pack. Canberra was a small city though, at least compared to most.

Still holding his ribs, the vampire backed away and then ran for the far exit of the service alley. Kyle struggled with the scent of the girl's blood. He swallowed a need to give into bloodlust and rip her apart.

The best he could hope to do for her now was to put her out of any pain she was in. Never one to leave an animal or human to suffer, he gritted his teeth and approached, trying not to breathe in the scent of her rich blood.

He wasn't entirely sure if other werewolves had the same reaction to blood, though they all seemed to like a good fight or chase and could smell blood for miles if it was upwind.

When he knelt beside the girl, he nearly swooned at the richness of her warm blood. He felt like a starving child walking into a restaurant, the scent of foods and spices thick in the air. The only problem was, his needs were for human flesh and blood.

"I don't want it," he told himself. He could do perfectly well on normal human food. He'd even gone vegan for a couple of decades to see if he could. No problem, although it had been harder to resist human blood and flesh on the full moon.

The young woman's mouth opened and closed slightly, almost as if hiccupping, her body still fighting to survive despite the odds.

"I'm so sorry," he said. "I tried." She didn't seem to be aware of his presence or even hear him. It was a pity, she was beautiful. Polynesian heritage most likely, watered down a little, but still there in her bone structure and skin tone. And her scent.

The artery in her neck pulsed with blood, keeping her alive for a little longer. Gently, he reached for her face, placing his hand over her mouth and pinching her nose closed.

"Shh," he whispered. "I'm so sorry, but it'll be over soon."

"Hey!" someone yelled from across the service alley.

Kyle snarled instinctively, claws extending at the sound of shoes pounding toward him.

Instinct merged with bloodlust and for a heartbeat he lost his senses. He bit the girl to claim her as his own, his distending canines punching through her white shirt and into her flesh where her shoulder joined the neck. He nearly howled in ecstasy at the taste. He hadn't tasted human blood or flesh in more than a century, and the last time it had been in self-defence.

"Hey! What are you doing?"

He barely got control of himself as the man ran at him. Although his instincts told him to attack and defend his prize, he found enough clarity to stand and sprint out the same exit the vampire had taken. Across the road he saw a tree-lined car park. Shops to his left and right. He went left, as there were more buildings that way.

It took nearly a minute of sprinting before the consequences sunk in. If the girl survived... He skidded to a stop when no one pursued him. A sickly feeling came over him. He had to go back and kill her. He needed his bag, too. He'd left it in the alley, and it could be used to identify him.

"Shit." Not even one day on the ground, and he was already in more trouble than he'd managed in a century.

CHAPTER 3

Darkness from the heavy clouds now hiding the full moon hid Kyle as he hunkered down on the dusty red tiled roof a couple of stories above the service courtyard. He was opposite the rear entrance to the bar, obscured by the trees as much as the darkness.

People rarely looked up anyway, and although city light illuminated the underside of the clouds above, it didn't reflect back enough light to reveal him. There weren't any tall buildings around either, so he was safe from anyone looking down from an apartment.

Below, the alley ends were blocked by police cars, with officers directing curious pedestrians away. Several bar patrons stood around with drinks in hand, trying to get a glimpse. An ambulance was parked close to the girl he'd bitten, the paramedics still working to save her life.

The longer they worked, the higher his anxiety rose.

"Stupid, stupid, stupid," he cursed under his breath, his anxiety heightened thanks to the moon which had already put him on edge. That edge was probably why he'd been stupid enough to try and save her. He sighed. No. He'd have done that anyway. No blame necessary.

It left a problem, though. He had to kill her, and hated the thought. Even so, he was surprised the girl had survived this long. His bite must be keeping her alive, the tainted lycanthropy that had kept him young for centuries now coursing through her blood and keeping her on the edge of life. With the medical attention she was receiving, the chances she'd die of natural causes grew slimmer each moment.

He closed his eyes, trying not to think about what he had to do, and the risks. He might be better off jumping down there now and killing her in front of witnesses than risk confronting her after she'd healed. She might have been an innocent girl who didn't deserve this, but he couldn't let her live. She might infect others.

At least he'd had time to get his bag before the humans swarmed the place. Everything he needed was in his bag, though his passport was the main concern. He had enough money in his pockets for a couple of night's accommodation, but that was about it. He liked to travel light. His bag held a couple of changes of clothes, toiletries, spare money, and little else.

At least with his passport back in his possession, he didn't have to worry about being identified or keeping a low profile for the next decade or two.

The girl was the problem now, assuming she survived the broken neck. His gut instincts told him she would. Even without his promise to Kimbriel he couldn't risk her survival. She could infect others until the whole world was full of immortal werewolves. It would become a stagnant world, the magical Creatures dying off due to the lack of lifeforce that humans provided, and no humans left either.

The dusty clay tiles he crouched on were fairly old considering the city was so young, probably one of the first buildings built when Canberra had been established. Rather than being upgraded with metal sheets or a flat rooftop to house air conditioners, the roof had retained its old-fashioned appearance. It looked and felt at least a century old and was probably heritage listed.

He'd seen the name while climbing up here. The Melbourne Building, named after another State's capital city. Across the wide road behind him was the Sydney Building, nearly identical, though closer to the city centre. Compared to modern buildings they were elegant, with white pillars and arches fronting a covered walkway and shopfronts.

The night air was a little gusty on the roof, but Canberra smelled much cleaner than Sydney, more like a country town than a big city. He held still as someone glanced his way, although the trees in the service alley obscured the roof where he sat. Still, it was unlikely he'd be seen even if the clouds cleared and flooded the city with moonlight.

"Moron," he muttered to himself as guilt bordering on terror filled his stomach. He was growing more and more certain he'd created another Creature like himself, something he'd promised never to do. He was a species unto himself, and now he had unleashed an immortal werewolf on the world, a werewolf that was far more infectious and powerful than any other werewolf. Deadlier, too. Like him.

Unlike normal Creatures, he wasn't bound by his promise, and now the consequences of that lack of accountability lay on the hard ground below him. He should have snapped the girl's neck instead of trying to smother her.

The two paramedics finished bracing the girl's neck and upper body before lifting her onto a gurney. A police officer seconded into medical duties helped by using a hand pump to force oxygen into her lungs. The medics carefully manoeuvred her into the ambulance where he lost sight of her, which only increased his anxiety.

One of the paramedics jumped in the back and took the hand pump from the cop as the other shut the doors and walked around the vehicle to climb in behind the wheel. The wrong side, of course. He didn't think he'd ever get used to that.

A young man with mousy-coloured hair climbed into the front with the driver, a regular human by the way he moved and held an ice pack to the back of his head. Kyle quickly recognised him as the guy who'd been unconscious when he'd entered the alley. The girl's boyfriend, perhaps. That would explain why he'd been silenced first. Predator strategy. Take out the stronger prey while you had the element of surprise, or otherwise separate the weak from the strong.

She'd put up more of a fight than most people would, at least, though she'd been no match for a vampire.

Kyle could smell the young man's blood from here, carried upward on the swirling breeze caught in the service alley, but it was the girl's he'd tasted, and it tasted good. He could survive well enough on human food, but when the full moon rose the hunger came on, and it was best to be alone then. That had never gone away. He took a long breath and released it slowly. It didn't help.

Perhaps it was time to dose himself with more garlic. He should have crushed a couple of garlic tablets and thrown the dust into the vampire's eyes. That would have changed the fight's outcome.

Predatory instincts still rising, Kyle hungrily watched the ambulance being let through the police barrier, and had to fight the urge to follow. It wouldn't be hard to find it, though. Canberra couldn't have too many hospitals.

He took another deep breath and covered his face with his calloused hands, regret fighting off the hunger, at least a little. He should have gone to see Kimbriel as soon as he'd arrived instead of looking for a beer. If he had, he wouldn't have to face killing the girl now. She'd already be dead and he'd never have known. He couldn't remember the last time he'd been in a worse mess.

Tiles shifted behind him. He stiffened at the sound, but tried not to give himself away. It had to be the vampire he'd fought earlier. He stood and spun on an adrenaline spike... and nearly fell from the roof in shock.

"No. Not possible," he whispered in disbelief as he beheld Taenorah's Welsh features and long dark hair. But his wife was gone - centuries dead.

The woman smiled, and it was a smile he only saw in his dreams now. "Hello, lover."

Lover? "No," he whispered.

"Yes," she replied.

"Taenorah?" he said louder. "You... you're..." He'd buried her himself. She was more beautiful than he remembered, her skin a little paler, lips red and inviting. Her eyes, oh God, her dark, beautiful eyes. Dark and wide set, transfixed on him the way he remembered her watching when he'd been pounding hot metal in the smithy.

It couldn't be her, yet this woman was Taenorah's height and build, and she had the same brown eyes and high cheekbones. Her long hair was free of any kind of binding, just the way Taenorah had preferred it in private. The woman before him was the same age Taenorah had been when she'd been murdered, too. It was the softness in her eyes as she watched him that made him sure, the knowing way Taenorah had.

"Did you really think I was dead?" she asked, a hint of surprise touching her expression as if she'd always believed he'd left her.

If she really was his wife, she must have been turned before he'd buried her. There'd been nothing to indicate it, just a bloody corpse with her throat torn out. He knew enough about vampires to know how they reproduced, and that didn't fit. They have to drain a person until they're almost dead and force them to drink the vampire's blood before killing them properly. The full process took days. Bleeding the victim out would undo everything though, and she'd certainly bled.

"You couldn't have been turned."

"He changed his mind after turning me. He never told me why. I must have had just enough blood left in me to finish the process. It took weeks though, not days, and when I woke I..." she shook her head.

This... Creature before him wore black clothes to match her hair, tight-fitting dark jeans, calf-high boots and a singlet top. He remembered Taenorah in plain peasant dresses, all a country blacksmith could afford, though he could afford more than most. The last time he'd seen her, the front of her prettiest dress had been bloody, her throat shredded. It was a stark contrast.

He turned from the memory, though he was too old and experienced to turn his back on a vampire, even his wife. Despite the soft look in her eyes, her casual but ready stance radiated danger, evident in the predatory way she watched him now, unafraid, yet interested in a very unsettling way.

In a world of Creatures that tolerated different species only in passing, she'd obviously survived on her wits and cunning. He'd known other Creatures like her, Creatures who'd watched him the way she did now, and they were all dangerous despite the welcome in their eyes.

She smiled. "I thought you were dead too. You can't imagine my surprise when I saw you take on Rake."

Rake? The vampire in the service alley. "I think I can, actually."

She sniffed the air, trying to catch his scent. "What are you? You smell like a dog, but dogs are mortal."

The insult hurt him far more than he'd have thought it might. He'd been called a dog by plenty of Creatures, yet the casual disdain in her voice stung. It was the lack of anything resembling respect, suggested she wasn't likely to want to rekindle their centuries-lost relationship. Her eyes were turning predatory as she assessed him, her instincts no doubt telling her he was now a threat.

"Tae?" he asked as gently as he could. He knew that look, but it was what came next that concerned him.

That hardness deepened, friendliness leaving her expression. "You shouldn't have come here, Kyle. You need to leave Canberra. Understand? Never return. You won't get another warning."

Her Australian accent didn't match the Welsh one in his memory, but then his own had evolved too. He didn't recognise the gleam in her eyes either. It was a look he'd only ever seen on the faces of Creatures used to manipulation and lies and getting their own way. They took what they wanted and never looked back with regret.

"It was Vincent, wasn't it?" he asked, hoping for a reaction to confirm his suspicions. Vincent Morrell, the vampire who'd tried to kill Kyle as well. Nearly succeeded. Should have succeeded. "Did he turn you himself, or force one of his lackeys to do it?"

She smiled as if staring into fond memories. "It was Vincent." She touched her throat, a finger moving back and forth to indicate the damage that had once been there. There was no sign of it now. She glanced around, a hand indicating the city. "This is my turf now, Kyle. You should go for your own safety." She met his eyes once more, a hint of that softness returning. "There's trouble brewing and believe it or not, I still care about you. You don't want to get caught in it."

She'd been stunningly beautiful, and more so now. A prize on Vincent's arm to show off, although Taenorah had always been her own woman, even as his wife.

"Turned. Sired. Whatever. I could sense him, so no doubt he could sense me, yet waited for me to dig my way out of that hole you buried me in. He could have opened the grave at any time or had one of his dogs do it, but he left me there for weeks. You didn't have to make it so deep." She sounded as if she carried a grudge against Kyle, not Vincent Morrell.

"I..."

"What are you, Kyle? Dogs aren't immortal." She seemed genuinely curious now.

"Tae," he whispered. "I'm so sorry for what happened to you. I'd have come looking for you if I'd known."

She glanced toward the service alley, then back to him. "I almost came to help you while you were fighting Rake, but he backed off. You must have hurt him pretty bad, which isn't easy to do. Where have you been these last few centuries?"

The whole attack didn't make sense. "Why did he hurt the girl? Vampires don't need to kill to survive."

She pursed her lips to reveal a trace of her old self, but the rest of her expression wasn't anything he recognised as she considered the question. Gone was the caring, devoted wife he'd known, the woman who'd wanted children so badly but miscarried three times, devastating her.

"You've landed in the middle of a... consider it a play for dominance. Two vampire clans and their dogs in an uneasy treaty. North and south. The city centre is supposed to be neutral territory, but Rake likes to stir things up. He probably thought he'd blame the girl's death on Vincent's mob. My people."

The news hit him hard. "You *still* serve Vincent? Even now? I thought you'd have broken his hold after all these centuries. You said this was your turf."

She shrugged. "Give me a few more decades and I might be strong enough to break his hold, but I started out weak and for now I'm his, and his alone. You'd do well to accept that and leave town, Kyle. I'll look you up in a century or two."

"But-"

She met his eyes, and there was a hardness there he wished he could erase with gentle fingertips. "Clear out, Kyle. This city's trouble, and it's going to get a lot worse before it settles."

"Taenorah-"

She spun, ran, and leapt over the ridge of the roof. A moment later he heard her jump to the ground beyond it. Tempted to follow, his legs gave way and he collapsed to the dusty tiles instead. Taenorah was alive? And a vampire? His world wasn't likely to settle for years.

It was several hours before he realised most of the police cars had gone. A couple of cops continued investigating the scene with the entrances to the alley still blocked off. His legs growing stiff, Kyle stood, wondering what to do now. Getting to the hospital and dealing with the girl was his first priority, though she'd be difficult to get to tonight. He'd make some inquiries to see where she'd gone and sort it out tomorrow.

Taenorah and the questions she'd raised would have to wait too. If it wasn't for the girl, he'd go straight to Kimbriel's place and then clear out of town, preferably on a flight back to the States.

A police officer chanced to look up and see him. "Hey! You up there!"

Kyle swore. He grabbed his bag and followed Taenorah over the far side of the roof, scaring the crap out of a couple of young party goers as he dropped several stories and landed just a few feet from them. The guy gave a cry of fright, but shoved his girlfriend behind him, regardless.

"Smile!" Kyle said brightly. "You've just been pranked. Someone will be by shortly to get your details so we can show the footage on our new reality show called Shit Stirring. Have a nice day."

CHAPTER 4

Kyle dumped his bag inside the door of the cheap motel he'd found near the city centre. Looking around, he realised it was cheap for a reason. It wasn't nasty, but it was tired. The furnishings and carpet needed replacing, and it smelled old and musty. It had a double bed with clean sheets, but the floral curtains didn't look like they would close properly, and the window was sealed closed. The room had a strong overlay of body odour and stale alcohol.

At least he didn't have to share common facilities. He opened the bathroom door and found the cream tiles and old toilet could use a makeover, but despite a faint moldy smell common to most bathrooms, it seemed clean. It was all he needed.

He ran the water, stripped off and stepped into the shower. Heaven.

As the hot water washed over him, he put his forehead against the tiles. Taenorah was alive. The thought wouldn't leave his head despite his other pressing concern.

Their conversation played over and over as water pounded over his head and back. What else didn't he know? Or did he know? Vincent Morrell was still her master, his hold still strong. He knew that much. Vincent must be old then. Very old to still be able to keep control of a vampire hundreds of years old herself.

Kyle didn't want to think about what Vincent might have done to Taenorah over the centuries. What he'd made her do. She was a different person now to the one he'd known. Colder. Harder. Perhaps more cunning. Although it was obvious she still cared about him, she didn't seem to want to rekindle their relationship or even let him get involved.

He blinked water from his eyes. One problem at a time. The girl. If he could, he'd kill her tonight and never think about it again. He could do it. He really could, he told himself.

If she died under suspicious circumstances the hospital would have security camera footage of him entering her room and moving through the corridors. Creatures might be a problem, too. He'd have to be careful and avoid the cameras. Garlic should mask his scent and keep the vampires away, though it may not fool werewolves.

Regardless, he needed to do it tomorrow, and he needed to make it look like she died naturally. No bruises or other marks.

He softly bumped his forehead against the tiles, thinking through his options. She'd be closely watched now, most likely undergoing scans to determine the extent of her injuries. Perhaps he'd be better off finding something lethal to inject her with. After that, he needed to forget all about Taenorah and leave town.

He reluctantly turned the water off and dried himself with the threadbare towel, dressing in his regular clothes so he could leave quickly if he had to. At least he had a plan. Tonight he'd visit the hospital to get a feel for the place and find out where the girl was. Tomorrow he'd... fix his mistake.

He made a coffee, cupping it in both hands as he leaned against the wall of the kitchenette, his head circling back to the conversation on the roof and trying to come to terms with the fact his wife was alive. Her life was certainly far more complicated than his own.

He could almost see how Vincent Morrell must have found her after he'd left Kyle to suffer and die. No doubt he'd prowled through their house and found the young widowed wife, an innocent victim for him to hurt and resurrect and spend centuries corrupting and twisting. The malignant bastard.

Taenorah, at least, was still herself, or part of her was.

Kyle backed away from the three hostile men, picking up a hammer as he moved. They noticed. One greying man was bleeding profusely from a head wound and seemed to be having trouble staying upright. Another cradled his left forearm close to his body, the hand limp. A massive bruise was forming just above his wrist, while his right cheek was swollen.

Kyle hadn't touched them, but they seemed to be blaming Kyle for whatever had happened.

Kyle edged away from the tallest of the three, a big red-headed fellow with just as much muscle as Kyle, but a good four inches taller. Tavoner, by name, and a giant of a man in comparison to Kyle. In a fair fight, Kyle was sure he'd lose.

"There was nothing wrong with the blade I made for you," Kyle said, hefting his hammer defensively. "I stand by my work."

Tavoner moved closer, but not close enough to take a blow. He was almost snarling in anger. "It didn't work!" He slammed his fist down on a workbench, making some of Kyle's tools jump.

Kyle backed another step. "Did it break? If you're questioning my workmanship, show me the blade. If the fault's mine, I'll re-forge it. Gladly."

Tavoner jumped forward and punched Kyle without any provocation, catching him across the jaw. As Kyle staggered, Tavoner caught and twisted the hammer from Kyle's hand, gripping Kyle's leather apron in his other huge fist.

He leaned in close, his breath strong with onion and meat. "The blade didn't kill him." Tavoner head-butted Kyle, catching the bridge of his nose.

"Ahh!" Kyle cried, stumbling back and falling to the stone floor. He put his hands over his face, far too late to protect himself. He was sure his nose was broken.

"Get up, Smithson!"

Kyle's eyes were watering so badly he couldn't blink his sight clear. He was still too shocked to feel angry. His head felt like it had been kicked by a horse.

A heavy boot slammed into his thigh. "I said, get up. We're all dead men because of you!"

Kyle pulled himself up by the workbench, desperate not to take another kick or punch. "I've got no idea what you mean! I can't fix anything if I don't know what that problem is."

"The stamp you put on the blade. You did it wrong." Tavoner's voice was quiet now, but it only made it more ominous. The huge man swung again, but Kyle staggered back, the blow missing by an inch.

"Stop it! Talk to me," Kyle said, palms facing outward even as his nose bled freely. "What does a stamp have to do with the quality of a blade?" He was beginning to fear for his life now.

Tavoner swung again, a glancing blow to Kyle's cheekbone that made him stagger another step. Kyle dodged the next swing and drove his right fist into the man's stomach with a whoosh of air.

As the man doubled, Kyle slammed his left fist into Tavoner's jaw, breaking teeth.

Kyle grunted with delayed pain, holding his fist up. Bone protruded from a gash on his knuckle, one of Tavoner's teeth lodged there. More than a little sickened by the sight, Kyle clenched his jaw in pain and pulled it free, blood welling from the wound. It wouldn't be the first tooth he'd knocked loose, though he tried not to get into fights. Some men seemed to want to try their luck against him because he was a smith, his chest and shoulders huge from his profession. A matter of pride, perhaps, or ego.

"Enough!" someone yelled from the doorway.

Kyle glanced up, though he was reluctant to take his eyes off Tavoner. A nobleman stood there, dark hair slicked back and a heavy fur coat over his shoulders, his breath steaming from the cold outside air. Barely as tall as Kyle, his presence nevertheless commanded respect. The two men with Tavoner instantly backed off, and even

Tavoner looked fearful as he climbed to his feet, blood dribbling over his chin.

The nobleman held up the blade Kyle had made and strode into the smithy. Half a dozen well-armed men followed, though none wore armour.

"So this is the smith you recruited for your insurrection, Tavoner?"

"Recruited?" Kyle asked. "They commissioned a blade, nothing more."

The man glanced his way dismissively, then returned his attention to Tavoner.

Tavoner wiped his chin with the back of his left hand, giving Kyle a filthy look. "Bastard wasn't worth the coin we gave him."

Despite the insult to his work, Kyle held his hands up, offering no resistance. "I'm not part of anything. They paid for that blade. I made it. Nothing more."

The nobleman strode over to Kyle's forge and threw the blade onto the cooling coals. The leather-bound hilt immediately caught alight.

He gestured to the three men who'd confronted Kyle. "You betrayed me."

"Master," the man with the broken arm began, but a single glance from the nobleman cut him off. The man dropped his eyes as if he'd been slapped.

"I expect loyalty from my dogs. Loyalty and obedience. If you can't give me that, I have no use for you."

The man with the cut to his forehead dropped to his knees. "I'm sorry, Master. I should never have listened to-"

"Quiet," the nobleman said softly. Clearly struggling to control his anger, he held out a hand, fingers spread. He rested it on the man's head. "I took you in and gave you a home, Will. I've protected your wife and children since you came to me, haven't I? How do you thank me?"

"Please-"

"Quiet!" He took a deep breath and released it slowly. "If you can get to your home before Greenus does, I'll let you and your family live. Get there too late and your wife and children will already be dead, and Greenus will kill you, too."

The kneeling man glanced at one of the noble's guards, fresh fear on his face.

"Start running, Will."

Will clambered to his feet and sprinted from the smithy. "Give him a count of a hundred." At a nod from the nobleman, Greenus, a smallish man with dark hair strode out after Will. Even with the broken arm Kyle doubted it'd be a fair fight, but Greenus didn't seem concerned.

Kyle shifted his weight, hoping he might be able to slip to the rear door unnoticed, but the nobleman caught the movement.

"This isn't my fight," Kyle said. He wasn't the kind of man to pick one, anyway.

The glare the noble rested on Kyle said enough. Fearing for his life and Taenorah's, Kyle spun and ran for the rear door, but another man tackled him to the ground before he got half way. He struggled, but more men joined in until three of them kept him pinned, one forcing Kyle's face hard against the stone floor, making his nose throb even worse.

"Lord Morrell," Tavoner began. "I-"

Someone drew a sword, the sound alone enough to silence Tavoner. Despite his strength, Kyle struggled to get any leverage.

"Kill these two," Lord Vincent Morrell said. "They're the ringleaders."

Chaos erupted as the two men tried to fight back, but blades cut them down in moments.

"Use silver. Remove their heads if you have to and bury the bodies in a field."

Close to panic, Kyle struggled again, but couldn't break the hold.

"And you, blacksmith. What did they promise you? Gold? Unlikely. They have little. No. They promised to make you into one of them, didn't they? And you couldn't resist the temptation."

One of what? "They offered a fortnight's wages for a blade with a design stamped on it. That's all I know. They haven't even paid all their debt yet. Barely half."

"Make him stand."

The men forced Kyle upright, pinning his arms painfully behind his back. Despite his strength, Kyle couldn't get his hands free. "I had nothing to do with this," Kyle said again, trying to free himself again. "I'm just a blacksmith. I've no idea what this is about."

"I was told otherwise by someone I trust far more than you." The man took a small wooden bowl from Kyle's workbench and emptied it of horseshoe tacks. "You wanted to be one of us. I'll make you one of us."

What he did next shocked Kyle. He drew a small blade across his wrist and let his blood dribble into the bowl.

"What are you doing?" Doing something like that wasn't right. There was something wrong in the man's head.

When done, the noble wrapped the wound in an old rag. He then drew a small bulging leather pouch from an inside pocket. "Garlic powder," he said. "Rarely fatal to my kind, but very nasty, nevertheless. Inhaling it can put you down for hours, and I certainly wouldn't recommend swallowing the raw stuff."

With gloved hands he sprinkled some of the powder into the bowl, leaning back as he did so and holding his breath. The blood thickened and went black, bubbling for several seconds before settling down. He stirred it with a nail from the bench.

"Force his mouth open."

One of the other men grabbed Kyle's jaw and drove fingers like iron into his cheeks. Kyle cried out and struggled, but couldn't help but open his mouth.

"You wanted to be a Creature? Then I'll give you what you want." Vincent approached with the bowl and poured the foul-smelling blood into his mouth. It burned like a hot coal had been dropped in. Kyle cried and tried to spit it out, but Morrell clamped a hand over Kyle's mouth and pinched his nose, cutting off his breath.

Kyle struggled and writhed, but was forced to swallow it, the thick liquid scorching his throat. It tasted like iron and burned like a hot poker.

They released him as convulsions took him and he fell to the ground. Every breath seared his lungs and his stomach seemed to contract in on itself, first going cold and then painfully hot. It felt like he'd been stabbed, or what he guessed being stabbed felt like.

He reached out for something to help. Anything. "Water," he whispered, his voice strained with pain. He got a kick in the guts. He doubled up, pain spreading through his veins like molten steel. "Help. Please," he gasped. "What did you poison me with?"

"When his heart stops beating, cut it out and burn it. Bury the body with the others," Vincent said.

Kyle lay gasping in agony, desperate not to cry out in case he drew Taenorah's attention and she came to the forge to investigate. The men left him writhing on the stone floor where he struggled to breathe through the longest night he'd ever endured. As dawn approached, he managed to uncurl, though his cramped muscles fought him. By noon he could stand again, his fears for Taenorah growing with every second. She should have found him hours ago. Dawn at the latest.

He felt a little stronger now the sun was at its zenith, almost as if the sun had weakened whatever poison coursed through him. Wheezing and still in agony, he supported himself on a workbench.

"Taenorah," he whispered, the word like blades tearing through his throat. He feared the reason she hadn't come for him.

He managed to stagger from the smithy to the house. The fire was out, the kitchen quiet. "Tae?" He barely breathed the word as he looked around in dread. He found her bloody body on their bed, her throat ripped out as if an animal had clawed it open, a blade through her chest and her dead eyes staring at the roof. Their bed was covered in her blood. He dropped to his knees beside her, sobbing over her lifeless body without caring that her blood was everywhere.

Despite his agony, he managed to bury her before the afternoon's warmth left the ground, but it took everything he had. He collapsed to his knees beside her grave, leaning on his spade. Even that didn't keep him upright for long, and he collapsed across the soft dirt. He lay there until nightfall, knees drawn to his chest in pain, his body growing numb as the sun began to set. As the full moon rose above him, he noticed a man he didn't know standing a dozen yards away, watching, but doing nothing to assist.

"Help me," Kyle whispered. "Please."

The man, a big guy with a dark beard and peasant clothes, merely watched. A knife at his side remained sheathed.

As the night wore on, Kyle felt his heart thumping harder and harder, as if his blood were thickening and going black like the blood in the bowl. Its beat grew slower and slower as it strained to keep him alive.

Breathing grew ever harder, his body wheezing and suffocating. It got worse until all he could do was gasp, and even that wasn't enough. Body sweating and aching, his veins burning like ice, he felt something deep inside himself give way and pass from existence. He took a final shallow breath, held the precious air for as long as he could in the certainty he'd never get another, and breathed out one last time. "Taen," he whispered, her name passing his lips like a prayer, though he didn't know if it was a prayer for him or her. He felt his heart thud one last time, but even then he didn't die.

Like a corpse he was unable to move or even blink, and stared at his watcher's feet. He was dead, he was sure of it, but his body refused to acknowledge the fact.

The man finally kicked him onto his back, unsheathed his blade and punched it into Kyle's chest.

All he felt was relief as the man forced his hand in and ripped Kyle's heart out.

CHAPTER 5

"THIS IS A GOOD SIGN, Ms. Ranger. I'm surprised you're even conscious."

Zannah tried to focus on the doctor through a haze of drugs and pain. It took her long seconds to work out what he'd said. He was surprised at something?

"Do you understand me, Ms. Ranger? You nearly died, although things are looking surprisingly... better than expected."

She'd nearly died? She had a vague memory of doctors talking, but he was the only doctor here. He'd obviously been trying to explain this for longer than her concentration was good for. Days, perhaps. Years, maybe. Whatever happened must have been bad.

Talking was beyond her. Her neck was painful. Swallowing was... impossible. Growing dizzy with the effort of concentration, she briefly closed her eyes and felt herself drifting off.

"Your neck is badly swollen and bruised. There's a lot of damage. Under normal circumstances we'd have you on a respirator, but you're breathing unassisted. It's... surprising, but a good thing."

Neck? She remembered him saying the same thing to her mother while they thought she was asleep, and again to her brother when they'd discovered she was awake. He was trying to tell her again, as if she didn't understand she'd been hurt.

She didn't remember what had happened. Her head was too foggy to think it through. She remembered being at work and booting out some underage girls, but that's it.

"The antibiotics are working, it seems," the doctor continued. "No infection from the bite."

Bite? She'd been attacked by a dog? She liked dogs. No dog had ever bitten her before. Had she fallen and hit her head too? That would make sense.

As if teleporting in, her mother leaned over her from the other side of the bed. "Honey?"

Relief that her mother was there almost made her cry. Had she been here the whole time? Zannah tried to speak but couldn't. It was hard to focus. They must have given her strong painkillers.

"Blink if you understand me," her mother said.

Zannah blinked after a few seconds, though it took time to put the words together.

Relief crossed her mother's face. "Do you remember the service alley? Blink once for yes. Twice for no."

She blinked twice. Why couldn't she move? Was it the drugs? No, her neck was... Emotions swept her down a desperate and fearful path, dragging her into the memories of the dark service alley behind her work. She'd been scared, really scared, only she couldn't remember what she'd been scared of. The dog attacking her, perhaps. She felt tears forming and couldn't wipe them away. That only made everything worse. She couldn't feel anything but dizziness and pain and the haze of drugs.

Something dabbed the corner of her eye. Her mother, wiping the tears away.

"Ms. Ranger, have you had any sensation in your extremities at all? Fingers? Toes?"

It took several seconds to derive meaning from the words. Zannah blinked twice. She couldn't feel anything but the pain in her neck, a deep ache barely dulled by the drugs. The doctor met her eyes for a moment and then moved out of her vision.

"Honey, you're going to be okay, understand?" Helen, her mother, was crying too, and she was crying because she knew it wasn't true, Zannah was sure of that. The damage was worse than they were telling her it was. Was her neck broken? Oh God, please no! She didn't want to be a quadriplegic. She blinked tears away again, tears her mother mopped up for her. Tears she couldn't touch with her own hands. She couldn't feel her hands. Her eyes blurred and she wanted to cry properly, yet she couldn't make a sound. Just tears.

Memories from this morning's drug-addled bedside discussions slowly returned, though it took a moment to sort them into order. They'd tried to induce a coma, but despite the medication she'd woken up. She'd been in and out of consciousness ever since, her head slowly getting clearer despite the painkillers they were pumping into her.

"This is actually quite incredible. Very exciting. Despite everything we expected, she's doing extremely well." The doctor seemed to be speaking to her mother now, as Zannah couldn't see him just then. He was a weedy man, balding and hyperactive and not her type at all, but he seemed smart, which was good. Smart and excited. A better combination. "I'd almost say that what we're seeing is impossible, though I have seen some pretty amazing recoveries in my time," the doctor said. What was his name? Had he told her? Harold? William? Ed? It was an old name, but one that escaped her memory.

Other memories came to her. There'd been dozens of doctors swarming around her shortly after she woke, trying to figure out why the induced coma wasn't working and why she was alive at all. They'd come to the conclusion it was her own quirky genetics and metabolism.

She would probably be more worried if her head wasn't so foggy. She could feel a solid brace pushing uncomfortably against her chin and jaw and wanted it gone. She wanted everything gone and to be gone from here. She ached for the coma she couldn't have and the blessing of oblivion. She wanted to wake up and remember this as a scary, freaky dream and nothing more.

Or not wake up at all. That might be better.

She caught the word *operation* from the doctor, but he was whispering now, neither him nor her mother in sight. No, no, no. She didn't want an operation. She needed to tell them that. She needed to recover or die quickly so this whole thing would be over. She tried to focus on what they were saying, desperate for knowledge. Almost as if her ears could tune into their voices like a radio signal, they became clearer the more she focused.

"Stability is more important than knowledge at the moment. We don't want to rush in and cause more damage by moving her for the sake of a few scans. One of my colleagues believes it's best to do as little as possible while she's the most vulnerable, allowing her body to stabilise and recover somewhat before we attempt anything more. I'm not a hundred per cent on board with that. I'd like to know what's happening, but he's got more experience. You can talk to him this afternoon when his shift starts. For now we'll keep her stable, offer pain relief, and let her recover as much as possible."

So they didn't have any idea how badly hurt she was, or even what she needed? A bullet to the brain, if she had any say. She didn't want everyone cheering if she managed to grasp a spoon again and feed herself. She couldn't put her parents through that.

Where was her father? Did he know she'd been hurt? Had he been here? His aftershave lingered in the air, suggesting he had. She tried listening to the doctor again, letting the sounds of the hospital fade away until all she could hear was the medic and her mother.

"The scans we did when she first arrived show significant trauma-"

"Please don't use vague terms like *significant trauma*," her mother said, with uncharacteristic acerbity. "Significant trauma could be anything."

The doctor continued. "Think of it this way, then. Spinal columns are like toothpaste. Squeeze some onto your toothbrush and it looks great. Nice and smooth. Just a tiny touch though and it gets messed up, and no matter how hard you try, you can't put it back the way it was. Judging by the way her neck was broken, our best guess is that the two halves are barely connected. Healing will occur, but it's like trying to reshape toothpaste with a fingertip. What feeling and movement returns is largely up to her body now. We can operate to stabilise her spine, but rushing into anything could be worse than doing nothing."

Zannah closed her eyes and stopped listening. She'd been right. She was better off dead. Unfortunately, her body seemed determined to survive despite her wishes. Her best guess was that she might get enough feeling again to speak or twitch a finger to control a motorised wheelchair. She'd be a burden to everyone.

"We'll see what happens when the swelling goes down and how much feeling she retains, if any, but considering the way her body is dealing with the trauma I believe there's every chance she could get some movement back..."

She stopped listening. She didn't want to know about how one day she might be able to wiggle a big toe or scratch her own nose. She didn't want anyone to have to wipe her ass or empty her urine bag either. She didn't want to be alive if it came to that. Couldn't they just kill her now and pretend she didn't make it?

Yesterday, she'd been looking toward a future full of travel and a great career. Now she faced constant care and someone to mop the drool from her chin. From the corner of her eye she could see the window and the late afternoon sunshine rushing in. How long had it been since the damage? Was it last night or several nights ago?

Her parents didn't need this. Her mother would have to quit work just to be a full-time carer. Better to give everyone the gift of a sharp shot of grief than remain an invalid requiring twenty-four-hour care. She'd seen too many medical shows to know the realities of what she faced. Reality shows sucked, she realised. She was a quadriplegic and would be lucky to intimidate pedestrians on the sidewalk in her motorised wheelchair, if her parents could even afford one.

Her mother returned and sat next to her, reaching out and... oh God, she was holding Zannah's hand and she couldn't feel it. Her mother might as well have been holding the edge of her bed, for all Zannah could tell. She wanted to tell her mother to leave and never come back, to let her die.

"Suzannah?" Helen said. "Zannah? You need to listen."

Listen? To who?

Helen stood, clearly too much nervous tension and fear driving her body at the moment, and Zannah finally realised her mother's eyes were red from crying, exhaustion, and despair. Helen must have sent Zannah's father home to get some rest. He'd always been the soft one. He'd be a mess judging by her mother's face. She wanted to hug both her mother and father. She wanted to hug anyone. She'd hug a pig in mud if she could.

Zannah felt tears building again and blinked them away, though her sight remained blurred. The doctor was saying something about doing scans and blood work. She didn't need tests to tell her what she couldn't ever do again. She ignored the man until he left.

Her brother, Jimmy, came in shortly after that, holding hands with a girl. Jimmy had a girlfriend? When did Jimmy get a girlfriend? The girl was stunning, way out of Jimmy's league. Tallish with light-brown hair and a sweetness in her features that Zannah couldn't see Jimmy going for at all. She even smelled pretty, like flowers or something. Earthy. The world really had gone crazy. Jimmy looked like he'd been crying and even the girl looked upset. She must be really nice to put up with her brother.

"Mum," Jimmy said. "Go home and get some sleep. I'll stay with Zannah until Dad gets back."

Her mother sat down again, clearly exhausted. "I'm fine. I'll sleep in the chair if I have to."

Jimmy walked around the bed and put his big hands on their mother's shoulders. His girlfriend, eyes trying to look everywhere but at Zannah, stayed close to him. Jimmy was so much bigger than both Zannah and their mother now, though Zannah was a few years older than him. He was barely sixteen and already a giant, well over six foot tall. Six three or four, she guessed.

"Mum, please. Take a couple of hours to catch a few z's in your own bed, refresh with a shower and come back a little more awake. I'll be here. I'll call if there's any news."

After an angst-ridden moment, Helen shook her head, her

posture stiff and defiant even as she rubbed her eyes with the heels of her hands as if trying to push the tiredness and emotions aside. "I understand what you're saying Jimmy, but I just don't think I can. What if... What if something goes wrong and I'm not here? I need to stay with my baby girl."

"I'll call the moment we get any news. I promise. Please, just go home and get some rest, even if it's only taking a break from the hospital."

Helen shook her head. "I can relax here."

"Mum," he said with a little too much sternness, like he was the adult for a change. "It's noisy here, there's people coming in and out, and that chair will kill your back. Besides, you've been awake for well over thirty hours. You're exhausted. You need to be able to think straight if the doctors have more questions for you."

Helen sighed. "I just wish... You know I won't be able to sleep even if I do go home, right?" She stood as if she were eighty years old. After a long moment of debate with herself, she leaned over Zannah. "I'll be back in a few hours honey, okay? I promise." She carefully kissed Zannah's forehead, her lips warm and soft. "I love you so much."

Zannah blinked tears, wishing she could speak. If she could, she'd organise to be dead by the time her mother returned in order to spare her any more grief. At least then they'd all have a chance to move on.

When Helen was gone, Jimmy looked Zannah over. "That's a hell of a lot of tubes and monitors," he said. "How are we supposed to get you out of here with all this stuff attached?"

What?

Zannah felt a sudden rush of panic as all her thoughts about wanting to die evaporated.

He must have seen the fear on her face. "It's okay, Zannah. We're going to make you better."

We? Better? What the hell? Nothing could make her better.

He took his girlfriend's hand. "This is Sellendria. She's got this way to heal people, but she can't do it here."

Sellendria moved closer, that downcast, submissive expression and posture gone. Holy shit. Sleeping Beauty had turned into Xena the Warrior Princess.

"The longer we leave it, the less I'll be able to do for you. Do you understand, Zannah? I can't heal a scar, so the more you heal naturally, the worse off you'll be in the long run."

"Maybe it would be best to wait another day or two, even so," Jimmy said. "I understand the earlier the better, but there's no point if we kill her."

This girl was definitely way out of Jimmy's league, like she was an actual princess or something. Psycho princess if she was dating her brother and thought she could heal Zannah. She didn't look like a psycho, but she sounded like one. She was far too perfect, and there was something entirely wrong about her as well, and not just her smell. Her voice sounded odd, and... just everything, like she'd been designed in a computer and grown in a lab.

Sellendria held her hand over Zannah's neck, concentrated, and frowned. "We have to do it now," she said. "She's healing rapidly, and if she heals like this she'll stay like this."

How the hell could she know that? What the hell was going on?

Jimmy brushed his tousled hair back from his face. "Are you sure?" he asked. "I've got no idea what will happen if we get caught."

Zannah tried speaking, but her throat was so badly swollen no sound came out.

Despite the protests she glared his way, Jimmy nodded in agreement with Sellendria. "We're going to have to turn off the monitors first, so no one comes running," he said. "Any idea how?"

Panic building, Zannah stared in disbelief as Sellendria moved toward one of the monitors near her bed. No. They couldn't! Her mother would die if Zannah disappeared from the hospital. Her father, too.

Jimmy's hand was slightly sweaty as he touched Zannah's face. "You'll be fine," he said softly, staring into her eyes as if that ensured she understood.

Unlike Zannah, who had her father's dark brown eyes, Jimmy's were a pale blue, like their mother's.

"I promise. Remember that time I was gone for nearly a week? Sellendria saved my life then. She can do the same for you."

Someone knocked on the door, and in moments the smell of David's aftershave reached her. Oh, thank God! He'd stop them from doing something stupid.

"Um, do you mind if I have a bit of time with Zannah? Alone?" David asked, as Jimmy and Sellendria froze like a couple of guilty children stealing sweets from the jar.

"Um, sure," Jimmy said, giving Sellendria a meaningful glance.

Sellendria nodded, her expression as neutral as she could make it. "How about we grab a coffee?" she asked Jimmy.

Jimmy nodded, relief and fear on his face. At least he looked appropriately guilt-ridden. Sellendria didn't. "Sure. We'll be back in ten minutes. That enough time, David?"

"Plenty. Thanks, Jimmy."

Zannah had never been happier to see her brother leave. She had to find a way to tell David what they were planning. As he moved up beside her bed, she mouthed the word 'help', but he didn't notice.

"Geez, babe. You..." He scratched his head, looking anywhere but at her. "Look like shit, to be honest."

What? She suppressed the hurt. He was supposed to say he loved her. The scent of his aftershave sparked an unexpected memory from the incident. They'd been arguing, though she couldn't remember what it was about. Is that why he'd come? To apologise?

"Listen, Zannah, I can't do this. Not now. Not ever. I didn't sign up to nurse a cripple."

She stared, shocked, as heartbreak crushed her. Her eyes filled again until she could feel tears running towards her ears.

"Yeah, I'm sorry. I really am. But, you know, I figured it was better to say it now than in a month or something."

Blinking rapidly, she looked away as best she could. She wanted to yell abuse at him, to tell him to get out and never come back. She wanted to break his neck so he could feel what it was like in her position. She wouldn't have abandoned him.

"I'd want you to move on if the situation were reversed. It's just, you know? It's such a frigging shame. You were... never mind. I just hope they get the bastard. I gave the police a full report. He belted my head pretty hard, though. Cops said I was concussed when I told them it was a man. They say a dog attacked you and you broke your neck when you fell. Total bullshit. It was a man."

He glanced at her and away again, not game to meet her eyes and tears. "Anyway, I'll come back and visit and all that, but, you know," he sighed, shifting his weight as if keen to leave. "I should probably wait for Jimmy to get back, but there's plenty of nurses and doctors about to look after you. Talk later, huh?"

He hesitated for a few seconds as if he knew it was too abrupt, but left anyway. Shattered, she stared at the painted concrete roof, vision blurry, and really wished she could kill herself. It wasn't more than a minute before she heard someone else enter the room. Heavy footsteps. A man's tread. He smelled... not quite normal. Musky, like a dog who'd just been bathed. She crinkled her nose.

Expecting to see a doctor, she felt surprise when she saw a heavily muscled man in his early twenties step into her view. Short for a guy, really short, he had longish dark hair roughly brushed back.

She remembered those eyes, remembered him leaning over her. He'd bitten her! What the fuck?

CHAPTER 6

KYLE MET the girl's eyes, abject fear in them. Shit. She remembered him. He cringed inwardly, wishing he'd been able to sneak in and kill the girl with all the mercy unconsciousness could offer, and leave without anyone noticing.

The fact that she was awake and scared of him tore like a wound. He wasn't ready for this. Although he'd been in a fair number of scraps and thought he was prepared, killing wasn't something he'd ever cared for. Killing an innocent girl only made it worse.

The way she stared at him, transfixed with terror, made him wish she could scream so at least he'd have a reason to do it quickly. Or run. Could he do it while she watched him? Could he do it regardless, even if she'd been unconscious? In the heat of a fight and its aftermath perhaps, but if he was honest with himself, he doubted he'd be able to do it even then.

Looking for any excuse to delay, he leaned close and sniffed, watching her eyes widen with the horror of not knowing what he was going to do. Did she remember being bitten? It was rare among werewolves to remember, but it happened.

It was there in her scent, just beginning to come through. Musk and ice. His own unique blend of werewolf tainted with vampire. Regret pierced him. He had no choice. He had to kill her now.

"I'm sorry," he said gently, trying to convince himself it was the right thing to do. "I can't let you live. I know you don't understand why, but... it's something I have to do."

She seemed to be trying not to cry, though enough tears had already coursed trails on her skin to make it difficult to tell. She was such a beautiful girl, too. An absolute tragedy.

His hand trembled as he placed it over her mouth, her skin warm but clammy. Steeling himself despite every inclination he felt, he reached for her nose with his other hand. "I really am sorry," he said, as if apologising once more would help him find the courage to murder her before she fully transitioned.

With his finger and thumb ready to pinch her nose closed, he found he couldn't take that last step. "Shit," he muttered. Despite his promise, he couldn't do it. If he'd been a normal Creature, his promise would have forced him to comply, but he wasn't.

He withdrew his hand. "Dammit!" he swore.

He wasn't even sure if suffocating her would do the job. Not now, not so long after the bite. The only way to be sure was to snap her neck properly, and even then he had doubts. He ran a hand through his hair, considering his options. Perhaps Kimbrel might be able to help?

"Hey, who are you? Where's David?"

A boy and girl entered the room, holding hands. They watched him with suspicion, the girl in particular. He caught a strange scent and focused on the girl, a cold shiver passing through him. She wasn't human. He couldn't tell what she was, but she wasn't a Creature he'd ever encountered, and he'd met just about every type of Creature there was.

She looked more wary of him than afraid, which was telling. She wasn't giving anything away either. That made her both smart and dangerous. She moved like she knew how to fight, too.

Judging by her boyfriend's scent and his features, he was related to the girl in the bed and entirely human, but the girl with him... He sniffed the air again, staring at her. She looked human, but then most

Creatures did. What was she? Maybe a dryad? It was unlikely, but she had an earthy scent.

She narrowed her eyes as if recognising something about him, too. She glanced at the girl on the bed, then back at Kyle. "You're the one who bit Zannah, aren't you?" she asked, though it wasn't really a question. "I thought there was something wrong with her aura."

She could see auras? What kind of Creature could see auras? Any number of them might. Could his visit to see Kimbriel get any more complicated?

"Jimmy," the girl said as her stance subtly changed. "Go get help. Quickly. Call for Longbow, too."

Shit, she was preparing to fight. Expecting it. If she'd ordered the huge boy away, then she was far more deadly than any human. She slowly reached for her necklace, of all things. Was it some kind of talisman?

The big kid glanced at her, then back at Kyle, a challenge in his posture. He clearly wasn't intimidated by Kyle or the girl's order. "Why?"

"He's a Creature, Jimmy." She glanced at the girl on the bed again. "You can't take him on. I think he's the one who bit Zannah, which is why the doctors say she's recovering so fast. Her aura's already different from a human's. I thought it was just the trauma, but it's more than that. She's changing into whatever he is." She nodded toward Kyle.

The kid was big, certainly big enough to cause trouble, yet the girl seemed to be in charge. Kyle stared, more than a little tense, as he tried to think of a way out of this without causing a fight.

He hadn't met a Creature he hadn't recognised in decades. Her lack of fear suggested she had quite a bit of power. She gripped the necklace at her throat tightly, watching Kyle with caution. And yet, if she was going to attack, she would have by now. She didn't want to fight either.

"What are you?" Kyle asked the girl. Hopefully, he could talk his way out of this mess and avoid any violence. Violence would create attention, so if he could get out without a fight, he'd consider it a win.

She watched intently, her stance ready. Shit. She really did know how to fight. He could tell by her posture. She was a killer if ever he'd seen one.

As Jimmy prepared to leave, Kyle caught his eyes. "Raise an alarm and I swear the girl won't live long enough for it to matter." It was a bluff, but anything to prevent an entanglement with the authorities.

A ball of light flared in the girl's free hand. Her lips tight as if afraid to take action, but she was prepared to.

"What the...?" Kyle stared. Magic? Only Kimbriel and her disciples could access magic... Oh shit. She knew Kimbriel? Was she one of her disciples? What else could it mean?

"Go, Jimmy," the girl said.

"Wait!" Kyle said, raising his hands and taking a slow and cautious step away from Zannah. "I'm not here to hurt her. She'd be dead if I'd intended that."

"Then why are you here?"

He glanced at the doorway. "This hospital is rife with Creatures. Vampires, mostly. The place reeks of them. I've caught the scents of ghouls and at least one incubus or succubus. The moment any of them realise she's changing, they'll kill her or take her to whoever's in charge. That won't go well."

Jimmy didn't seem the least bit surprised that his girlfriend was holding a ball of light, and neither of them reacted at all when he mentioned vampires and ghouls.

"What are you?" Jimmy asked Kyle. "Why did you hurt my sister?"

The question was telling.

Kyle kept his hands up to try to placate the kid. Jimmy was huge, head and shoulders taller than Kyle, making him seem older than he probably was. "I tried to save her from a vampire last night, but the bastard broke her neck. There was blood..." He took a calming breath as the memory brought up unwanted desires. "Instinct took over, and I'm sorry for that. I doubt she'd have lived more than a few minutes otherwise, so believe it or not, my bite saved her."

"I don't believe you," the strange girl said.

"She's alive, isn't she?" Kyle asked, still staring at the magical murder ball or whatever she held. "We have to get her out of here before the local werewolves notice her scent's changing." A good sense of smell was one of the few advantages of being a werewolf.

The girl spared her boyfriend a glance. "Jimmy, if Zannah's been bitten by a Creature, I can't heal her, not that part of her, anyway." The ball of light in her hand winked out as she looked Kyle over again. "If you truly intend to help, what do you propose?"

He almost sagged with relief. "I have a friend," he said, suspecting she might know Kimbriel anyway, but not wanting to give that information up when he knew so little about her. "She might be able to stop what's happening to Zannah. Help me get her out of here and I'll take Zannah to her."

"What are you, first?" the girl asked.

How was he supposed to answer that question? Unfortunately, he didn't seem to have any choice if he wanted her trust. "Unique. A werewolf tainted by a vampire's essence, accidentally created. What are you?"

She raised her chin as if a little surprised by his revelation, the moment holding as if she were reconsidering her position here. "Not of this world," she eventually said.

"Right..." he whispered slowly, stretching the word out as he hoped she'd elaborate. She didn't.

If she wasn't a Creature and wasn't human, then what was she? Were aliens real? He'd met an elemental fire dragon once who said she could travel to other worlds. Maybe this girl was a dragon too. Not attuned to the element of fire, though. She smelled earthy, so that was probably it. The simplest explanation was always the most likely in his experience, and considering she didn't seem afraid of him, it fit. A dragon could rip him apart. Hell, from what he'd been told, the greatest of all dragon-kind, a draken, could wipe out a modern city of millions of people with almost no effort.

The young couple looked at each other, but it was the girl who nodded first.

"Okay," Jimmy said in agreement as he pointed toward Kyle. "We'll help you get Zannah out of here. I'll keep a watch while you two disconnect all the monitors and... tubes and whatnot."

Someone passed the door then, a figure Kyle recognised. Rake. He met the vampire's eyes with a shock of fear and adrenaline as he saw the recognition returned. He held his breath until the Creature continued on, as if nothing were amiss.

"What?" the girl asked when she noticed his reaction, her tone soft and deadly.

"The vampire who attacked Zannah is here, probably to finish the job." Kyle leaned over Zannah and spoke quietly. "Here's the deal, child. I'm going to take you to a friend." He refrained from mentioning that Kimbriel would probably still demand he kill her, but one problem at a time. "Before we can do that, I'm going to cut myself and dribble my blood into your mouth. It will help you heal. Not instantaneously, but much quicker. By tomorrow morning you should be back on your feet. Maybe sooner. The more you drink, the faster it'll work. Understand?"

She blinked once, but her expression showed horror.

"Good. Are you two okay with that?" He asked Jimmy and his girlfriend.

Jimmy appeared revolted, but the inhuman girl only nodded as if it were the least Kyle could do for Zannah. "Do it," she said. "Hurry."

Kyle held his right wrist up to his mouth and forced his canines to grow and sharpen. He punctured his wrist with a wince of pain and held it over Zannah's mouth. Blood splashed onto her lips, and despite the disgust on her face instinct took over. Whether she wanted it or not, her lips parted and ecstasy filled her expression. He held his wrist against her mouth and she sucked as if parched.

"That's disgusting," Jimmy hissed.

"I thought you were supposed to be keeping watch?" Kyle said. If a vampire came in and they weren't prepared, this whole thing would be over very quickly.

The inhuman girl approached the monitors, staring intently at them as she gripped the necklace she wore. Without hesitation, she began switching machines off before removing the tubes and sensors attached to Zannah.

Zannah began making moaning sounds, desperate, hungry noises, her lips slurping at his wrist. He wasn't sure how much to give her, having never done anything like this before, but the more the better.

It took a few minutes to fully disconnect her, and by then Kyle was beginning to feel light-headed from his own blood loss. He pulled his wrist away and Zannah moaned in anguish. He could sense her now, like a limb he'd never used. She was a part of him, yet separate at the same time. So that's how vampires controlled their newly made offspring?

"More," Zannah whispered. "Need more."

Jimmy rushed to her side. "You can speak?"

"Hungry. Thirsty. Need more." She licked her lips clean, a drop of blood still on the side of her mouth.

Jimmy had tears in his eyes. "Oh God, Zannah. This is incredible!" He glanced at Kyle. "What if I give her some of my blood? Will that help?"

Kyle held his hand up, palm out. "No. You'd get infected too, and she might tear a good chunk out of you as well. A wheelchair would be useful though."

"Wheelchair. Got it. You okay here, Sellendria?" he asked, clearly forgetting the fact they'd almost come to blows with Kyle.

"Yeah. I'll check Zannah over while you're out."

Jimmy left, almost running.

"The bruising and swelling have almost gone," Sellendria said, checking as much as she could around the brace. "I'm surprised it worked that quickly."

"More," Zannah whispered. "Please!"

Sellendria raised an eyebrow at Kyle, and he had the feeling he wouldn't want to cross this inhuman girl. "Are you going to be able to control her? There's a rage and hunger in her aura I've never seen in a

Creature before, even you. She'd probably have a go at me if she could move."

"I sired her. If it works the same way as for vampires, she has to obey me. Her hunger will settle in a few years."

"Years?" Zannah whispered with a moan.

"Vampires are different," Sellendria said, and he wondered just how extensive her knowledge of Creatures was. Where had the girl got such knowledge from? And power, too? She couldn't be more than sixteen, yet she seemed to have more knowledge than most Creatures ever accumulated. Humans who'd been turned into Creatures generally looked a little older.

"I can sense Zannah already. She's... I won't let her harm anyone, if that's your concern."

"It is." Sellendria met his eyes again. There was no compromise.

Jimmy returned with a wheelchair, breaking the tension. "It was down the corridor," he said. "I hope no one needed it. Longbow's on his way too."

Between Kyle and Jimmy, they managed to get Zannah's limp form into the wheelchair, but before Kyle could wheel her out, Jimmy grasped his forearm. He had big hands, and he was strong too. He'd have made a good blacksmith.

"I know Zannah didn't have many prospects as a quadriplegic, but she's still my sister. If you-"

Kyle gripped the kid's shoulder with his free hand as he met his determined stare, and didn't mind looking up to do it. "I understand. If my friend can help her, Zannah will be much better off." Kyle pulled his arm from the kid's grip, not wanting to say what would happen if Kimbriel decided not to help, or couldn't. "I'll do whatever's best. I assure you."

With an uncertain look, Jimmy moved aside and put his arm around Sellendria's shoulders. "Can you do anything?" he asked the girl.

She shook her head. "I'm sorry. Zannah's a Creature now. That puts her beyond my help."

With a final frown at Kyle, Jimmy stood back and let him push his sister in the wheelchair, the siblings locking eyes but neither saying anything.

"We'll watch your back until you're out of the hospital," Jimmy said.

Outside the room, Kyle hesitated at the sight of a young man with long blonde hair tied at the nape of his neck. He had a similar smell to Sellendria, and a similar cast to his features. They weren't related, he was sure, but part of the same race, whatever that was. He shivered as he realised they may both be dragons. Some dragons were shapeshifters, he'd been told.

Longbow. That was his name. He was a little taller than Jimmy, with a wiry look and a stance that suggested he knew how to fight even better than Sellendria.

"How many of you are there?" Kyle asked Sellendria as she followed him out of the room.

"He's my protector."

Kyle gave Longbow another once over, noticing Sellendria hadn't answered his question. He was probably better off not knowing, but his curiosity was burning. What were they? If not dragon shapeshifters, then what?

Leaving the hospital was almost anticlimactic. Kyle pushed Zannah out the front doors, and with Jimmy's help he got Zannah into a cab.

Sellendria put her hand on Longbow's arm like a princess to her protector. "Go home. I'll meet you there." Despite the misgivings on his face, the guy gave a brief nod and started jogging toward the main road. Kyle was happy to see him go. He had the feeling he was more dangerous than he looked, and he looked very, very dangerous.

"Go easy," Zannah muttered, as they positioned her unresponsive body in the cab, the injured young woman's face pale and showing pain. "I've got a broken neck, remember? The brace is my friend, not my guarantee."

"Sorry," Kyle muttered, distracted as he tried to look everywhere at once while he put the seatbelt around her. He'd caught the scents of at least half a dozen vampires and werewolves as they'd left the hospital, but none followed or seemed to watch. What was their game then? Why allow him and the girl to leave?

Something was up. He was certain. It was far too easy.

CHAPTER 7

ZANNAH WINCED as the tingling in her extremities began to hurt from the vibrations and bumps of the moving taxi. Her left arm jerked involuntarily as pain shot through her shoulder, and she let out a moan as it settled into a dull ache. She wished she could move her arms to ease the pain. When would the ride end? She'd rather a trip to the dentist. Almost.

At least she had control over her breathing and could speak a little, though speaking killed her throat. She didn't care what she was becoming, despite Jimmy and Sellendria's concern over what they called Creatures, which she still didn't understand.

Werewolves and vampires? She'd have called bullshit if she wasn't thirsting after blood. Jimmy, in particular, smelled really tasty. It sickened her that she felt that way, yet she wanted it nevertheless.

Was she a serial killer then, or going to be? She didn't want to be a serial killer, or a killer of any variety. Hell, she was a vegan. Sometimes. It was more of an ideal than actual practice, but still. It was a philosophy she'd tried to get into a few times.

Serial killer it was then.

Maybe she could just eat bad people, like lawyers and politicians? And dentists, the sadistic bastards. She really didn't like dentists.

Okay, that wasn't fair. Lawyers had some redeeming qualities. Probably.

Either way, being a Creature was far better than what she'd been facing, and at least Kyle appeared to be doing right by her. He had bitten her though, and had been intending to kill her. But he didn't. A blessing and a curse. She'd take it for now. Kyle looked her over from his seat by the other door, Jimmy between them. Her big little brother didn't seem to want to let Kyle get too close. Sellendria sat in the front next to the driver.

"You okay?" Jimmy asked. "You look better."

Pain was better than no feeling whatsoever. "Hands and feet are tingling. Stinging," she amended. She took a moment to swallow in a throat that felt like the first time she'd had tonsillitis. Razor throat, she'd called it. "I'm getting hungry, too. Real hungry." Her stomach growled like an exclamation mark making a statement, though she couldn't tell him it wasn't a burger she craved. He really smelled good. The taxi driver smelled better. Sellendria now smelled like a clod of dirt mixed with manure. Yuck.

Sellendria, sitting in the front seat, turned around. "Pain's good. It means your body's healing." She had a funny look in her eye when she added the next words. "Getting you something to eat... could be an issue, though."

How did she know what Zannah was thinking? "I hope not, because right now I'd be happy to take a chunk out of a hit and run pedestrian." The woman driving the taxi smelled like a banquet, although the scent of her skin was tainted by a mix of soaps, deodorant, hair spray and perfume. At least she had earphones in, the steady thump of music masking their conversation. It didn't seem very professional, though.

"People don't smell like food," Kyle said, as if it were one of the Ten Commandments. "People don't smell like food to you anymore."

As if the words held power, her hunger dissipated to a quiet ache and the taxi driver began to smell just like any other person. She couldn't help showing her surprise. "Wow. That is really cool. And scary." He really could control her as he'd alluded to in the hospital, which didn't bode well for the rest of her life if he turned out to be an asshole. It didn't bode well, no matter what.

Sellendria seemed to be thinking the same thing. She narrowed her eyes at Kyle.

"What?" he asked. "You want her to eat someone?"

Sellendria's eyes narrowed further, and Zannah wished she could see Kyle's face.

Despite the brace, Zannah still needed to prevent herself from accidentally severing her own spinal cord simply by turning to look out the window, so she did her best to frown at Kyle from the corner of her eye. She couldn't see him past Jimmy, though. "How did you do that? I mean, actually do it? I know what I smelled just a moment ago. Is it like hypnosis or something?" She swallowed again, and winced. Razor throat.

Kyle leaned forward until she caught a glimpse of him, then back again so she couldn't even see a hint of him from the corner of her eye. "I'm your sire. It... gives me influence over you. It'll be several centuries before you're strong enough to resist whatever I say and break my hold. I guess. It's how it works with vampires. If I were to say you feel tired, you'd feel tired, though your resistance to my commands will strengthen in time."

"Not fair," she whispered, not daring to challenge her throat with full-blooded insult. "I'm your slave now?" Was slavery any better than being a quadriplegic? Fuck, yes. She hoped. What if he made her do kinky things? Or hurt people? "Wait, did you say centuries?" Maybe it would be worth it. Was she going immortal? That would be so awesome.

"Yes, and I didn't make the rules about the obedience thing."

She shrugged, or tried to, and failed. "Better than dying, I guess. You planning on treating me nice? I am a spoiled brat, you know."

He leaned forward again at that, and he actually appeared worried. She guessed he was a good guy then, judging by his frightened reaction. "At this stage, I'm just hoping my friend can help."

"And if they can't?" she said more coldly than she'd intended, her throat clearly getting better now. Talking didn't hurt quite as much. "Considering you can command me to do anything you want and I'm hardly in a position to fight you off anyway, why don't you just tell me to be happy about it?"

He frowned past Jimmy, who was studiously and uncharacteristically not saying anything as he stared ahead. "Is that what you want?" Kyle asked. "To be commanded to be happy?"

"As if you can command emotions," she muttered before thinking it through.

"Be happy." It had the tone of a command. Challenge accepted.

Her anger abruptly fell away, and she felt... happy. "Holy shit! That really worked. I'm actually looking forward to doing whatever you command now. Can I be your beer wench, please?" Despite the happy feeling imbuing her, she laced it with as much sarcasm as she could.

Even Sellendria turned at that, but it was Jimmy who spoke. "He said be happy, not nasty. Shit. I wished it worked for me. I'd tell you what you could do, that's for friggin' sure."

Zannah wished she could glare at her big little brother. The last thing she needed was attitude from him. "He said nothing about sarcasm or the fact that I can still think for myself. But yeah, I'm feeling pretty good about being his undead slave dog."

"You don't sound very undead," Jimmy muttered.

Kyle stared resolutely out the windscreen. "And your sarcasm's not endearing."

"Oh. Why didn't you say so? Remind me to work on that." Why was she so pissed off all of a sudden? She never liked being told what to do, but still... Maybe it was the fact her body was quite literally changing. Hell, that'd cause a hormonal imbalance if anything would, not to mention a bit of anxiety. She shouldn't be surprised her emotions were all over the place.

Kyle sighed. "I didn't plan this, and I don't want to be responsible for you anymore than you want to have a broken neck. However, neither of us have any choice about it. So please just... be nice."

At least he'd said please. It wasn't a command. "Lucky me." She really shouldn't be complaining though, but her mood was darkening again.

He stared toward the front of the car. "Happy, remember?"

"Put a clock on it next time. I got over it."

"I liked it better when you couldn't talk," Jimmy said before Kyle could respond.

"Then tell my new lord and master to make me stay silent." Shit. She shouldn't have said that. Kyle really could tell her to never talk again.

Jimmy stared at her, frowning in annoyance. "He saved your life, remember? And he's trying to help you now. Show some appreciation."

When the hell had Jimmy got all wise and mature? He was right, though. She really shouldn't be angry with Kyle or anyone else but the fucker of a vampire who'd broken her neck. "Yesterday, I was a normal human being. Today, I'm a crippled Creature thingy bound to obey someone I don't even know. How's your day, Jimmy?" Dammit. Anger and sarcasm again. "Sorry," she added. At least Jimmy didn't take the bait.

Kyle spoke. "Last week was better for me, too," he said softly.

They rode along in uncomfortable silence for nearly fifteen minutes. "Hey! David's home is in the suburb just up ahead," Zannah said, before she remembered his hospital visit. Heartbreak caught her off guard and almost overwhelmed her. She fought it down with a few slow breaths. "We should at least tell him about... If someone's after me, he might be on the hit list too. He's a jerk, I realise that now, but I should warn him."

Jimmy looked incredulous. "Seriously?" he asked.

"Wouldn't you?"

Her brother shook his head. "I never liked him, and he never treated you well. You deserve better."

"Wow," she said. "People might think you give a shit about me."

Kyle leaned forward enough so he could meet her eyes. "I heard what got said while I was waiting. I agree with your brother."

Loyalty ran deep in Kyle, clearly. It must be rubbing off because she really wasn't sure why she felt such a strong need to warn David, but it seemed necessary. "We really should tell him. Please?"

"Call him," Jimmy said.

"I don't have my phone." Where was her phone anyway? At work, along with her purse, she realised.

"And I don't have his number in mine," Jimmy said, resignation in his voice. "Do you know his number?"

"No," Zannah said. "I don't know anyone's number. I just push a button on the screen."

Kyle met her eyes. "You're serious about warning him, aren't you?" When she didn't respond, he sighed. "Fine. What's the address?"

Sellendria caught the taxi driver's attention, and when she removed her earphones, Zannah told her the address. The woman nodded, played with her GPS for a moment, and then put her earphones back in.

Zannah turned her attention back to her sire. Weird term, sire, but she supposed she was going to have to get used to it. "Hey, Kyle?"

"Yes?" He didn't lean forward and look her way, and sounded like he'd rather be alone.

"Can we start over with me being appreciative of the fact that you didn't kill me, don't actually want to, and are trying to help me?"

This time he did lean forward, clearly wondering if she was serious, judging by his expression. After a moment, he nodded. Win, win.

They rode in silence until the taxi pulled into David's driveway behind his crappy old brown Mazda, the paint oxidised in places. David must have gone straight home after seeing her. Kyle paid the driver, got out and opened her side as Sellendria unbuckled Zannah. "Wait here," Kyle told the driver.

Zannah grimaced as he prepared to lift her. "You know what, I don't need to be involved in actually seeing the ass-wipe face-to-face. Can't you just tell him for me? I can wait in the cab."

Kyle frowned. "I'm happy to leave now, if you don't want to face him."

She sighed. "Fair enough. Lift me up then, sir knight."

Getting picked up hurt like hell, but that was good. Hopefully the pain was the forerunner of a genuine ability to sing and dance on tables again, not that she'd ever done that. Sober. He carried her up to the door as the taxi abruptly reversed out the driveway and drove off. "Shouldn't have paid her," Kyle muttered.

At that moment, butterflies began dive bombing from all directions, moving between Zannah's stomach and throat. She really didn't want to face David now that she was about to see him. Not ever.

"This was a stupid idea. Why did I let you talk me into it?" she asked Kyle.

Kyle paused, meeting her eyes. "Are you kidding?

"No. How about we leave, find a bar and drink to new beginnings?"

He held her gaze for a while longer. "Um, no..."

"Hey, have you got some sort of super strength working for you, because I reckon I'm about six or eight inches taller than you, and I'm fairly solid for a girl as I used to do a lot of sports. You're not so much as making a grunt."

"I used to be a blacksmith." Kyle knocked on David's door with a foot as Jimmy and Sellendria moved up behind them.

Zannah gave Kyle a genuine smile. She really should be nicer to him. "I thought you looked pretty buff under that shirt. Here I am, pressed up against a hard-muscled man, and I can't feel anything but pain. How crappy is that?"

He seemed uncomfortable at that comment.

"You a bit old school?" she asked. "No sex before marriage?

"What?" he looked sharply at her. "I'm not talking about sex with you."

"Prudish or what?"

He focused resolutely on the door as heavy footsteps approached, completely ignoring her last comment despite a flush to his cheeks. She smiled, hoping to make him uncomfortable in a nice kind of way whenever she could, considering she was likely to be stuck with him for a while. Centuries. She liked the idea of centuries. "You are kind of cute."

His jaw clenched and her smile deepened. When David opened the door, her ex's mouth made movements, but no sound.

"Mind if I bring her in?" Kyle asked. "She's kind of heavy."

David just stood there, staring.

"Please," Zannah added, looking up at him. "Yeah, I can speak now. You're a dick."

Almost as if on autopilot, David moved out of the way, his mouth still open.

Kyle shifted Zannah in his arms, sending a jolt of pain through her neck before he walked past David. He sat Zannah on one of David's reclining chairs facing and the huge television. She almost felt bad when she realised she was in David's favourite seat. He'd never let her sit there before.

Screw him.

David followed the four of them into the room, clearly confused. "What are you doing here? Wait. That's not what I meant. She should be in hospital!" He glared at Kyle, then Jimmy and Sellendria. "Are you stupid? You could have killed her. Why did you bring Zannah here?" He looked Sellendria over a second time. "Who are you?" He shifted his eyes to Kyle. "And who are you?"

Zannah cleared her throat, and when she had David's attention, she glanced Kyle's way. "He bit me, so now I'm his bitch. Can we move on to important matters now?"

"Bitch?" Kyle asked, a hint of exasperation in his voice. "You realise we're werewolves and that's the kind of word other Creatures use to insult us?"

She dropped her eyes. "Sorry. I'll try harder to be funny." The guy was way too serious. But then again, so was David. Why did she always go for the serious guys? Maybe she liked teasing them.

David put a hand on his head, staring from one to the other. "Anyone care to fill me in? You know, like how is it possible that Zannah's talking?"

"I'm here too," Zannah said before Kyle, Jimmy or Sellendria could speak, waiting until she had David's attention. She mustered her courage in the form of a deep breath, or as deep as she could manage. It hurt. "Apparently the world is filled with vampires and werewolves and other supernatural Creatures. It was a vampire that attacked us last night, and he was at the hospital not long ago, apparently getting ready to clean up the mess he made when I didn't die. I figured you might be on the hit list too, and despite the fact that I think you're a complete jerk and I hate you, I wanted to warn you to prove I'm not an ass-wipe like you." She glanced at Kyle. "Anything you'd like to add?"

Kyle stared at her with almost the same expression as David did, although with more embarrassment. Jimmy looked like he wanted to laugh while Sellendria smirked. Sellendria leaned closer to Jimmy. "Why didn't you introduce me to your sister before? I really like her."

Weirdly, that made her feel surprisingly good.

Kyle stared at David. "Any questions?"

David's lips formed several words before he found some. "Lots. Who are you and what's really going on?" He glanced at Jimmy before focusing on Sellendria. "Who's she? Haven't I already asked that?"

Sellendria merely raised an eyebrow, completely unfazed. Princess Asskicker, that's for sure.

"Zannah's obviously high on morphine or something," David said. "And anyone stupid enough to take her out of a hospital deserves a long rest in a prison cell. I'm calling an ambulance. I suggest you three be gone when it gets here because I'm calling the police straight afterward."

Zannah glared at David. "Don't be a jerk. I was telling the truth."

He met her eyes. "Vampires and werewolves? I'll believe that when you get up and walk around."

"I'm looking forward to it," she muttered. She'd punch him in the face the moment she could.

The doorbell rang.

"I wouldn't answer that," Kyle said quickly, as Sellendria grasped Jimmy's hand, keeping him still with a slight shake of her head. If vampires and werewolves were real and Sellendria seemed to know all about them, what did that make her? Zannah had thought she was a regular girl at first. A weird girl, considering she was dating her brother, but still human despite her earthy smell. Not anymore. She really did smell wrong.

David gave Kyle a *piss-off* look and opened the door. A man stood there, someone Zannah had never seen before.

"Uh, hi. What can I do for you?" David asked.

"May I come in, please? My name's Jaque."

"No!" Kyle and Sellendria almost shouted in unison to drown out any response from David. Kyle gripped David's shoulder, drawing him back a half step. "Don't invite him in, whatever you do."

Jaque narrowed his eyes at Kyle, sniffing slightly. His expression darkened. The man's scent finally reached Zannah. It had a cold, sharp edge to it that she didn't like at all. David gave Kyle a look. "What do you want, Jaque?"

Jaque returned his gaze to David. "I'm here to give fair warning to your..." He glanced at Kyle before his eyes found Zannah. "Friends."

"Warning?"

Jaque returned his attention to Kyle. "I haven't seen you around, so I'm assuming you're either a feral or part of Samira's crew?"

"Who's Samira?" Zannah asked. Sellendria gave Zannah a warning glance, and despite herself Zannah obeyed and kept quiet.

There was a brief silence when nobody spoke. Jaque broke it. "You've got five minutes to get your asses back on the road and to the south side of town. Take your newly minted bitch with you. We kill ferals around here."

Kyle had been right about that then. She was the only person allowed to call herself a bitch, and when she did, it had far different connotations. "Asshole," she muttered, drawing Jaque's glare, his eyes narrowing slightly. She had the feeling he was very dangerous.

David went to move forward, but Kyle caught him. "Okay, Jaque. I'll call a cab. We'll leave as soon as it arrives. Good enough?"

Jaque held Kyle's gaze for long enough to ensure they all knew who was in control. "I'll be watching."

Kyle slammed the door in Jaque's face and turned to David. "Pack some clothes and get out of town for a few weeks. You don't want any trouble from that lot. I know their type. And whatever you do, don't invite anyone in unless you know them."

"I take it this is bad?" Zannah asked. "Vamp politics?"

He nodded. "Not as bad as it could get. Let's go straight to Kimbriel's house. We'll figure out our next step afterward. Kimbriel's on this side of town, at least. If nothing else, she can protect us and help us get out of town."

"Kimbriel?" Jimmy asked as if he were familiar with the name. Sellendria stared with similar incredulity.

"Who's Kimbriel?" Zannah asked.

The doorbell rang again. Kyle glanced at David. "Remember, don't invite anyone in," he said.

David gave him a filthy look before he opened the door. "Shit!" He jumped back before it was half open, his face going completely white.

"What?" Zannah asked, as she tried to see past David and Kyle.

Kyle turned toward her. He seemed almost as shocked as David. "Jaque's body is on the porch. Someone punched through his back and ripped out his heart." He swallowed. "I didn't even hear them. We're in a lot of trouble."

The scent of blood reached her, overpowering. It had a sharp, icy edge to it, but for all that it was even more enticing than Kyle's. Like a top shelf spirit that she could never afford more than a sniff of.

Kyle closed the door again. "Believe me now?" he asked David, who looked like he was about to retch. Her ex backed up until he hit the wall, and it was probably the only thing keeping him upright.

Zannah felt as sick as David looked. A vampire, murdered just a few metres away? What would happen when the cops got involved? What would they even make of it? Would an autopsy be able to tell the difference between a human and a vampire? The universe had shifted sideways in the last couple of days, and just did so again. She didn't recognise anything anymore.

Kyle met her eyes. "We're getting drawn into something. Local politics, and we'll be the next ones to suffer unless we get out of town." He turned and waved his hand in front of David's face to get his attention. "Your car? We have to go. Now."

David seemed to come to his senses a little, though he still appeared pale. "Keys are on the kitchen bench."

"Good. I'm going to borrow your car so I can get Zannah, Jimmy and Sellendria somewhere safe. I take it you're coming?"

Zannah glanced at her little big brother and his girlfriend. Neither seemed particularly surprised nor bothered by the murder. What the hell had they been up to, if this was normal to them? She met her brother's eyes, questioning, but he just gave her a slight shake of his head. She'd find out. Just not now.

David glanced at the front door and seemed to go whiter. "Yes."

"You're smarter than you look. Let's go. You can drive."

CHAPTER 8

Rake watched from up the street, as far away as he could park and still see the house. He didn't want them to notice him or chance the werewolf might smell Jaque's blood on him and come investigating, but more importantly, he didn't want any of Vincent Morrell's Creatures to see him on this side of town. That would cause complications, the least of which could cost him his life.

The garage door finally lifted from the inside to reveal a short man, the werewolf he'd fought in the alley and who'd taken the girl out of the hospital. Who the hell was he? A Creature, certainly, but he wasn't so sure he was a werewolf anymore. A strangely powerful one, even considering the full moon.

Rake narrowed his eyes and slid lower in his seat. If the dog had shifted form in that alley Rake was certain he'd have been killed, and even with the dog in human form it had been a close match. Too close. A feral dog nearly as strong as a vampire his age? It seemed to be impossible.

Rake didn't have a werewolf's sense of smell, but he was fairly certain the Creature had smelled a little strange for a dog. Perhaps he'd been bred for purpose, like a pit-bull for dogfighting, though what that purpose was he couldn't tell. Except for his strength and speed, he appeared to be a normal dog.

Jaque hadn't seemed to know the dog when he gave the werewolf orders to clear out either, so he wasn't one of Morrell's. He had to be a feral. Unfortunately, he'd bitten the girl who could identify him, giving Rake two problems instead of one. While neither would be a significant problem under most circumstances, he couldn't afford loose ends right now. Blaming them for Jaque's situation would help, but only if they cleared out of town or couldn't speak the truth.

He couldn't even bring his own dogs in to help, and not just because he was on the north side of town and well beyond his territory. There were rules against killing among Creatures. Bodies drew attention, and not just from the human authorities. Dying Creatures drew more attention, and that was a bigger problem. He was in a big mess if he couldn't quietly deal with the ferals or at least run them out of town.

Jaque was his insurance policy if things didn't go well.

Rake stayed low even though the streetlights were coming on, soft pools of light beginning to spread from them. The werewolf cautiously peered up and down the street, his eyes lingering on Rake's distant car. Rake kept low, watching through his steering wheel. After a moment, the werewolf's eyes moved on.

They ignored Jaque's body as they prepared to go, leaving the vampire on the porch and sensibly staying away. Rake hadn't destroyed Jaque's heart, so the body still lived and would be dangerous if they touched it, but not for much longer. A vampire without a heart wouldn't survive beyond dawn. The werewolf seemed to have plenty of experience with vampires, and clearly wasn't stupid enough to take any chances by moving the body.

"Why are you here?" he murmured. Just a casual bystander helping someone in trouble, or something else? He needed more information.

He pulled out his phone and dialed, speaking softly. "Hey," he said. "The dog from last night is still around. Seems he bit the girl I thought I'd killed. Now he's picked up some human companions as well. They're heading somewhere. If it's out of town, I'll call them lucky and let it be. Otherwise, we'll have to deal with it." He didn't want the hassle of disposing of the bodies. The less work he had to do, the better.

He pulled his ear away from the abuse coming through the phone.

"Bullshit!" he hissed back. "I'm not a dog, and certainly not your Creature to command. I'll follow them and try to figure out what they're up to, but that's it. This is your side of town. You need to deal with it if they don't piss off."

He pulled the phone away, wincing at the additional abuse. "Yeah, I love you too," he muttered sarcastically before hanging up.

He stayed low as the werewolf and his companions got into the car, reversed out of the driveway and unsteadily took off down the street, almost bunny hopping. The human was driving, and he seemed nervous, unsurprisingly. He'd probably only just discovered there were Creatures in the world and wasn't enthusiastic about the concept.

If nothing else, Rake had found a weak link.

Kyle gave David the address in a suburb called Charnwood. "How far is it from here?"

"Only five or ten minutes." David glanced over his shoulder at Zannah as if expecting confirmation, but she merely narrowed her eyes at him. David returned his attention to the road. Judging by his expression, he seemed more than a little uncertain of himself. Kyle glanced Zannah's way and found she seemed satisfied with herself, as if torturing David was helping her feel better. It was a tiny bit spiteful, but Kyle didn't like the guy either.

"Just go straight there. No detours," Kyle said.

David glared via the rear-view mirror. "I got it the first time." He was still looking pale and frightened, but seemed to be dealing with it for now. Not well, but dealing. He turned left onto a slightly larger street, and Zannah grimaced at the shift in her bodyweight. She was still in a lot of pain, though she didn't say anything.

Despite the sarcasm and graveyard humour, she was tougher than she probably knew, and more vulnerable than he suspected she'd ever admit to.

Kyle didn't quite have the same sensitive smell of a mortal werewolf, but enough of it to tell David was too scared to try anything stupid, and Zannah too pissed off to admit she was hurting.

Jimmy and Sellendria remained silent, making it seem too quiet. He needed to break the silence. "Doing okay?" Kyle asked Zannah. He didn't want to get attached, but being polite wouldn't hurt.

She winced at a bump in the road. "Alive, if not kicking. The tingling's hurting a lot, so that's awesome. The death threat's bugging me a smidge though."

"Death threat?" David asked. "You mean what happened to that guy on my porch? I can't believe someone's after me."

"Yeah," Zannah answered. "It's all about you. Hey, I think my leg just twitched! Like, voluntarily." Her expression became animated and excited.

Kyle smiled despite himself. She was probably the only girl he'd ever met who would take this so well, though he suspected a lot of what she said was just her way of coping.

He put his head back against the seat and closed his eyes. He hadn't slept much last night, and he had a suspicion tonight wouldn't be much better. Sleep, even a catnap, wouldn't come. Only memories...

...Kyle gasped as air hit his face like a hard slap. He squeezed his eyes shut as painfully bright light, the first he'd seen in decades, seared his vision.

Hard packed earth kept him pinned, far too much of it to let him move, let alone dig himself out, but he could taste air again. The sweet air filled his nose and throat, but only a little considering the crush of dirt and rock on him.

It came with the scent of human flesh. Hunger, a constant dull pain, flared fresh at the scent of humanity. He gritted his teeth, wishing he could take a full breath to clear the pain. Earth crushed his chest though, allowing him only the smallest amount of air, yet it was the most wonderful air he'd ever breathed.

"It's good to see you're finally awake. I've been sitting here for hours." It was a young woman's voice.

Kyle tried to see beyond the glare of light filtering down through the narrow hole above his face, but nothing resolved within the white light.

"You look desiccated."

He swallowed, the movement both painful and exhilarating. It took him three attempts to speak. "Please," he whispered, his painful voice sounding like sand scraping over rock. "Help me." He tried to move, but the hard packed earth felt like stone.

"Help? How?"

The brightness was slowly beginning to reveal shadows. "Thirsty."

"Sure. I can do that."

Liquid rained down on his face, the sweetest, most amazing water he'd ever tasted. He opened his mouth as wide as he could, drinking it in and filling his desiccated stomach until he felt bloated. Maybe two full swallows.

There must have been more in the water than he could taste, because strength returned and his vision cleared.

A young woman's face stared down at him, a slight frown marring very ordinary features. She could be any village girl from the region. Unremarkable. "I'd like to help if you'll let me, but I'd prefer it if you didn't try to kill me or anyone else. That would be awkward."

He tried to remember how he got here. He'd been a smith. Married. Tortured. Mostly all he remembered was pain from hunger and despair. "What happened?"

She glanced away as if looking into memory, her brows crinkling a little. "It appears you cut your fist punching a werewolf in the face which infected you with lycanthropy, and then a vampire forced you to drink his tainted blood. The result seems to be a hybrid of some sort. Never thought it was possible, as magic rarely mixes well. I suspect it was a combination of the aggressiveness of the new lycanthropy infection and the weakness of the vampire blood. They seem to have reached an equilibrium despite the fact they cut out your heart. That alone should have killed you. Makes little sense, but then, magic rarely does."

He didn't feel very alive, and stared at her as if she were an angel. She had blonde hair and while not beautiful, there was something about her eyes he'd never even seen in Taenorah or any other woman. More than intelligence or certainty or determination. It seemed to be a sense of assurance and a complete lack of fear or concern. He didn't believe a word of what she'd said though, and yet here he was, buried, and buried deep. The hole she spoke through was maybe six inches wide.

"Can you get me out of here?"

"That depends on you."

What did that mean? "Please? I can't move."

"I'm disinclined to release something as powerful as you seem to be, but I wanted to at least talk with you."

Powerful? His sense of desperation was growing stronger now he could taste freedom in the air. "Please? I'll give you anything."

She seemed to consider that for a long moment. "Anything? How about a promise?"

He might be trapped, but he wasn't stupid. "What promise?"

"Promise me you won't turn anyone."

Turn anyone? "I've got no intention of doing such a thing, whatever that means."

Even with what little he could see of her, he could tell she shook her head. "That wasn't a promise. Promise me you won't make any Creatures like yourself. If you do, even accidentally, promise me you'll kill them."

Creatures like himself? He guessed he was buried and still alive, so perhaps he was some kind of Creature. "I promise to make no Creatures like me, and I promise to kill any I accidentally make."

She watched him for a moment, considering. She didn't seem to take his promise at face value. "If you break either promise, I get to return you to your grave and fix any problems you create. Fair?"

That didn't sound promising, but it was better than staying here. "Sure." Anything to get out. "I'm fine with that."

Earth exploded upward in a hail of rocks and dirt. He closed his eyes, expecting it to rain back down on him, but there was nothing but the blessed release of pressure.

"No Creatures," she repeated. "Something like you has the potential to bring on the apocalypse."

"No Creatures. I promise."...

...The car rocked as it turned into a driveway. Kyle looked around, barely remembering where he was. He'd made a promise, and he had to keep it. Kimbriel wasn't the forgiving kind. Well, that was his impression of her. Uncompromising was a more appropriate term.

Zannah stared at him, her body still slumped, but with a smile on her lips and her eyes bright. "Guess what? I can move my pinkie!"

She seemed so sweet. How was he supposed to kill her if it came to it?

CHAPTER 9

ZANNAH STARED in mild dismay at the nondescript house through David's grimy car window. Ugly chocolate-coloured bricks backed a dried lawn that seemed to be more weeds than grass. A dying carport at the side seemed to be held up with little more than peeling paint, and a faded metal garage just past it in the backyard had probably been brown once, but had been baked over successive hot summers until it looked more dirty than brown. A few rust streaks ran down the front to the left of the decrepit-looking roller door.

Three cars were parked on the front lawn, two with weeds growing out from under them. One had cobwebs stretching from the driver's side mirror to the door. The two with weeds were also decorated with bird droppings, while the third, an ugly beige thing which might actually get used occasionally, had paint peeling off the roof and bonnet.

To say she wasn't impressed was overstating her opinion. "Your powerful sorceress friend lives here?" Zannah asked, trying to sound like she wasn't looking down her nose at something brown and steaming. "I've seen better-kept rubbish bins."

"Uh-huh," said Kyle softly in a tone suggesting non-committal agreement with her. "This is the right address though." He looked like he wanted to double-check his information.

"This place is like, I don't know, three streets from mine," Zannah added. "The local high school's just a couple of turns up the road, yet it's like we crossed into a different country."

"This is the place," Sellendria said, getting out. "Everything you see is an illusion. It's actually quite nice."

"Illusion?" Zannah asked.

"Oh yeah, I forgot about the illusion," Jimmy said as he got out of the car as if illusions were normal things, giving Kyle the room to do the same. He ducked down so he could see her through the car door. "I can only see it now if I concentrate. I guess I've spent too much time here."

Zannah glanced at Kyle, his expression of disbelief matching her own. "Do you know about illusions?" she asked.

"Not so much," Kyle said as got out of the car and came around to open her door.

"Such a gentleman," she said with a raised eyebrow at David, who still sat behind the wheel as if scared to move. Considering everything he'd seen, she didn't really blame him. That much. She was scared too.

Jimmy was already out and holding Sellendria's hand. She'd trust Jimmy to pick her up considering how big and strong he was now, but he seemed hesitant to interfere, like the whole matter was well beyond him.

"I would have opened the door for you," David said a little too late, but it sounded forced.

"Of course you would have, like you always did before."

He frowned. "He got there first."

Pain shot through Zannah's neck as Kyle reached in and his thick arms jostled her, but she bit her lip and managed not to cry out. The pain settled into a throbbing sensation down her left arm and shoulder, but she couldn't feel much more of her body beyond the ridiculously painful pins and needles.

"Sorry," Kyle said as he lifted her out and carried her to the front porch.

David hurried to get out of the car and ahead of them to ring the doorbell. Jimmy and his girlfriend hung slightly behind, heads close and whispering. About what? What were they up to?

The doorbell didn't work, forcing David to knock.

"What do you know about all this?" Zannah asked Jimmy, raising her voice so it would carry. Obligingly, Kyle turned so she could see him.

Rather than answer, Jimmy glanced at Sellendria. His girlfriend remained silent. "Err..." Jimmy tried. "Um-"

A huge bald man with dark skin and broad shoulders opened the door. Kyle turned back so Zannah could see him properly. The man looked them over, frowning at David. "Who are you?" he asked before noticing Jimmy and Sellendria. He raised an eyebrow at them.

What was her brother into? Was he a werewolf too? No, he didn't smell like one. What about Sellendria? And why was Zannah just beginning to find out about all this supernatural stuff?

"Uh, I'm David. I'm Zannah's-"

"Ex," she cut in. She'd grill Jimmy later. "He dumped me at the hospital when he found out I was going to be a quadriplegic. Other than that, and the huge yellow streak down his back, he's a really great guy."

"What?" David asked. "I'm not a coward-"

Anger flared, hot and almost physically painful. "You fucking-well ran to try to save your own skin when that vampire came for us," Zannah said coldly. "Only we didn't know he was a vampire. I remember."

The big bald guy kept his attention on David, his gaze direct and unsettling. "Yes, you did," the man said. "It's in your aura. The cowardice, that is. Come in, Kyle and Zannah. You're welcome too, David. My name's Mal. I assist Kimbriel."

Kyle carried Zannah in and sat her on an ugly three-seater lounge, the purple fabric worn and stained and smelling of old tobacco and sweat. Yuck. It had probably been taken from the local dumpster or saved from landfill. She couldn't figure out why anyone would bother. It wasn't worth the price to cart it away. Was everything inside the house an illusion too? If it was, it was convincing.

A dangerously-balanced television rested on a broken stand. The stand had been clamped to a coffee table made from an old door and a couple of wooden boxes.

The curtains were yellowed lace, backed by ancient venetian blinds that had probably been installed soon after the house was built. The carpet was worn and threadbare in places, and there was an odour to the place which suggested it hadn't been cleaned in months, if not years.

It made the modest home she'd grown up in seem like a palace.

"I smell your brother and his girlfriend," Kyle said softly to her, doing a slow turn as if he didn't quite trust his eyes. "They definitely know Kimbriel. Sellendria spends a lot of time here. I suspect she may even live here."

"Yeah, I guessed that already," Zannah said. "This is all wrong, though. It's like... what someone wants us to see."

David looked around, frowning. "We're supposed to be safe here?" he asked with a hint of disdain, if not downright disgust.

Zannah couldn't help but feel embarrassed by his presence. What had she ever seen in him? The place was run down, certainly, but despite that it had a comfortable, homely feel. It was a bit like one of those cafes she enjoyed going to while doing a group assignment, the kind of place set up in a run down old shop with half-renovated walls and concrete floors. There were always second-hand lounges around old coffee tables, often out the front and under shelter. In winter they'd bring out gas-fired patio heaters and rugs while you worked and drank your coffee.

"Yes, David. You're safe here," said a woman's voice. Despite the youthfulness, there was an air of maturity in it, and a hint of disapproval.

Although the voice came from behind, it had to be Kimbriel. For someone rumoured to be so powerful, she sounded distinctly underwhelming. Normal. Human. She remained behind the couch where Zannah couldn't see, damn it.

Zannah hadn't heard the woman enter either. She had to be content with seeing her shadowed shape on the screen of the blank television. From the reflection, Zannah could tell Kimbriel was short, but that's about all. Mind you, with her own legs out of commission, everyone was taller than Zannah.

"Kimbriel!" Kyle grinned and rushed around the lounge. She heard them embrace and saw it mirrored in the television screen's reflection. Kyle had finally found someone he topped for height. Good for him. "It's been far too long."

"Buttering me up for the inevitable begging and pleading, huh?"

There was a drawn-out moment of silence. "Maybe just a little. Do you blame me?"

"You know I don't like to interfere, but I've been watching."

They embraced again, fabric against fabric, but only briefly. The woman had a peculiar smell Zannah couldn't place. An old smell, but not grandma old. If anything, it suggested experience, weird as that was.

"So you already know what happened?" Kyle asked. He didn't sound surprised about it, more like he'd expected it.

Zannah saw Kimbriel's reflection nod. "You should have killed her at the hospital, Kyle. You've put us both in a very awkward situation."

"What?" Zannah asked with sudden fear, and couldn't help the sense of betrayal she felt. Where had Jimmy and Sellendria gone? They hadn't followed her and Kyle in. "Kill me? That's not nice."

Kyle spoke up for her, at least. "Come on, Kimbriel. You know, I've always had a soft spot for tall girls. Surely you can make an exception just this once? I've honoured my promise for hundreds of years now, and... and I really don't want to kill her."

Fuck. They were serious. Where the hell was her brother? She felt trapped and exposed. "I don't want him to kill me either. Him or anyone else," Zannah said. "Please don't kill me."

She almost screamed for Jimmy. David was standing off to the side, staring as if too shocked to contribute a word.

"Why don't you introduce me then?" Kimbriel asked.

"Of course."

The sound of footsteps traced a path around the lounge, and when Kimbriel finally walked into Zannah's field of vision, Zannah felt a little underwhelmed. She not only sounded ordinary, but she looked ordinary. Completely miss-able. She'd guessed her age wrong, too. Kimbriel barely looked like she was in her twenties, and wouldn't have any trouble passing for a teenager. The woman was even shorter than she'd expected, stick thin too, and her blonde hair was making escape attempts from the ponytail she kept it in.

Still, she had a certain presence, although that could have come from Kyle's deference more than anything to do with her physical appearance.

"Um, hi," Zannah said. "Please excuse me for not getting up or shaking your hand. I'm a bit broken."

Kimbriel gave Kyle a look, eyebrows raised.

"She caught me by surprise too," Kyle said.

Kimbriel returned her gaze to Zannah. "You seem to be in remarkably good spirits considering I can't allow you to live."

Zannah hid her fears, though she was freaking out on the inside. She really wished Jimmy were here. "Ah, pfft. You love me already," she said with false bravado, though her heart was racing.

She'd found out a long time ago that people liked people who seemed happy and cheerful, and right now it was time to go nuts on the concept. She wished she could shrug despite the fear she hid.

"A few hours ago I was wishing I had the strength to jump from a window, so the fact that I'm no longer in a hospital bed attached to tubes and wires is a step up." Fuck, she was rambling and talking too fast. Time to shut up.

"Meaning?"

Zannah thought a smile might be trying to play on Kimbriel's lips. Meaning what? There was an opening there, and she jumped at it. "I kind of want to live now. Prospects, you see." She gave David a look, and he had the grace to flush red and turn away.

Kimbriel nodded as if in understanding. "Yet I can't allow you to survive. You're far too dangerous."

"Dangerous? I can't even stand." There was something in Kimbriel's eyes though, a reluctance to state the problem. It seemed to be another opening of some kind. Zannah took a gamble and played on the guilt trip. "So, who's going to do it? You or Kyle?"

Kimbriel seemed slightly disappointed by the response.

"Kyle, of course. It's his mistake."

Zannah glanced at Kyle and saw the pain there. He clearly didn't want to, but she sensed it was more reluctance than defiance. Oh shit. She swallowed her fear, trying to figure out exactly what was going on. She needed to buy some time and get them talking. Maybe they'd drop a hint about how she could indefinitely defer her death sentence. "Mind if I speak to my Mum first? Maybe tell her a few sweet lies about how I'm in a government research facility helping scientists study the effects of puppy therapy? She'd like that."

Kimbriel sighed, clearly recognising the emotional manipulation and not moved by it. "Better a clean break. Kyle?"

Zannah laughed with false bravado. "Break. My neck... never mind."

Kimbriel just stared. God, where'd her sense of humour go? Zannah studied the woman's face, certain she saw compassion there, but no compromise to go with it. She wasn't hearing what she'd wanted to hear from Zannah, which meant there was still an opening. What, though?

She decided to take the direct approach and ask. "So how do I change your mind? That's what this chat's about, right?"

Kyle gave Zannah a slight nod, and he seemed to be relieved by the change in the conversation's direction.

"Let's not rule the possibility out."

Relief coursed through her, tempered by the fear she might not figure it out, but it was better than what she had a moment before. She needed time to think. "Great, because I'd hate Kyle to feel so guilty and heartbroken for the rest of his life that he'd probably want to kill himself too."

Kimbriel actually let a smile slip at that.

"Oh, come on," Zannah added. "You know what I'm asking. What do you want from me? If you don't tell me, I'm sure Kyle will curl into a ball and rock himself to sleep every night knowing he missed out on my thank you kiss. Think about Kyle. He needs me."

"Give her a chance. Please, Kimbriel," Kyle said. "Let me explain the rules."

Kimbriel faced him. "You promised you'd make no Creatures," she said. Kimbriel returned her focus to Zannah. "I'm sorry this happened to you, but I can't risk more Creatures like Kyle. I freed him on the condition he didn't make more of his kind, which presents a problem for you."

"You're going to kill her? Seriously?" David said, butting in.

At that moment, Zannah actually felt grateful to him. He wasn't a complete jerk, at least. Just an asshole.

Kimbriel ignored David and addressed Kyle. "Vampires have to drain their victims and make them drink their own blood in order to turn them. Doing so weakens them, sometimes for decades, as it dilutes their distilled lifeforce. They don't take such risks lightly. Werewolves transfer their curse through a bite, but their victims rarely survive the attack, so they don't often procreate. You, though, you're as controlled as any vampire, you don't go crazy on the full moon, and a single bite will almost certainly turn a victim. The potential to spread your kind is akin to that of a virus. Both you and Zannah could set off a chain reaction that would turn the vast majority of the world's population into what you are in a matter of months. The answer is no."

"What if Zannah makes the same promise I did?"

She shook her head. "Pointless. You can't be forced to keep it despite the fact you're a Creature, which is what I feared. She'd already be dead if you'd been bound to your promises as other Creatures are."

That seemed to anger him. "I'm not shirking my promise. I came to you because-"

"Hey? Don't I get a say?" Zannah asked. "It's my life you're talking about." She was certain she'd missed a chance to change Kimbriel's mind, but the option was still there. She was sure of it. What did

Kimbriel want then? No Creatures. How could Zannah guarantee that?

"I think that's fair," David added. "It's Zannah's life you're debating."

"Thank you, David," Kimbriel replied. "But please keep your opinion to yourself."

Zannah cleared her throat, realising for the first time that it no longer hurt to speak, but it gave her no comfort. "But Kyle said you could help me. So why not fix me and add some mumbo-jumbo whammy magic that stops me from being a virus?"

Kimbriel narrowed her eyes at Kyle. "He said that, did he?" Her body language changed, but Zannah couldn't work out why.

"Well, can you fix me?"

"I guess that depends on your definition of 'fix you'. Dead is fixed. Is that what you had in mind?"

The front door opened and Jimmy walked in, Sellendria behind him. Finally, a real ally or two.

CHAPTER 10

"Zannah?" Jimmy asked. Sellendria stood by his side, their fingers intertwined.

"Jimmy?" Zannah replied, not sure what else to say, but certain she didn't want to continue her conversation with Kimbriel without knowing more about what the woman might want. Was she even a woman? Human?

Jimmy reluctantly let go of Sellendria's hand and sat beside her. "What's happening?" he asked.

Zannah really missed being able to shrug, but it was the pit of uncertainty and fear in her stomach that bothered her more. "You know. Coffee. Cake. Kimbriel told Kyle to kill me. They're thinking of ordering a pizza later."

"Kimbriel said *what*?" Jimmy's face went white. He stood and turned on Kimbriel. "Not going to happen. She's my *sister*!" Jimmy held out a hand for Sellendria, as if her presence could somehow shield him from what he'd just heard. Despite what he'd said and his size, he looked like he wanted to back away from the diminutive woman. It wasn't exactly fear, but he clearly wasn't about to take her on.

Despite Jimmy's reaction, Kimbriel seemed bemused, a hint of a smile on her lips. "You know the rules, Jimmy. We've played this game before, haven't we?" The words sounded dangerous, layered with hidden meaning.

The tone as much as what she said caught Zannah by surprise, and that pit of fear in her stomach opened further. Their mother would die if something happened to Jimmy too.

"Jimmy? What did you do?" Sellendria asked, a little too quietly.

So she didn't know either? Zannah could see guilt or something like it in her brother's face. He dropped his eyes, refusing to look at either of them. "Did you make a deal with Kimbriel?" Zannah asked. When did he do it, and what were the consequences? Had he become a Creature too? Fuck. What if he had?

Instead of addressing them, Kimbriel glanced at Sellendria. "Surely you haven't forgotten how everything works?"

Sellendria pursed her lips, but didn't speak even as she raised her chin slightly. She'd obviously made some kind of bargain with Kimbriel too, though she seemed upset that Jimmy had done the same. Zannah glanced around. They'd all been keeping secrets from each other.

"What have you done?" Zannah asked again. "Is this like one of those 'be careful what you wish for' bargains?"

Jimmy glanced at Kimbriel. "Please, Kimbriel. This is my sister's life."

Kimbriel gave him a long look before turning back to Zannah, an eyebrow raised. "Well? Nothing to ask me?"

How had the conversation turned so quickly? She still had no answers, yet Kimbriel expected her to make a request based on a guess? "You want something from me, but... what exactly?" Zannah asked a little hesitantly, hoping to stall for time.

Kimbriel smiled, but it wasn't a comforting smile. "Not just from you."

Baffled, Zannah looked from one person to the other, even Mal, who stood quietly in the corner without contributing. "What are you asking for, Kimbriel?" Kyle said. "Please, just tell us."

Kimbriel looked like a teacher forced to deal with a disappointing and slightly daft student, but it was Sellendria who spoke. "She can't see the consequences of her actions. That's the problem. Fear of what she might accidently do."

Kimbriel glanced at Kyle. "You should know that. I can only see the consequences if you ask, and even then, only some. You've told me what you don't want. What do you want? Be specific, and be prepared, because there's almost always a price and I won't be able to tell you what it is beyond a guess."

Jimmy knelt before Zannah, biting the inside of his cheek as he took her hand like a marriage suitor, a disturbing thought considering he was her brother. "It's not a trick. She wants to help, but fears the consequences. If she messes with the universe, it just may mess back." His expression suggested he was talking from experience.

What the hell had he been through then? What had happened to make her brother so cautious and serious? "But you trust her?" Zannah asked softly. If Jimmy trusted her, then that was good enough for Zannah.

Before he could answer, Kimbriel put a hand on Jimmy's shoulder, drawing him to stand again. He towered over the woman, but he seemed the smaller in other ways. "You knew what you wanted, Jimmy, and you wanted it so desperately you were willing to pay any cost," she said, glancing at Sellendria. "Was she worth it?"

"Yes," Jimmy said without hesitation. His hand found Sellendria's again. She squeezed back, but her face was full of confusion and apprehension. It was clear they were going to talk later.

"What did Kimbriel give you?" Zannah asked, worried for him. "It was a love potion, wasn't it? You dumb shit!" Could it be that simple? She glanced at Kimbriel. "Was it a love potion?" How the hell else would Sellendria have fallen for Jimmy? He was a clumsy, annoying oaf. Sellendreia was a graceful, magical being from another universe. It made no sense otherwise.

"I can't mess with emotions or thoughts, at least not without that person's permission. Zannah, I'm trying to help you, but I..." Kimbriel took a deep breath. "I'm causing issues even hinting at possibilities. There are costs for that, and I'll be the one to pay them."

"What do you mean?" Zannah asked, a little worried now.

"There's already a filter on the future. I can't even see what might happen tonight, let alone a decade from now. Neither you nor Kyle are important in the grand scheme of things, but you're both good people and I want to help. What do you want, Zannah? Really want?"

Kyle shifted restlessly, and it was clear he didn't know what to say either.

Rather than charge ahead with a quick response like she'd normally do, Zannah took a moment to think it through. The answer came quicker than she'd expected. "The issue is Kyle's ability to make more of his... our kind, isn't it?" Zannah asked. "You want to ensure it doesn't happen again?"

She watched Kimbriel's face for confirmation. The woman gave nothing away, but Zannah had the feeling she was on the mark. Kyle sat next to Zannah, his presence comforting despite the fact she barely knew him. He had a distracted frown when he looked at Kimbriel.

"You foresaw this, didn't you? You've always known it would come to this, or something like it."

Kimbriel's expression was gentle. "My hindsight is perfect, but the further I look into the future the fuzzier it gets. I assumed you'd eventually find yourself in a situation like this."

"So you could have prevented it?" he asked a little harshly. "Me biting Zannah, I mean? Why didn't you do or say something?" Kyle asked.

"I'm not a God, Kyle. I can't force my will on the universe, let alone an individual."

"But-"

Her expression softened. "Kyle, you're a half-Creature, existing outside of every community you're almost a part of. I did nothing to prevent this, but only because I foresaw Zannah's death." She met Jimmy's eyes, and then Zannah's. "You're alive because I called for Kyle when I realised the chances were good your paths would cross, but I didn't steer either of you to it. The alternative was you and David dying at the hands of a vampire."

"You broke all your own rules?" Zannah asked, surprised at how much hope carried in her voice. "So you're not going to make Kyle kill me?"

Kimbriel met her eyes, almost as if reading Zannah's thoughts. "I won't tolerate you creating more Creatures like yourselves."

"What will it take?" Kyle asked without hesitation. "To ensure we can't?"

Wow, he really was batting for her. She resisted an urge to raise an eyebrow in David's direction. "So can you... neuter our bites?" Zannah asked. "Make sure it doesn't happen again?" She and Kyle would be the only two of their kind, but she was fine with that. She'd never really felt included in any group before, anyway.

"I can't do anything without your permission," Kimbriel replied. "And only if you ask. Just be careful what you ask for. Say it wrong and you could end up being turned into a frog."

A frog? She glanced at Jimmy for confirmation. "She's kidding about the frog thing, isn't she?"

He gave a hesitant shrug. "Maybe?" He didn't look confident.

Could she really turn someone into a frog? Zannah looked at the diminutive woman with newfound respect and apprehension. "Are you a genie?"

Kimbriel laughed, and it felt like a small victory to Zannah. "No."

"But you did engineer this, right?"

Kimbriel glanced at Kyle. "I've already said too much. Until this is resolved my foresight is useless. What are you asking for?"

"Oh," Zannah whispered, glancing at her brother in the hope he might offer some inspiration. It had started to make sense in a weird way, at least. "Can someone at least explain the rules?" she asked. Zannah's mind was already racing. "Like if I asked you to heal my broken neck you could do that without any problems, but I'd have to trust you?"

"I can only guess what you'll be satisfied with, but your neck will completely heal by the next full moon without any intervention from me. Would you like it healed before that?"

"The next time I need a lawyer I'm coming to you," Zannah said softly, slightly discouraged despite the hope she might be walking soon.

"Kimbriel," Sellendria began. "Why not just tell Zannah what you want from her and Kyle? You've already said your foresight's useless."

"I already told them. There can be no more Creatures of their kind."

"But if I get my wish wrong you could sew our mouths shut, right?" Zannah asked. "What if I promise not to bite anyone? Would that clear Kyle's promise so you won't make him kill me?"

"No."

The frog thing weighed a little more heavily on her. She raised her chin, trying to think everything through. What difference would it really make? If Kimbriel wanted to mess her up, Zannah doubted she could do anything to prevent it. "Fine. You have my permission to ensure I won't pass on through my bite whatever curse thingy Kyle gave me, so long as no werewolf-vampire hybrids are harmed or altered in the fulfilling of this permission slip."

She could have sworn Kimbriel wanted to smile despite a frown creasing her brow.

Sellendria leaned close to Jimmy. "Your sister's... odd," she whispered.

Zannah took it as a compliment.

"Kyle?" Kimbriel asked. "It's both or none."

"I can trust you, right?"

She raised an eyebrow. "I trusted you, didn't I?"

He agreed with a nod. "I really don't know how to phrase it any better. What Zannah said goes for me too. Good enough?"

"So long as it's your choice." There was a huge chasm left unspoken.

"Sure."

Kimbriel crouched before them and took a hand each. The movement sent a jolt of pain though Zannah's neck, but it eased off after a few seconds.

"You're not going to do the frog thing on us, are you?" Zannah asked. "I'm a little nervous about that. I don't think my wish ruled that out."

This time Kimbriel did smile. "No alterations, so no frogs Zannah. I suspect your brother wouldn't forgive me if I did."

Kimbriel concentrated for a moment. Zannah felt another jolt, this time like an electric shock, and then Kimbriel released her hand. Kyle's too.

Zannah waited, but she didn't feel any different. "That's it?"

"No werewolf-vampire hybrids were harmed or altered in the process."

So what exactly did she do then? "I don't suppose you'd mind fixing my neck too? I'd really appreciate it."

"I could do that, but only because you asked so nicely. Kyle?"

Kyle stood to allow Kimbriel room. Kimbriel sat in Kyle's place and put her hands on Zannah's cheeks. "This might tickle a bit."

Agony flashed through her entire body. She gasped, unable to exhale. The entire world seemed to go dark for a moment, and when she came around Kyle was holding her upright and Jimmy kneeling before her.

"Oh shit," she whispered. Her entire body trembled. She felt sweaty and nauseous. "I think I need a spew bucket."

"That's your nerves reconnecting all at once. It'll pass in a moment."

Zannah took a few deep breaths until she felt blood return to her face. She lifted a hand, forgetting that a moment before, she couldn't. "Hey, look at that. Can someone help me with this brace? I don't suppose you could magic me up some decent clothes too? Hospital smocks are so last night." She felt seriously out of sorts.

Sellendria helped her with the brace as Jimmy moved out of the way. "I have some dresses you can choose from," the strange smelling girl said.

"Dresses?" Zannah asked in dismay. "Can I get a corset, white gloves and a matching lace umbrella too?"

Sellendria paused, glancing questioningly at Jimmy.

"Sarcasm," he said. "I don't think she's worn a dress since she was six."

"I see. I have other clothes you can borrow. Something might fit," Sellendria said as she ripped the Velcro straps back. Zannah was free within a minute.

"Wow. You've got no idea how good that feels." She cricked her neck. "Feeling feels good. A dress will do fine if that's all that'll fit me, thanks."

She arched her back and stood. It felt like she'd never been hurt - no aches, no tenderness, no lack of coordination. Sellendria was tall, but Zannah was a little taller and far more solid. "Thanks, Kimbriel. In fact, I feel totally human. You didn't hit a full-blown reset button, did you?"

"No. Just compulsion. If you accidentally pass your... condition on, you'll be compelled to kill that person. If you fail to kill them, you'll kill yourself and pass your compulsion onto whoever you turned. I couldn't alter you, so I had to tie compulsion into the curse."

"What the crap?" Zannah lost her smile. It equated to Kyle's promise all over again, only this time with a big stick.

CHAPTER 11

DAVID SHIFTED his weight with an unexpected pang of regret as he watched the two young women disappear up the hallway so Zannah could choose a dress. He wanted her back, but he might have to wait until she got over her issues. It's not like she wouldn't have cut it off with him if he'd broken his neck.

He met Jimmy's eyes, but Zannah's brother returned a glare which didn't feel all that far from a physical blow. Considering how big the kid was, David did the wise thing and ignored the clear challenge in Jimmy's stare.

Mal, the big man, had disappeared, though David hadn't seen him go, but he noticed Kimbriel walking around the lounge and into the kitchen. He hesitated, but decided to follow her. Maybe she could sort out Zannah for him.

When he walked into the kitchen Kimbriel was standing behind a horrid lime-green kitchen bench which probably dated back to the sixties or seventies, though it was in good condition for its age with only a few scratches. The cupboards themselves had burnt orange doors, and the fridge was old and rounded and yellowed with age. The fridge probably predated the kitchen. He was surprised it still worked.

Kimbriel watched him curiously, as if seeing something nobody else could. It was a disturbing feeling and gave him the creeps. There was disdain in her expression too, though he couldn't understand why. It's not like he'd done anything to her.

He glanced around and tried to hide his distaste. He had no idea why such a powerful woman would choose to live in a place like this, though he'd heard something about it all being an illusion which was utter bullshit. He knew the suburb, and this place was in keeping with it, though on the crappier side of things. Zannah didn't live far from here.

He looked Kimbriel over again, curious now. Small. Petite. Blonde. Young, or at least she appeared young. If there was an illusion here, that was probably it. He'd seen her fix Zannah's neck so she could probably tweak her own appearance. What was her play in all this? Why help any of them? She had an agenda and he intended to figure it out.

She smiled warmly, surprising him. Zannah had been the only person that seemed to see through the hard protective shell he put up, so he guessed Kimbriel wasn't too bad after all.

"Zannah has you pegged as a heartless moron. I guess you're just a heartless asshole."

He felt his jaw drop at the insult, shocked and surprised anyone would be so rude. "What's that supposed to mean? You don't even know me," he said.

What if she could read minds and didn't like the way he dissed her home in his thoughts? He tried not to think of anything he didn't want her to know, like the collection of porn magazines he kept in the box in his wardrobe. "Can you read minds?" he asked, trying not to think of anything else he didn't want her to know, like the porn he watched online.

"I see the past, the present, and sometimes the future, but not your thoughts, David. I can read body language pretty well though."

At least his thoughts were safe from her prying. "What happens now?" he asked with relief. "If the world really is full of supernatural Creatures, what are the ones after us going to do now?"

Her expression gave away nothing. "I can barely see what's in front of me at the moment, let alone a clear path forward."

"What about me and Zannah then? How am I supposed to get back with her if she's some werewolf thingy? Are you just going to let her leave with me after we saw what you did?"

Kimbriel gave him a puzzled look. "You're both free to do as you wish."

"We can leave?"

"Front door's that way. Watch out for vampires and werewolves on the way out. I'm sure they'd love to snack on you. You're probably all they're after, really." The last was said with a good amount of sarcasm.

It was like she was intentionally trying to piss him off. "I didn't believe in all this shit a day ago."

"Neither did Zannah. She handled it pretty well."

"Yeah, but I got dragged into it when I didn't need to be. It's not right. How am I supposed to have a relationship with her if she's messed up?"

Kimbriel pursed her lips.

What was wrong with this woman? It was a fact. Zannah was cursed in some supernatural way.

"Most humans like you forget about the supernatural quickly enough. A month from now this will all be a hazy dream, if that. You don't have to worry about the trauma you're experiencing."

"Trauma?" He didn't have trauma. He had a girlfriend that needed a dose of cure-all to make her the way she was supposed to be again. "I have a question."

She leaned on the counter as if she'd been expecting it. "Of course you do."

"Could you, I don't know, lift the curse and make Zannah human again?"

"Sure, but only under the right circumstances."

He hadn't expected a straight answer, and it probably showed in his expression. He waited for her to continue, but she said nothing more. Annoyed, he took a deep breath. He seemed to rub people the wrong way, but suspected it was because they were all morons. "What circumstances?"

"She didn't ask. There's nothing more I could do." She picked up her tea and took a sip.

He tried to reason out her line of thinking. "So why didn't you just tell her you could make her normal again? She probably didn't realise you could fix her."

"You saw her walking around, didn't you? She's fixed."

"But... you could have made her properly human again! Normal."

Her expression hardened along with her tone. "She didn't ask." Her words were clipped, the tone precisely measured.

He really didn't like the patronising way she spoke. "I'm asking for her! Make her human again! I want her back the way she was."

"You're assuming Zannah cares about what you want?" Her sweet tone didn't match the words.

David glared in impotent anger before stalking out of the house, ignoring Jimmy and Kyle as he left. Outside, he stomped to his car and angrily pulled his car keys from his pocket, determined to sort out Zannah's problems when these idiots weren't around. What did he want with a stupid werewolf for a girlfriend, anyway? If he couldn't have her as a human, he didn't want her. At least that was decided. He'd talk her into getting Kimbriel to fix her properly later.

He heard a noise behind him and spun, but a fist thumped into his temple before he saw anyone. He dropped, legless. His head was spinning as his attacker took his own car keys and hauled him up by his shirt, threw him over a broad shoulder and carried him around to the boot.

Moaning in pain, he heard the boot pop open before he got dumped in, the top slamming down hard over him. As he lay moaning, the car reversed out of the driveway, and it was only with the onset of panic that he regained enough sense to thump uselessly on the roof. They didn't drive far. Maybe a few blocks. He kicked and thumped the entire way.

When the boot popped open, a fist slammed into his jaw.

Fearing for his life, he struggled as the man hauled him out of the car. He tried to get a look at his face to identify him later, but David got unceremoniously shoved into a smaller boot before the top slammed down, confining him in an even smaller space. He thumped and yelled until they drove off. He swore, fighting down panic and fear. It was all Zannah's fault. If she hadn't come to his house none of this would have happened.

They were going to kill him for sure. Probably eat him alive.

Taenorah slammed on the brakes, the Porsche's safety systems preventing a slide as the car jerked to a stop. She stared at the body across the street.

"The bastard wasn't lying," she whispered.

"Who?"

She gave the werewolf beside her a glare, silencing him before he could ask anything else. Partially hidden by shrubs and the darkness of evening, a body lay on a porch, its heart dangling from wind chimes.

"Jaque," she said under her breath, getting out and slamming the door.

Ferguson followed without the door slam. "Shit," the werewolf muttered the moment he caught the scent of blood. Taenorah gave the big dog another glare before walking across the road.

It really was Jaque. The smell of his blood kindled her hunger like a shark entering a feeding frenzy. She hadn't fed in days. If a human chanced to jog past, they'd be in some serious danger. She could have waited a moment until she calmed down, but approached regardless, risking the life of any human who appeared.

Ferguson, a huge dog who spent at least a couple of hours a day in the gym, was wise enough to keep his distance. Fortunately, werewolf blood had all the appeal of rotting seafood stinking out a bin in summer.

"Want me to look inside the house?" he asked, knowing she couldn't enter uninvited. Some strange quirk of a werewolf's nature prevented them entering a home when they changed form, but not as a human. The rules affecting other Creatures didn't seem to apply to them, at least not consistently. "There's quite a few scents out here. Hard to tell who might have done this."

She took a deep breath to try to control herself. "It was south siders trying to stir up trouble." She threw him her car keys. "Report in and explain what happened. I'll deal with Jaque."

The werewolf seemed about to question her, but another glare sent him jogging to her car. Once he was gone, she unstrung Jaque's heart from the wind chimes and stuffed the bloody mess through the hole in the back of his ribs.

Swearing at the muck on her sleeve, she pulled a pocket knife and jabbed it into her wrist, wincing at the pain before letting her blood dribble over the gaping wound. Very slowly it began to close over, the edges knitting themselves together.

This kind of damage would take weeks to heal. She could have just stuffed the heart back in and waited for him to regenerate on his own, but then Morrell would question her loyalty. He didn't like having his soldiers down.

While she waited, she used the tap to wash his stale, coagulating blood off her hands, and then ripped her sleeves off. She stuffed them in Jaque's pockets so he could dispose of the mess later, and then began pacing back and forth. About two minutes later, Jaque sucked in a breath.

"Oh, crap!" he said, his voice horse. "What hit me?"

"I'm not sure, but whoever it was tore out your heart. You're lucky they didn't kill you properly."

"South siders?" He winced, his pinched features hollowed out like a desiccated corpse.

"Probably, but without proof we'll be struggling to justify any retaliation. There's too many scents for my dog to identify the attacker."

Jacque winced as he carefully sat up and looked around. "Your dog? Ferguson? The big recruit?"

"Yeah. I sent him to report. He'll return in a bit, or he'd better, if he knows what's good for him. Your car nearby?"

"Yeah. A dozen doors up. There's a place for sale - looks like the owners have already moved out." He stretched, wincing, blood all over the back of his shirt. "Fuck that hurts. A human could take me down with a glare right now."

Taenorah helped him balance with a hand under his elbow. "Head home and get something to eat. I'll dig around here until my dog returns with my car. I might find something to implicate the south siders."

Wincing as he took a step, he shook his head. "Bad plan. I'll get my hide tanned for leaving you alone."

"You're useless, and I'm not going to take any risks. Go. You need blood or you're likely to attack anything. I'll be fine."

He nodded, and she helped him get down the steps. "Thanks," he said. "Would have caused a real bad situation if humans had found me."

"Anytime."

As he was hobbling up the street, her phone rang. "Yes?"

"*It's Rake. You discovered my handiwork yet?*"

"You're an ass, you know that?"

"*Your dogs killed one of ours last month. Seems fair.*"

"And we punished them. I take it you got both their hearts?"

"*You should have sent them to us alive.*"

"So you could torture them? Samira's a bitch. She'd have kept them alive for months. If you're going to put a dog down, at least do it cleanly."

"*Whatever. Bygones and all that. I've got a present for you, if you're interested.*"

"What?"

"*You still cleaning up my mess?*"

"More or less. I'm alone though."

"*Be there soon.*"

About two minutes later, a sleek grey BMW pulled up under the streetlight across the road. She stayed where she was as Rake got out and opened the boot, pulling out a struggling figure.

Whoever it was cried out, but a backhand from Rake knocked him senseless. Rake carried him to Taenorah.

"I didn't think you south siders were the gift-giving type," she murmured, eyeing the unconscious body of the young man Rake dumped at her feet.

"You'd be surprised."

"What's this blood bag of joy for?"

"This is his place. Some out-of-towners met him here. I was following when Jaque dropped by for a chat. I ripped his heart out while he was distracted."

"He's going to be calling for your blood, you know?"

"Only if you tell."

"What am I supposed to say to Morrell about this human, then?" She indicated the unconscious young man at her feet.

"Whatever you come up with. I followed him and his feral friends to a house not far from here, and nabbed him as he left. I thought you'd appreciate the gift."

"The feral stomping on your turf too?" she asked, surprised at her feelings of concern for Kyle despite the fact she hadn't thought of him in a century or more. "Or just mine?"

"Mostly just yours so far, though he came to Canberra Hospital to retrieve the bitch he made. Neutral territory otherwise, but we can't have ferals breeding like dogs, can we?" He pointed to the unconscious kid. "I can give you the address I caught him at."

"By rights I should kill you right now. The treaty says you're not allowed north side. Ripping Jaque's heart out gives us even more cause for retaliation."

He grinned as if she'd made a pun. "You want the address or not?"

She grimaced. "Fine, but you've got about thirty seconds afterward to clear out or I'm calling in the dogs. I've got to cover my ass, Rake."

"I can handle your dogs."

"A whole pack? What's the address?"

He told her, touched a couple of fingers to his forehead in salute and arrogantly turned his back on her.

"You're a shit, Rake. You know that?"

He laughed.

"Yeah, you know it," she muttered.

She stared at the unconscious boy. Young man, she amended. At the very least, he might make a decent blood donor.

When Ferguson returned, he had another dog with him. Euan Luckett. Lucky, the other dogs called him. Taenorah dumped the unconscious young man in her car's tiny boot. "Stay here for a bit," she said to Ferguson as she took the wheel. "Get in," she said to Lucky, and gave him instructions as she drove.

"Remember," she said as she pulled up outside the address Rake had given her. "Watch only. Don't interfere. I want to know what's going on, that's all. Stay out of any conflict and make sure you're not seen."

"I got it the first six times," he said. He was one of those werewolves that had to be put in his place every few weeks. If it had been up to her, she'd have put him down a couple of years ago.

"And lose the attitude before I rip out your tongue. Full moon's weeks away. You'll have fun trying to talk while it regenerates between now and then."

He dropped his eyes. Good. She was serious, and he knew it. When he was out, she returned to pick up Ferguson and headed home.

CHAPTER 12

Taenorah drove into the rear entry of Morrell's vehicle sales and repairs in Mitchell, the concreted service yard dark and foreboding, at least to a human. It was still foreboding enough for her considering she'd been talking with Rake on her own turf, and she hadn't shoved a silver blade between his ears.

Morrell would kill her if he found out, or at least make her wish she'd killed him. Half a dozen cars awaited repair in the yard, standing like sentinels against the chain-link fence to the left.

Light spilled through the rear roller door, which was fully up to reveal the ramp leading down into the workshop under the showroom and beyond.

For Taenorah it was almost as good as daylight even without the lights. Daytime was so bright she could barely see unless she squinted or wore sunglasses, probably the source of some of the vampire myths today. She certainly wouldn't burn up in the sun, though it could get pretty uncomfortable and kept her as weak as a human.

She was a little surprised the workshop hadn't been locked down already, and had half expected to have to park on the street and use the side gate. Someone must have given orders to leave everything open until she arrived, which was convenient but disconcerting. Something was going on. She hoped it had nothing to do with the mess Rake had made.

The offices upstairs were dark, but that was normal for this time of the evening, which suggested it had something to do with Morrell's crew. Vampire or werewolf?

Morrell used the workshop and second-hand dealership as a legitimate business to funnel money from other, less legitimate businesses. The cars awaiting repairs in the yard were all legit, as were those in the showroom and out front.

The second-hand sales and parts wrecking business made it very difficult to tell if money was being laundered, as did the rebirthing of stolen vehicles and parts onto legit chassis taken from write-offs. Outside of town, he had a wrecker's yard with around a thousand wrecks slowly being stripped back for parts. Great cash business.

In the front car yard there were several dozen second-hand vehicles that had been traded in, while the better quality vehicles were kept in the showroom. All would be sold legitimately, though there would be false mark-ups and additional features added post-sale. Even if Morrell lost a half his dirty money in taxes, he turned the rest into legitimate funds.

Taenorah drove into the basement workshop, parking her car beside Morrell's Ferrari and blocking in a couple of the werewolves' cars. It wasn't normally this busy. Something was definitely going on.

"Go tell Morrell I'm here," Taenorah said to Ferguson. She got out and opened the boot. The cramped young man was awake again and cowering as she opened it.

"Help me, please," he said. "Some guy-"

She grabbed his shirt and hauled him out. He gave a surprised cry and fought to break her grip.

"Keep it up and I'll break your arm kid, got it?"

He struggled harder.

She swept his legs out from under him and slammed him against the ground, holding him down. "Last chance, kid." She caught his left wrist and twisted until he cried out in pain. "Are you going to be a good little boy, or do I need to dislocate your shoulder?"

"I'll be good! I'll be good!"

She released his wrist and pulled him up, pushing him past her car and deeper into the workshop. "Far door. Go."

He staggered a few steps, looking over his shoulder as if hoping to make a break for it, but walked on when he saw her glare. She followed him to the door and pushed him through into the staircase going down to the basement.

"Why am I here?" he asked, the fear in his voice suggesting he was close to panic. "Where does this go?"

"Down. Move."

She gave him another easy shove and followed him to the basement, the cold smell of the subterranean area mixed with the reek of werewolves. The basement wasn't on any government plans, but despite that, it had been excavated and built along with the workshop. Getting it done was just a matter of bribing some people and threatening others.

As far as secret lairs went, it was hardly a secret, and it wasn't much beside that. Just a big basement area subdivided by walls, with a large wine cellar at the end. It was more of a concrete bunker that could be fortified than a lair, not that Morrell had done anything to fortify it. Taenorah could rip the stair door off herself if she wanted to, and the door at the bottom was already off its hinges thanks to some stupid dog crashing through it. Nobody had ever bothered to fix it.

The open area beyond the foot of the stairs had a pub-sized pool table, with a lounge and coffee table along one wall. A fridge filled with beer sat at the other end of the lounge and a few stools had been pushed up against the opposite wall.

Werewolves liked their games - a small investment to keep them happy, though it always smelled like wet dog in the basement. When Taenorah got her independence, she'd run things differently.

Three werewolves looked up as she passed, tension in their stances. One gripped a pool cue a little too tightly, a game already in progress. The other two held bottles of beer. Judging by the empties filling the flat surfaces and a couple of bottles of half-finished spirits, they looked like they didn't want to stay sober tonight. Shit. And they were the ones who could control themselves over a full moon.

Those who couldn't had locked themselves in cages for the duration, usually in their homes. The basement had its own version, though it was unused at the moment. Either way, it provided soundproof werewolf containment for the newbies.

"Mistress," they all said to her, bowing their heads. One of them looked distinctly more hairy tonight than normal, and she narrowed her eyes at him. Larry. He'd never had any trouble with the moon before. Whatever was going on definitely had them spooked.

She acknowledged them with a nod. Best to be polite. They had her back on occasion, and tonight they could be trouble if they banded together or shifted.

"The hallway. Go." She followed the kid deeper into the basement until they reached a large storeroom, the wine cellar just past it. The freaked-out look on the human kid's face suggested he wanted to run.

Taenorah tried not to show distaste as she pushed him into the storeroom. It was a junk room as far as she was concerned. Planks of timber, car parts, building materials and work tools lay about, some of the latter hanging behind a workbench. A compressor and hose had been shoved into a corner beside a mop and bucket, and there was an empty cardboard box on top of the bench for no reason she could see. It smelled damp thanks to a blocked sink filled with reeking water. Morrell needed to get a plumber, or have one of his dogs trained to fix it.

At the other end of the room, two vampires and a few werewolves stood around two people kneeling before Morrell.

Cain, she recognised. He was one of Morrell's dogs, but not the bitch at his side. A feral Cain had dragged in, probably.

"What's happening?" the kid asked.

Her own werewolf, Ferguson, took the kid by the throat and lifted him off the ground. The kid kicked and struggled, going red in the face as he tried and failed to break Ferguson's hold.

"Speak again and I'll tear your throat out. Understood?" the big werewolf said. The kid did his best to nod a reply, hands gripping Ferguson's wrist as his face went redder. Ferguson lowered him to the ground as if he weighed nothing. As soon as Ferguson let go, the kid dropped to his knees, gasping.

Vincent Morrell, middle-aged in appearance and barely taller than Taenorah, looked the kid over disdainfully before narrowing his eyes at Ferguson. The werewolf visibly swallowed and backed off to the side of the room.

Vampires, unlike most other Creatures, retained the appearance of their age when turned. Most other Creatures reverted to a youthful appearance, or if younger, grew up overnight.

Morrell looked like a middle-aged bachelor who'd never had the courage to speak to a girl when younger. He turned to Cain. "Explain the new bitch to me," Morrell said.

"We were kissing. It was an accident."

The girl glared at Cain. "You fucking bit me on purpose, you bastard! You said-"

Morrell backhanded the girl across the face with a solid crack. She sprawled and didn't move for several seconds, long hair over her face. She moaned.

"You made a Creature without my permission, Cain. I'm disappointed. You know the rules."

Morrell turned to Taenorah. "It seems we have a new pack member, dear. Her name's Shannon. Would you like to deal with her?"

Taenorah grimaced. She had her own issues to deal with. She caught David's jaw, making him look up at her as her fingers forced the blood from his cheeks, the skin white around her grip. "Stay still and shut up. Say anything and I'll kill you." She dropped his jaw and crossed the room, grabbed Shannon by the throat and hauled her up against a wall, pinning her there. Still reeling from Morrell's blow, the girl barely resisted, her mousy brown hair covering her face in a messy curtain.

"Never trust the word of a horny werewolf," she told the girl. "He just wanted his own bitch to play with."

Morrell strode over to the building supplies at the far end of the storeroom and took two steel rods used to reinforce support pillars in concrete or pin retaining walls in place. Each was about a metre and a half long. One at a time, he bent the ends over to ninety degrees, surface rust on his hands.

"They'd make good walking sticks, wouldn't they?" he said to Cain with a smirk, his tone jovial.

"Please, Vincent-"

"Mister Morrell to you! You lost the privilege of calling me by my first name."

"Mister Morrell. Please, don't do this to her. It was my mistake, not hers. Please, just let her go. She won't be any trouble, I promise. I'll look after her-"

Morrell raised his arm, preparing to backhand Cain, but held off. "The only reason she's still alive is the fact she hasn't turned on the full moon. She can control herself. That makes her valuable."

"Yes, Mister Morrell."

As far as Taenorah could tell, a werewolf's ability to control themselves on the full moon had little to do with age or experience and everything to do with the dog who turned them. It was a trait Morrell had been trying to breed into his pack for generations. There were always throwbacks to earlier generations or random traits. The ones who could control themselves were the ones Morrell bred from. The hit rate was about one in ten, which left a lot of carcasses to be buried. Fucking dogs couldn't even be trusted to pass on a simple trait or two.

Shannon finally seemed to regain her senses and began squirming in Taenorah's grip, but she didn't have a chance even if the full moon gave her strength. She was too new. Unless she changed form, she wasn't going to be able to match Taenorah for strength, and probably not even then.

Taenorah tightened her grip on the new werewolf's neck until Shannon became more concerned with breathing than freeing herself. Taenorah relaxed just enough to give Shannon some air. "Don't fight it," Taenorah said gently. "Really. It's not worth the angst."

Shannon sucked in big gulps of air as Morrell placed the blunt tip of the steel rod just under the girl's right collarbone and rammed it through. She screamed in agony as the steel punched through the wall behind her. Morrell pushed the rod all the way in to the bent down end, holding Shannon in place like a butterfly pinned to a specimen board.

Her head slumped forward, unconscious.

Morrell turned to Cain. "You shouldn't have done it, Cain. You really shouldn't."

Taenorah moved aside and took the girl's other arm, holding that side up slightly as Morrell drove the second rod through under her other collarbone. "Tae, would you be a dear and go bend them down on the other side of the wall? I don't want her working her way free."

She kissed him on the lips. "Sure, honey. Want a bottle of red while I'm there?"

He nodded. "Something old."

She entered the narrow cellar, bent the bars down on the bare wall and grabbed a dusty bottle of Grange from the rack opposite it before returning.

Cain, still on his knees, didn't dare look at Morrell now, and none of the other werewolves standing around did either. Taenorah hid a smile. They knew their place even over the full moon. The reek of werewolf blood permeated the room from the dribbles running down Shannon's chest from the rods, a rancid smell that turned her stomach. At least the blood wasn't flowing freely.

Vampire blood sometimes turned her on and human blood could send her into a frenzy, but werewolf blood always stank and turned her stomach.

"Do you see what you've done, Cain? You brought her into this. You turned her. *You defied me!*" He took a deep breath and slowly let it out. "Baxter, give him your knife."

Baxter, a young female werewolf Morrell trusted above the others, glanced at Morrell and then Cain as she pulled a silver-bladed knife from a sheath at her hip and tossed it to Cain. It hit the concrete floor after the hilt bounced off Cain's knee, but he wisely didn't make a move for it.

Baxter didn't look pleased at the loss of her knife. "You'll get it back in a moment," Morrell said. "Don't look so morose."

Cain glanced at the knife and then back at Morrell's feet.

"Here's my only offer, Cain. You're a good dog and I've never had any trouble with you before today, so I'm going to give you a choice. You can shove that blade through your girlfriend's heart, or you can shove it through your own. You decide."

Cain paled as he gingerly took the knife, careful to avoid the blade as his hand closed around the hilt. He stared at it, hand trembling slightly. "Please, Mister Morrell. It was a mistake. If I'd known-"

Morrell held up his hand, cutting Cain off as he took the bottle of Grange from Taenorah. "Tae, if one of them isn't dead in two minutes, kill them both. I'll be upstairs."

"No!" Cain yelled, lunging at Morrell.

Morrell sidestepped and punched Cain in the head. The blade clattered free as the werewolf dropped to the ground, the weapon skittering away from Cain's hand. Morrell stomped on the back of Cain's neck with a crunching sound, the other werewolves backing away, even Ferguson, too scared to intervene.

Casually, Morrell picked the blade up and slammed it through the back of Cain's skull for good measure. The body didn't even twitch. "Anybody else feel like making Creatures without my permission?" Morrell asked.

He didn't wait for a response but moved to Shannon, placed his palm on her forehead and pushed her head back. She gazed at him with dazed eyes through her hair, barely conscious and clearly in a lot of pain.

"I've just created a new opening in the pack. Join up by the next full moon or clear out of town. They're your only choices. This is my turf. You can live here only if I say you can, and I only say you can if you do what you're told. Understand?"

She made a noise, winced and cleared her throat, and tried again. "I understand."

"You have until the next full moon to decide." He let her head go. "Righto, you lot. Clear out. Entertainment's over. Taenorah, with me. You too, Ferguson." He focused his attention on David with a slight frown. The kid looked terrified. "We have something else to discuss, apparently."

CHAPTER 13

THE PACK DISPERSED QUICKLY, even those in the poolroom and upstairs, most of the members heading off to their homes. Taenorah doubted many would be in a mood to party after what they'd just seen. Cain had been well liked. Killing him might have been a mistake, and the last thing she needed was a pack of werewolves questioning their loyalties.

She told herself it didn't bother her, though she couldn't think of any way to use it to her advantage. Morrell still controlled her, a dozen other vampires, and every one of the wolves. If he exerted his will on her, she'd comply before she even realised he'd made her do it, and she didn't seem to be any closer to breaking his hold than when she'd been newly made. Until that changed, she needed to agree with everything he did. Appearances were everything in this game. The appearance of trust.

Taenorah followed Ferguson as he dragged the terrified kid up to Morrell's office. After the big werewolf dumped him on the ground, Taenorah poured herself and Morrell a glass of Grange, took hers to the black leather three-seater across from his desk and sat, legs crossed, as the young man found the courage to stand.

"His name is David."

David had appeared scared before, but now he might be ready to puke. Pale as a fresh snow drift, he didn't seem to know whether to keep his eyes down or look for an escape.

Morrell picked up his glass and sat on the edge of the desk. "Jaque seems to think we've got a feral problem. How's this human involved?"

Taenorah turned her attention from the kid to her master. He could compel her to answer anything, but he rarely did. He'd trusted her for more than a century now, and she'd done everything she could to ensure that trust didn't slip. "A feral and his newly made bitch went to see the kid. I don't know why."

"I-" David began.

Ferguson drove a fist into David's stomach and the young man dropped. "You don't speak until someone tells you to," Ferguson said.

Taenorah gave the big werewolf a look and he backed a step, but she didn't reprimand him.

"I understand," David gasped. It took him a moment to climb back to his feet. He seemed unsteady.

"Now, tell us what you know about this feral that's wandered into my city," Morrell said.

David, still struggling to breathe from the blow, dared to meet Morrell's eyes. "I know you're going to kill me. Why should I tell you anything?"

Ferguson stepped closer for another blow and the kid cringed, but Taenorah gave Ferguson a slight shake of her head. He let it go. Morrell, however, seemed amused at David's defiance. "You know, that's a fair question. Ferguson, what do you think about it?"

The werewolf glared at David. "I think we should just kill him and clean out the ferals ourselves. We don't need this little shit."

Morrell smiled. "You see, David, Ferguson has my trust, which is why I brought him into my crew. In turn, I don't abuse that loyalty. The same goes with all the other members of the pack. I'm loyal to them, they're loyal to me, and as long as everyone follows the rules there's no problems. So, how about I extend the same courtesies to you and you take them at face value? Fair?"

David risked a glance at Taenorah as if hoping for some guidance, clearly wondering if there was a trap being set. "Okay, I guess?"

Morrell smiled. "I have no intention of killing you, David, so long as you're honest with me. Does that seem like a fair deal to you?"

David glanced at Taenorah again, and then to Ferguson, then back to Taenorah as if expecting another blow and hoping to avoid it. He swallowed hard.

"You can trust his word," Taenorah said.

David gave Morrell a tentative nod in response. "What about my... what about Zannah? You going to hurt her?"

Morrell glanced at Taenorah, eyebrow raised questioningly.

Taenorah shrugged. "I think she's the bitch the feral made when he got here." It was disheartening to be thinking of Kyle as 'the feral', but she couldn't afford not to.

"Ahh," Morrell said, returning his attention back to David. "Zannah's fate isn't something you should be thinking about right now. Consider your own, instead. Tell me what you know."

David swallowed nervously. "I want to know what you're going to do first."

Taenorah almost grimaced. Stupid kid. For a snotty shit he had a seriously over-inflated sense of his self-worth if he thought he could demand that Morrell answer his questions.

Morrell sighed. "Ferguson, bite him. I don't care for his attitude."

"What!" David cried as Ferguson grabbed the kid by the throat, took his arm and bit the kid's bicep.

"Ahh! Ah!" David yelled. "Get the-"

Ferguson let go and backed away as David dropped to the ground, clutching his arm to his chest.

"You bastard!" Tears ran down his cheeks. "Asshole."

His arm bled, and Taenorah had to close her eyes so she didn't see it. She'd never been good at controlling herself around blood, even blood now infected by a werewolf's bite. She could still smell it as human blood, and tried to stay calm as she reluctantly inhaled the scent.

Hurry up, hurry up, hurry up, she chanted in her mind. The scent of his blood would change in a moment thanks to the werewolf taint, and that would be enough to turn her off. Stay calm.

It took a few minutes, but the scent of his blood finally began to change as the werewolf curse took hold.

David simply sat there, rocking back and forth as his eyes glazed over and the memories of the last few minutes became foggy. She'd seen it many times before. Lycanthropy didn't like to reveal itself to its host, and some dogs wouldn't even believe they had it without coercion.

"Thank you, Ferguson," Morrell said as he pushed away from his desk.

He dropped to one knee before David, took a handful of hair and forced the kid's head back until he met his eyes. "Now David, I want you to know you're a werewolf now. Technically not until you've changed, but let's not quibble. For some reason compulsion works far better on werewolves than humans, which is why I had Ferguson bite you. Say you understand."

"I understand," David said, staring Morrell in the eyes with his mouth slightly open. Taenorah though he might drool.

"Good dog. Now, I want you to tell me everything you know about the feral werewolf, his bitch Zannah, and anything else you can think of that might be of use to me. Do you understand?"

"Yes," David replied, his voice distant.

"Good. Start talking."

"They will push the limits, won't they?" Taenorah said as she reclined back on the lounge. "If we didn't need humans to survive, we could get rid of them and rule the world."

David had finished telling them what he knew, the kid almost comically baffled over it all. Ferguson had then locked him up in one of the empty basement cages.

Morrell didn't seem to hear her, staring into nothing instead. Her attempts to read his expression were futile, though it didn't bother

her. He was relatively straightforward, brutal at times, but generally easy enough to manipulate.

He took a sip of his wine, winced, and put the glass on his desk. "That tastes like shit."

She smiled, waiting for him to get around to what was really on his mind. He often took the conversation on a tangent as he got his thoughts in order. "You're the one who told me to get used to wine. Eating and drinking human food in public helps us blend in, although it's been a decade since we actually ate in a restaurant. How about tomorrow night? We can get dressed up, turn heads, and you could buy me the most expensive meal in the city. Humans will stare with envy."

He pushed the glass aside and gave her a look. "You want to go out and eat food? With all this shit happening?"

It wasn't about the food. It was the attitude. The intent. "Do as I say, not as I do, huh?" she asked. She held up her own glass, swirling the wine around, the recessed lights reflecting from it in several places. She wouldn't say she enjoyed wine, red or white, but she'd grown used to it. It was far better than solid food, at least. Any liquid went down easier with a little blood, though. Pity Morrell had turned the kid. The fresh blood would have been nice instead of the stuff on ice from the local Catholic-run Calvary Hospital.

"What do you want done about Cain's bitch?" she asked. "I guess she's an orphan now with her sire dead."

He shrugged as if the matter were already behind them. "If she wants to join the pack, let her. She'll keep the boys distracted when things go quiet. If she wants out, kill her and burn the body. I don't need a feral problem. Another feral problem," he added.

She turned her glass in her fingers, watching the play of light as he drifted into silence again. It was time to take a risk. "I saw Rake today," she said.

Morrell held still for a long moment, taking his time to focus his full attention on her. "You went south?" There was a dangerous tone in his voice. A buried threat. She ignored it. She'd been defying him since he'd first turned her, though she'd never let him know that. Use the truth like a weapon.

"No. He came north side. He seems intent on stirring up trouble. Who do you think ripped Jaque's heart out?"

Morrell's eyes narrowed, but he didn't seem to be surprised or particularly annoyed. She'd hoped he'd escalate things. Push for retaliation. He seemed to be mellowing as he aged, though. "Rake and Jaque have a long history. I take it you spoke to him?"

She allowed a seductive smile to cross her lips as if she were flirting with danger and liked it. "Apparently he caught the feral's trail at Canberra Hospital on the south side and followed the dog north side. I guess he couldn't pass up the opportunity to piss Jaque off when he spotted him. If we don't do something, Rake and his mistress might start thinking they can act with impunity on our side of town." Another barbed hint.

She watched his reaction closely, prepared to move if the cold fury in his eyes exploded into action. He'd lashed out at her more than once over trivial things, yet this time the conflict seemed to amuse him. Calmly, deliberately, he picked up his wine and took another sip, grimacing. "Let the dogs know what happened. Tell them to watch their backs."

"You don't want to retaliate? You'll look weak."

He met her eyes, and a little spike of fear made her wonder if she'd overplayed the situation. She liked playing the part of his bloodthirsty enforcer, but it wasn't always possible to judge his intent. What she did kept him from seeing deeper into her plans and allowed her to get away with a lot more than his other vampires.

"I'm planning on giving Rake something to think about. Samira, too. We'll do something a little more vicious than sending his pets home with bruises."

She smiled as if the brutality he was hinting at was her only goal. "You want me to gut the shithead and send his heart to Samira with a bunch of red roses?"

He actually smiled at that. "No. Let's see how far we can push before Samira pushes back. Kill a couple of her dogs for now, tear them apart, and make sure she knows it was us. Do you know if Rake has any pets he's particularly fond of? It'll teach him and Samira to keep their shit on the south side of town."

She smiled. "You know I'm going to enjoy that, don't you?" He was so easy to manipulate.

He stared at her. "I'm counting on your enthusiasm. Make it bloody."

He moved to the couch and dropped beside her, a hand on her leg. She gave him a slow, steady smile and sidled closer, encouraging him. "A father shouldn't be treating his daughter like this, you know?" she said, raising an eyebrow at his hand even as she opened her legs. "You could get into trouble with the authorities. We're talking serious jail time." She placed her hand on the back of his, gently guiding it further up her thigh.

He took her glass of wine with his free hand and put it on the side table. "I'll risk it." He kissed her, long and sweet, the taste of Grange still on his lips. She kissed back and ripped open his shirt as his hands began removing her own clothes. In moments they were making heated love on the couch, and then a second time more slowly. When done, they lay naked together, his chest pressed against her back and a hand cupping a breast.

"Do you believe what the kid said?" he finally got around to asking. "I've never heard of a hybrid before."

"Impossible," she said, having no trouble with the lie. She'd been lying to him for centuries now, though cautiously, as he still had power over her. She had to be careful. She'd recognised Kyle for what he was the moment she'd seen him, though. He smelled like a dog, but to be alive after centuries? That required more than lycanthropy. He couldn't have been anything else. "The kid must be confused. Or stupid. Certainly ignorant."

A long time ago, Morrell had told her what he'd done to Kyle. She'd been bitter and angry for years, certain he'd only told her because her reaction amused him. After a while, she forgot about it. She and Kyle had only been married for a few years, after all. She'd been with Morrell for centuries.

Kyle was her first love, but she'd changed since then. She didn't particularly want to see him dead, but she had her own life now and he wasn't a part of it. She wanted her freedom and her own turf to rule. This turf.

"That's the only thing that makes sense to me, too."

She turned in his arms so they were face-to-face. "Why did you turn me?" she asked. "I mean, turn me yourself? I was nothing to you then. You could have had one of your dogs bite me, or even forced another vampire to create me. Why you? Weakening yourself like that was a big risk then, particularly after what you did to my husband. It would be now, too." He'd tried to undo it afterward, draining her again to get his precious blood back, but the event itself still seemed out of character.

A slight smile passed across his lips, his amusement reflected in his eyes. "There was a defiance about you. You were scared, desperately, but you didn't scream or run. It was the challenge in your eyes. I had to break you myself. Afterwards, I regretted it and took my strength back. I never thought you'd survive. Perhaps when you find the strength to leave me, I'll find another girl just like you. I love a good challenge."

She laughed, genuinely amused. She couldn't ever remember being innocent or sweet, but she did remember the defiance. The only difference was that now he didn't see it. "I bet you're seriously disappointed in me now, the simpering beauty in your arms?" She kissed him as she lifted a leg over his thigh, feeling desire creep through her again. She could do this all night, and being a vampire, so could he. She moaned as he responded in kind.

CHAPTER 14

Kyle shook Jimmy's hand as Zannah embraced Sellendria and then Kimbriel. It turned out some of Sellendria's so-called fighting clothes did fit. Jeans, boots and a slightly too-small t-shirt that showed off Zannah's figure a little too well for Kyle's comfort. It was like walking around with a supermodel and certain to draw attention.

"I'll look after your sister," Kyle told Jimmy. "I promise." He still couldn't believe how big the kids were growing these days. Jimmy was easily head and shoulders taller than Kyle, maybe six three or four, and the kid was only sixteen and yet to fill out. Even Zannah could see clearly over Kyle's head, and then some.

Jimmy glanced at his sister, his expression full of hope and regret before returning to Kyle. "I'll explain things to Mum. Just get Zannah's car from Nikki and clear out of town for a while. Stay in touch and we'll let you know when it's safe to return."

"I understand, kid. I really do. There's a turf war brewing here, and I've seen too many to want to get caught in the middle of one."

Jimmy's concern was clear on his face, though Kyle had a feeling he and Zannah fought more often than not.

"Zannah seems to trust you, but don't think that means I'm okay with it. She's always had crap taste in guys." He softened the words with a smirk. "But Sellendria thinks you're okay and I trust her instincts."

Jimmy held a hand up as he glanced at his sister, thumb and pinkie extended to indicate a phone. "Stay in touch, huh?"

She smiled. "Apparently vampires tend to cluster in bigger population centres. That leaves plenty of country to explore. We'll be fine."

Jimmy and his sister embraced. "You better get in touch soon. I don't think Mum's going to buy a lame story from me."

Kimbriel put a hand on Kyle's shoulder. "You know I can do a lot more for you."

"You've done more than I asked for already. Thank you." He embraced her and stepped back, but she kept a hold of his hands.

"Any time you need advice or assistance, let me know."

"I will, but we're good, thanks to you."

She glanced at the front of the house as if seeing something he couldn't. "You're still in a lot of danger. You don't know how much, and the future's still pretty clouded, but they're going to be looking for you. Don't delay heading out of town, okay?"

He wanted to dismiss her concerns, but she was right. "I know that look. It's the 'ask me' look."

Kimbriel smiled. "Well?"

"Do you have any advice for me?" he said, almost formally.

Her smile broadened. "You should ask more often because yes, I do. There's a werewolf outside, watching. I have no idea about his intentions. I suggest you avoid further confrontations with the local wildlife though."

"Wildlife. Right. Thanks, Kimbriel. Anything else?"

"You'll always be my favourite half-breed werewolf, you know that?"

"Oy!" Zannah said from across the room. She clearly had werewolf hearing already. "I thought I was your favourite?"

Kyle gave Kimbriel a lopsided grin. Kimbriel returned the smile. "You better go. Mal will drive you to Nikki's place so Zannah can get her car."

Zannah grinned as if this were all a fun adventure with no real danger or risk. "Thank you again, Kimbriel, for everything. I promise not to bite anyone who doesn't deserve it," she said with a cheeky smile. "Except Kyle, though to be fair, I owe him at least one bite."

"Just make sure you rip their head off if you bite anyone else but Kyle, or you'll be ripping your own off. I'm not kidding."

Zannah gave Kyle a worried look. He nodded in confirmation. "You really don't want to bite anyone without killing them too. I mean it."

Kyle led Zannah out to Mal's car, and within twenty minutes they'd driven halfway across town and pulled into Nikki's driveway, the home in much better condition than Kimbriel's appeared to be.

"A vehicle is a valuable possession to be lending to a friend," Kyle said to Zannah as Mal pulled the handbrake on.

Zannah gave a shrug. "It's a rust bucket. Besides, I was working and Nikki needed it. Do you think I'll be able to come home in a few years? You know, if someone kicks the vampires out or something?"

Mal gave her a look. "Kimbriel is against open warfare. I'm sure you two can sneak into town on occasion, though. You better go," Mal added in his deep voice. "The sooner you're out of town, the better."

"Sure thing, Mufasa," Zannah said.

"Huh?" Kyle asked.

"He sounds like James Earl Jones. Mufasa. From The Lion King."

Kyle shrugged.

"Darth Vader? Surely you've heard of Star Wars?"

"Movies aren't my thing."

She rolled her eyes. "Heathen."

They got out and Kyle walked with Zannah to Nikki's front door. Zannah knocked as Mal reversed out of the driveway, the house blending in with the neighborhood. It had a few shrubs in need of care, a lawn dying from the heat, and a side gate leading to the backyard. Kyle kept watch in case anyone had followed, but saw nothing.

At least it was a quiet street and there seemed to be no sign they'd been followed.

Kyle turned around as he heard a squeal of delight when Zannah's friend opened the door. There was lots of hugging. Kyle tried not to listen in or watch, but couldn't avoid hearing Nikki's surprise at seeing Zannah. "I heard you broke your neck! I was planning on going to the hospital tomorrow. What really happened? Did they misdiagnose you?"

Kyle walked over to Zannah's car, which was parked before the tired side gate, trying not to listen into the reunion. It really was a rust bucket. He was surprised it was roadworthy. Even the tires were barely a revolution away from complete baldness.

"Who's this?" Nikki asked as she and Zannah walked over to Kyle. Like most people these days, Nikki was taller than him, but she seemed interested despite the height difference, giving his chest and arms an appraising look. It made him feel both good and awkward at the same time, like he was betraying Zannah. Nikki wasn't half the looker Zannah was, but with braided strawberry blonde hair and a figure to turn heads, she was definitely good looking.

Zannah grinned, and surprised Kyle when she put her arm across his shoulders in what seemed to be a possessive way, almost as if she'd picked up on her friend's interest. He stiffened, liking it despite the fact it made him feel even more awkward. "This is Kyle. He helped me out recently. Long story. Don't ask. I'm just here to grab my car and get going."

Nikki gave Zannah's arm a sharp glance as if she wasn't impressed by the casual possessiveness, but tossed Zannah the keys as if it didn't bother her. "All yours. I even vacuumed it. Dad said not to wash it in case it fell apart, and forbade me from ever driving it again." Nikki grinned.

"Aww, thanks." They hugged once more. Zannah opened the driver's door to a wash of heat. The inside was a furnace, and Kyle knew furnaces. He grimaced. Zannah ignored the heat and got in before unlocking the passenger side while Kyle reluctantly walked around. He was sweating just thinking of getting in. Zannah rolled the driver's side window down as Kyle opened the door.

Nikki stepped back. "You've gotta tell me how come you're not a vegetable. Later, I mean."

"Vegetable?" Zannah said, clear offence in her tone, though it sounded fake. "I wasn't brain dead, Nikki."

Nikki snickered. "I disagree. In fact, you might still be a vegetable."

"I love you too," Zannah said with a grin, casually brushing the insult aside as if it were a compliment.

A minute later, Zannah was driving like road rules were optional. "Gotta get some petrol. We're on fumes," she said.

Blind luck and a fair amount of determination from other drivers to avoid getting hit, more like it. He gripped the seat with both hands. "Perhaps you should slow down to double the speed limit?" he suggested.

She screeched into a petrol station and nearly gave him whiplash while stopping. Before he could say anything, she bounced out of the car and opened the fuel cap.

"What have I done?" he wondered aloud. "She thinks she's impervious to dying in a horrible fireball."

"I heard that!" Zannah called. "Lucky we're not in something with some grunt!" She bent down and looked through the window, a big grin on her face. "Besides, it doesn't go any faster."

At least it had been vacuumed and didn't smell too bad. "We need to get some supplies," he said when Zannah got back into the car. "Some food, at least. I can't be certain how you'll react, but I'm fairly sure your body's going to be going through some major changes over the next few days and weeks. As we're predominately werewolves, you'll get hungry. We'd better have something on hand rather than risk you wandering off and eating a little old lady."

"I'm not going to eat anyone," she said, giving him a look. "Certainly not a little old lady. Too scrawny. Hell, I feel entirely human except that I can hear and smell better." She sniffed. "Actually, I am pretty hungry. I could really go for a beer or three as well. There's a supermarket around the corner. We can get whatever you need there."

"Beer? I thought you were hungry?"

She shrugged. "Liquid steak."

Taenorah's phone rang, an old-style ringtone she liked from the first landline telephone she'd owned. That antique would be worth a bit if she still owned it. Straddling Morrell with him deep inside her, she glared across the room at her jeans, the pocket of which held the offending modern technology.

"Better get that," Morrell said. "Might be your mother."

"Asshole," she muttered as the phone continued its incessant ringing, but extracted herself from Vincent's groping arms and strode naked across the room to her jeans. She pulled the phone from the pocket and glanced at the caller ID. It was Lucky. "What?"

"They're at Cooleman Court."

"South side?" she asked, surprised. "How the hell did *you* get south side?" She held up a hand for silence as Vincent raised a questioning eyebrow.

"I stole a car."

The asshole was going to get caught one of these days. "Keep watching, but stay clear and out of sight. If you get caught, Samira's crew will roast you over a slow fire. I'll be there in twenty minutes." She hung up.

Vincent gave her a steady smile. "A minion's work is never done, I see."

She pursed her lips in distaste at the term. "So I've graduated from harem girl to minion? The opportunities for advancement here are endless." She pulled her lace underwear on, quickly followed by her jeans. "I'm going to refresh your memory about my promotion to minion the next time you beg me for a fuck."

"You'll fuck me because you love it."

"Or perhaps I'll tell you to take that new werewolf girl for a spin."

He gave her a look that implied she'd just suggested bestiality. "I think I'll book you in for some surgery. Turn your peaches into double-d melons."

She gave him the finger and picked up the rest of her clothes before stalking out half naked. It would give the male werewolves something to talk about when she went through the workshop. The couple of females too. "Gotta keep 'em motivated," she muttered to herself.

CHAPTER 15

JIMMY FELT sick as he took Sellendria's calloused hand for his own comfort and opened the front door to his house. "I still don't know what to say," he whispered. "Are you sure Dad's not home?"

She squeezed back, far too strong for an average girl, though he doubted it had anything to do with the fact she wasn't human. She practiced using her sword with every spare moment, and her body was as lean and hard as a professional athlete.

"Yeah. I can't see any fresh traces of his aura. I don't think he's dealing with Zannah's accident too well."

He looked around the home's interior, its familiar appearance not comforting. Neat, tidy, and a little run down. "So, what do I tell Mum?"

Sellendria looked away as if thinking something over. "I could show her what I really am?"

He almost forgot she was supposed to look human. He'd been seeing through her illusion for too long now, and had to concentrate to see it. There wasn't really all that much difference between Sellendria and a human if you ignored the violet eyes and softly pointed ears that twitched and moved like an animal's.

He gave her a concerned look, not sure he was prepared to agree to his mother seeing her as anything but human. "I'd like to avoid people knowing about you, even my parents. Enough people know about you already. Any other ideas?"

"She's your mother. She should know what's happened, and if dropping my illusion helps, I'm willing to try."

"Let's see how the explanation goes." Whatever that happened to be. He still hadn't thought of anything.

As Jimmy and Sellendria walked into the combined family room and kitchen, Helen came out of her bedroom rubbing sleep from her eyes. She was still dressed in the same clothes she'd been wearing when she went to the hospital and must have woken at the sound of the door. She looked like she could use a shower to freshen up.

She stared at them uncomprehendingly for a few seconds, and then her expression dropped. "Oh no," she said, shaking her head and taking a step back as her hands went to her mouth. "She's dead, isn't she?" She shook her head too fast. "No, no, no!"

"Mum!" Jimmy said. He rushed to her side and caught her in a hug, supporting her even as she seemed ready to fight him off, perhaps to rush to the hospital. "Zannah's fine. It's okay, Mum. Zannah's okay. In fact, I think she's going to be better than okay."

Helen had lost a lot of weight in the last few months, and she seemed to have lost more over the last day or so. He could feel her thinness through her clothes. He would have to watch her and make sure she ate properly considering his Dad was spending more and more time away. Neither of his parents had said anything, but they weren't getting on as far as Jimmy could tell, and the fact his Dad wasn't here now wasn't a good sign.

As his mother calmed down, he guided her to the lounge, knocking a newspaper to the floor as he helped her to sit. Sellendria gathered up the mess for him.

"Why aren't you at the hospital?" Helen asked as if she'd suddenly realised no one was with Zannah. "You're supposed to be watching her. What's happened?" Her tone rose with anxiety. "Someone should be there. I have to go to her!"

She tried to stand, but Jimmy kept his arms around her. She was so small compared to him now. He had no trouble keeping her on the lounge, not that she fought him for more than a moment. He had a lot to explain and couldn't do it if he was chasing her out the front door. She remained stiff, though.

"Jimmy, let go of me now!" Her words conflicted with her actions. She didn't seem to want him to let go.

Jimmy met Sellendria's eyes, and she gave him a nod to say she supported whatever he chose to say.

What was he going to say? "Mum? I want you to listen to me," he said, struggling to come up with a plausible explanation for his sister's remarkable recovery. "The doctors have injected Zannah with an experimental stem cell therapy which is speeding up the healing process. It had to be done within twenty-four hours after the break, and we only just found out. You weren't there, so I signed the papers. They say she's going to be able to walk again."

"Really?" Helen seemed to buy it for a full three seconds, but then her expression turned to anger. "Do not lie to me!" This time she managed to break his hold, but he caught her wrists and refused to stand with her. "Jimmy, let me go now or I swear I'll ground you for a decade-"

"Mum! She's really going to be okay. I promise."

Helen struggled against his hold until he let go, her face furious. "She has a broken neck, Jimmy! She'll never be okay again! There is no wonder drug, so stop lying to me. You're not helping."

She stomped to her bedroom.

"Mum! Wait!" Jimmy said, standing with the intention of following her, but Sellendria caught his arm.

"You can't let her return to the hospital," Sellendria said. "We don't know what will happen if there are vampires controlling it, as Kyle suspects. They'll have already covered up Zannah's disappearance. They might kill your mother to tie up loose ends."

Helen returned from the bedroom with her handbag and car keys, so he crossed the room and got in her way, preventing her from getting to the front door.

She glared up at him. "I know you're twice my size now Jimmy, but so help me, get out of my way or else!"

Jimmy caught Sellendria's eye, pleading for inspiration.

"We have to," Sellendria said to Jimmy. "I think she should know anyway."

Helen turned on Sellendria, her anger overflowing to her. "Know what?" she asked, the anger abruptly turning to abject fear. "Zannah really is dead, isn't she?" Her eyes filled with tears and she collapsed like an unsteady toddler, sitting hard.

Jimmy helped her to her feet, though she seemed dazed. "No Mum, Zannah's fine. Sellendria's not human." Zannah wasn't either, for that matter. Not anymore.

The dazed look resolved itself into an exasperated look. Under any other circumstances he'd have sided with her after what he'd just said.

"Move. Now."

Although there was a sob in her voice, her tone implied *imminent murder*. It was a tone he knew well and had feared since childhood for good reason. No one messed with his Mum, not even Jimmy's father, and his Dad was bigger than Jimmy.

Light flared, too bright to look at directly.

Helen turned away and squinted as Jimmy did, but the brightness rapidly dimmed to reveal a ball of white light floating above Sellendria's hand.

It morphed into a blue flame before turning into stardust, which fell upwards, where it spread across the ceiling and became a tropical forest canopy high overhead. The room dissolved entirely. Helen stared as if trying to work out what she was seeing.

"That's just an illusion," Sellendria said. "I'd like to show you something real, if you'll allow it?"

Helen seemed to have trouble tearing her eyes off the ceiling until the canopy faded, but she finally managed to meet Sellendria's eyes, her mouth open. She didn't say anything as she glanced at Jimmy, but she seemed to be looking to him to confirm he'd seen it too, her expression halfway between fear and shock.

"You should probably sit, Mum. I suspect I know what Sellendria's going to show you." He didn't like the necessity, but he couldn't think of anything else.

He guided his mother back to the lounge where they sat, her back stiff. "How did you do that?" She glanced at the roof again, then at Sellendria. Jimmy sat beside her, placing an arm around her bony shoulders. She leaned into him, too shocked to resist.

Sellendria knelt before them both. "I can do it again if you like, but right now I want to show you what I really look like. Jimmy wasn't lying. I'm not human and the world is... far more complex than you believe."

"You're going to prove you're not human?" Helen sounded doubtful. Suspicious even, as if this were just another delaying tactic.

Sellendria smiled. "I wasn't even born in this universe. There was a war which tore open the fabric of the Veil, and... that's a different story. Let me show you what I really look like." Sellendria reached behind her neck and unclipped the gold necklace she wore, piling the links and the sword charm it held into her right hand. "When I give this to Jimmy, the illusion hiding my appearance will vanish. I'll still be the same girl, but I'll appear different. Okay?"

"I think she's trying to ask you not to freak out," Jimmy said. "Can you not freak out? I'd really appreciate it if you don't freak out."

Helen looked like she was about to freak out. "Okay. I won't freak out. I promise."

Doubt on her face, Sellendria nevertheless tipped the necklace from her palm into Jimmy's. As the last link slid into his hand, the glamour faded from her features.

Her blue eyes changed to their natural violet colour, and her ears morphed into soft points. Her features, though still much the same, took on an alien cast that marked her as being a little different from a human, though with sunglasses and a hood Jimmy was sure no one would notice if she didn't draw attention to herself.

Helen seemed almost relieved. "I was expecting tentacles."

Jimmy couldn't help it and laughed, breaking the tension.

Sellendria pushed her hair back, fully revealing ears that looked more like a dog's than a human's, though without the hair. She moved them.

"Okay, that's a little freaky," Helen whispered, leaning back. "Please don't do that again."

"Here," Sellendria said, reaching out to take Helen's hand and guiding her fingers to her face. "I don't bite."

Her hand shaking slightly, Helen touched Sellendria's right ear, holding it between her thumb and forefinger for a long moment before running her thumb down the side.

"It's warm," she said with mild surprise in her voice before withdrawing her trembling hand. "And kind of soft. Please tell me what this has to do with Zannah? Did she get zapped into... what you are?" She swallowed nervously.

"Zannah's hardly a princess from another universe," Jimmy said as he handed Sellendria her necklace back.

The illusion returned. His mother stiffened slightly, but then seemed to relax a little. "You're a princess? Really?"

"Aren't all girls?"

Helen glanced at Jimmy. "Are you really dating a princess from another universe?"

"It's not the weirdest thing that's ever happened," Jimmy said. "Trust me." Jimmy caught his mother's hands. "You know all those stories about magical Creatures like dragons and unicorns and mermaids? Well, they're true. Embellished a bit maybe, but magical beings do exist, and some of them live on our world."

This time there was doubt on Helen's face. "Mermaids and dragons?"

Sellendria nodded, confirming Jimmy's words. "Yes. Succubi, dryads, sprites, and many other kinds of magical Creatures. Vampires and werewolves as well."

"Are you trying to tell me that Zannah's...?" her eyes going to Sellendria. "A dryad or something?" She looked Sellendria over again. "Are you a dryad? No. A nymph. I imagine a nymph might look like you do."

Sellendria appeared slightly offended at that. "I'm not a silly nymph, and dryads aren't the nicest of Creatures, though they're not unpleasant. They do need to kill to survive, though."

Helen's eyes widened.

"Many Creatures do," Sellendria added.

Jimmy caught his mother's attention by waving his hand before her face. "Sellendria's more like... a regular person who can use magic. That's all. She also happens to be a princess from another universe, but that's a story she can tell you later."

Helen appeared doubtful again. "Another universe." She glanced at Jimmy and then back at Sellendria again. "I thought you might be kidding about that."

"No," Sellendria said.

"How many universes are there?" Her voice was small, as if she feared the answer.

Sellendria shrugged. "Two that I know of."

Jimmy took a deep breath, gathering his courage as he turned the conversation back to his sister. "Zannah got attacked by a vampire, Mum." He expected a bigger reaction than silence. "Mum?"

"Zannah got attacked by a vampire," Helen repeated. She looked Sellendria over again, apprehension clear. "And that means what?"

"You remember that bite on her shoulder the doctors weren't sure about? The one they thought was a dog bite, even though the bite wasn't anything like a dog's?"

"And now she's a vampire?"

If he pushed too hard now, he wasn't sure what she'd do. "No. A werewolf saved her. His bite saved her life. He did it to help her after the vampire broke her neck." Okay, that was a bit of a lie, but not entirely untrue. "She was stable when she got to the hospital, remember? They were going to operate, but held off because she was breathing on her own despite the broken neck."

Helen nodded, clearly uncertain. "I remember."

"She's up and walking now, and she's with the werewolf who bit her. He's helping her. By now she'll be almost normal." She was never really normal, but as normal as Zannah ever got.

"How normal is normal?" Like a moth drawn to a streetlight, Helen glanced uncertainly at Sellendria again, more than a little fear on her face. "Does she have animal ears too?"

Jimmy answered. "Yes, but only on the full moon."

CHAPTER 16

Taenorah pulled to a stop on the far side of the car park across from Cooleman Court, reversing into the last row so she could watch the shops. Ferguson sat beside her, his muscled bulk taking up too much space. She felt crowded.

Lucky sat in his stolen family wagon a couple of rows ahead and off to her left, the slightly beat-up car blending in well in the suburb. It was probably more chance than actual intelligence that had seen him steal the wagon, though.

She stared ahead as Lucky got out and strolled over to her window, chewing gum, the scent of peppermint strong. Apparently chewing gum helped werewolves cope with the city's scents, particularly in dirty areas like car parks.

"They came out of the supermarket with a case of beer about five minutes ago and then went back in. I haven't seen them since."

Taenorah got out, looking around the unfamiliar territory. It wouldn't be hard to get outnumbered by Samira's dogs here, though she could easily handle a few on her own under normal circumstances. A few more with Ferguson and Lucky. If they had a vampire with them, though, she'd be in trouble.

"Idiot," she muttered, and Lucky cringed, though the comment wasn't directed at him. She'd warned Kyle, even told him to get out of town. It seemed like he was taking her advice, but was too slow in implementing it. By rights, she should kill him. Morrell would expect it.

Taenorah had something else in mind though, a lesson Kyle would never forget. With two werewolves here, she couldn't very well let him walk without doing something. For appearance's sake, she'd have to kill his new bitch at least.

Ferguson got out of the car and slammed the door before glancing her way, ready to follow her lead. She began to walk toward the shops, but Lucky grabbed her arm. She turned on him, hand raised to strike, but he backed away, arms raised to protect himself and real fear on his face.

"I-I just, um. There's more, that's all."

She lowered her arm, glaring. "What?"

"I saw two of Samira's werewolves sniffing around. I think they caught the ferals' scents. They're loitering near the shop doors and trying not to be obvious about it." He pointed them out.

One was a lean woman with unkempt long blonde hair, sitting on a bench and dragging on a cigarette. She looked like a vagrant, typical of Samira's dogs.

The other, a male, was a fairly solid-looking werewolf. He was leaning against a post not far from the female as if waiting for a friend, turning his phone over and over in his hand like it was a nervous habit. Taenorah swore under her breath. Another complication.

"I say we kill Samira's werewolves, then the ferals," Ferguson said in his deep voice.

Taenorah studied Samira's two werewolves for a moment longer, making sure there weren't any more around. "I have a better idea. Let's kill Samira's werewolves and make sure the ferals get the blame," she said. "Ferguson, go left and get the guy. Lucky. Go right and get the girl. When you're in place, I'll run straight at them and try to split them up. More than likely they'll go in different directions the moment they see me to ensure at least one of them gets back to report. I want you both ready to chase them down. Go now."

They jogged away in opposite directions. Taenorah gave them a head start and then ran at Samira's werewolves. The werewolves caught sight of Taenorah and bolted in opposite directions, the female toward the Presbyterian Church and parkland beyond it, the male for the main street.

She followed the male to the right. Ferguson wouldn't have any trouble taking the female down, but for Lucky it would be an even match, if that.

The male glanced back, saw her coming and almost pissed his pants by his expression.

He sprinted around the corner, taking it close, and slammed headlong into Lucky. Two people nearby backed away and then ran as the two werewolves got to their feet. Lucky caught the guy, but only succeeded in ripping his shirt off before Taenorah crashed into the dog, dragging him to the ground.

Before he could cry out, she slammed his head into the concrete. Not a fatal injury, but good enough to put him down for a few hours.

The two young men they'd spooked watched from the other side of the street, shocked and backing away. She ignored them. They might file a police report, but that was only an inconvenience.

Something within the natural order of things hid the activities of supernatural Creatures from regular humans. Within hours their memories would begin to get hazy, and without proof of a crime, they'd begin to doubt themselves and put it down to seeing a scuffle. In a month or so, they'd have completely forgotten what they saw. It was one of the world's hidden gifts to Creatures, just as a Creature's inability to enter human homes and places of worship seemed to balance it out.

Lucky stopped by her side, still clutching the shirt as if it were a prize.

"I wonder if Ferguson did any better than you?" she asked acerbically. He looked away, cheeks flushing.

She stood and walked off.

"Um, what do you want me to do with him?" Lucky asked.

"Why don't you leave him there?" She suggested with as much

sarcasm as she could get into her voice. "I can't think of a single reason we might have chased him down otherwise."

He almost seemed to take her at face value, but something got through his thick skull.

"Um, I'll bring him then?" he said before hauling the limp body off the ground.

Taenorah already had her phone out.

She met Ferguson at her car, the limp body of the female werewolf across his shoulders.

"We should be more careful," Ferguson said. "There're cameras everywhere nowadays. We're probably being recorded."

"Good," Taenorah said. "This is Samira's turf. Let her pay off the cops."

"She might be the one who causes the trouble. I think she owns this shopping centre."

"At which point, we start turning cops into dogs until the problem goes away. Lucky knows all about that little perk, don't you? Been a long time since you wore a uniform."

Lucky stared distastefully at the two unconscious werewolves. "Are you baiting me, Taen?"

"Taen? Only one person ever called me Taen," she said, thinking of Kyle. "I'll kill you if you ever use that again, got it?"

He kept his eyes on the ground. "Yeah, I got it."

"Good, now rip the heads off these dogs and put them in the feral's car."

"And their bodies?" Ferguson asked without hesitation.

"Dump them in bits on the rock and hill over there." She pointed to a slope next to the shops, too rocky and steep to build on.

"Rip their heads off?" Lucky asked with distaste.

She raised an eyebrow.

"I mean, sure. Whatever you say, Taenorah."

"When you're done, park your stolen car somewhere close to our side of town and torch it, and then get back as quick as you can. I want the ferals blamed for this, not us."

"That's good thinking, Taen...orah," Lucky said.

She looked him up and down, his skinny body an excuse for a real werewolf. "I swear you were brain damaged before I found you."

She and Ferguson got in her car and drove to the edge of the car park, watching from a distance as Lucky brutally tore the werewolves to pieces, forced open the feral bitch's car door and dumped the heads in.

After he'd scattered the bodies, Taenorah drove off, smiling when she saw Rake's car pulling into the supermarket car park as Lucky left in his stolen car. Rather than take the nearest exit, she turned so she would pass Rake.

"What are you doing?" Ferguson asked as she slowed down. He gripped the seat as if expecting a crash.

"Making sure he sees me."

"What? Why?"

"Part of the game."

She slowed even more as her car passed Rake's, gave him a cocky smile and a nod, and then sped off. Her timing couldn't have been better.

CHAPTER 17

KYLE TRIED NOT to cringe as Zannah took a breath to ask another question. The way she took a breath and held it for a moment ensured he knew a question was coming. He'd been fielding questions the entire time they'd been shopping.

"Kyle, don't misinterpret what I'm about to say as being bloodthirsty, but shouldn't we be buying juicy steaks instead of fruit and canned stuff?"

He paid, grabbed a couple of bags and left the supermarket, walking through the small mall toward the car park. She quickly caught up.

"That meat section smelled *so* good, and I mean *really* good. You shop like a vegan." She hefted her shopping bags filled with fresh produce and long-life goods as shoppers walked around them, a long loaf of crusty bread nearly falling from one of her bags.

He gave her a look loaded with meaning, or at least what he hoped was meaning. "We don't need meat or blood to survive. We eat regular food, just like most other Creatures. Even vampires can eat normal food if they want to."

"Oh. But aren't I supposed to have the whole undead werewolf thing going for me now? Doesn't that mean meat and gore?"

"Undead?" he asked, stopping. He wasn't sure what to say to that.

He'd never considered himself or any other Creature as undead. "Do you feel undead?"

She looked slightly embarrassed. "Well, not exactly. But, you know, part vampire-"

"We're Creatures. We're still people."

She seemed a little uncertain, a frown marring her expression. "Can I at least turn into a real wolf? Not one of those upright Hollywood monstrosities. I mean proper paws and everything?"

How had he managed to bite the only person in the city who would be enthusiastic about it? He'd moped for a century before coming to terms with it himself. "Yes, well mostly. We turn into a kind of freakishly powerful wolf, but you can't do it before the next full moon. I've never made a Creature before, so I'm guessing, but that's how werewolves normally work."

"Full moon? But it's the full moon now. The next one's a month away!" She sighed. "I can turn into a wolf whenever I like after that, right? You know, like if someone was trying to hurt me, could I wolf-out and scare the bejesus out of them?"

He stared up at her. "Wolf out? Are you a puppy?"

"What do you mean?"

"A puppy. You know, all energy and tail wagging and no forethought at all?"

Her expression changed into a look that seemed to be genetically coded into every woman. "Of course not."

He chose the path of wisdom and pretended he didn't see *the look*. "So, by wolf-out, you mean kill?"

She shook her head. "Heck no. But, you know, intimidate. Scare off the vamps. I'm not your average werewolf, am I? I'm an enhanced version? Super-charged or super-powered. Super cool, at least. Could I just, you know, threaten a vampire or something? Strike fear into them with my bloodthirsty snarl?"

He tried to hide a smile. "Not really. They're faster and stronger than us, except on the full moon. Even so, there's a lot of other powerful Creatures out there, and vampires are hardly near the top of the food chain. Werewolves are definitely at the bottom though."

Her expression revealed disappointment. "So what should I do then? Piss my knickers and run?"

He did laugh then. "A better option. Besides, changing tends to... mess with your mind. You don't think rationally."

She frowned down at him. "So we're only kickass on the full moon, and even then we're mediocre in the grand scheme of things?" She seemed even more disappointed.

"Yeah. Sorry. You could probably intimidate other werewolves, though. Does that help?"

She gave him a lopsided grin. "Kind of."

"Every werewolf is a little different, so I don't know what traits you'll have, but you're likely to be more powerful than most."

"Traits?"

He started walking again toward the mall's exit. "Some can smell or hear better than others, some can resist turning on the full moon. I don't know what you'll be capable of, especially with the vampire taint we share. Creating you could have produced anything."

"But the wolf thing, that's a definite? I'll be able to shape shift, right?" She sounded so hopeful.

He shrugged. "You wouldn't be a werewolf otherwise, and I can smell it in you."

She grinned in delight. "I so want to turn into a wolf. Can I choose the colour of my fur like a chameleon? A white wolf in moonlight would be awesome."

He needed to dampen that enthusiasm before she got herself into trouble. "You'll have the same fur colour as your hair, which is good. You'll blend into the darkness."

"I can't wait!" She almost did a little jig right there.

"Tell me that when you're struggling to maintain control in a crowd of humans, or when I have to stuff a handful of garlic tablets down your throat," he raised his hands to do air quotes despite the shopping bags. "To stop you *wolfing out*. Transforming's painful. Intensely painful, and you tend to wake up the next day with a memory like you've been on a drunken bender. I do it as little as possible. I don't think other werewolves change on purpose either, except when they have no choice."

"Killjoy," she muttered, but with a grin. "Can I at least drink copious amounts of alcohol and not get wasted?"

He couldn't help but return the grin. "I can. Traits might vary, but we're basically the same."

"No way. Not even close. I'm a girl. That makes me way cooler." She grinned at his expression. "Hey, don't look so worried about it. Not everyone can be a woman."

He shook his head as they left the shopping centre, wondering yet again what he'd got himself into.

"What cool stuff can *you* do?" She got in front of him, forcing him to stop or go around her. "What's special about you that you haven't told me already?"

A scent caught his attention, and he stiffened. Blood. Werewolf blood. He glanced at the ground but saw nothing. He turned about, scanning the car park as he ignored her question. He couldn't see anything, but that didn't mean much. The air was still and hot and there was little breeze, yet the scent reached him anyway.

"Something's wrong," he said, sniffing the air and wishing his senses were as keen as a regular werewolf's. Werewolves had been here though, he was sure of it. Werewolves went to the shops just like regular humans, so it could be a coincidence.

"What?" she asked, sniffing. "All I'm getting is the still-warm smell of the car park, oil leaks, dogs, piss, manky food starting to rot, body odour and deodorant, stuff like that."

He turned around again, slower this time, watching the area as disquiet arose. He was far too old to ignore the feeling. He checked the few nearby cars and the surrounding area, but saw no one. They were being watched though, he was sure of it. "I can smell blood. Werewolf blood. It's richer than human blood. More complex."

Looking around once more, he couldn't find anything amiss. Hopefully it was nothing more than a couple of werewolves who'd had a scuffle.

"I see a car park with a bunch of cars, mostly."

"If they'd been looking for a fight, they'd have come at us by now. Something else is up."

She grinned. "Whatever. So tell me about... Well, us."

Pretending everything was fine for her sake, he watched the area without trying to be obvious about it. He started walking again, taking it slow to make sure no one could jump them as they passed cars.

"Okay. Like vampires, we don't age, but we can be killed. We're allergic to garlic, but not to the same degree as vampires. It won't drop us. Like any Creature we're allergic to silver too, but vampires are fairly resistant to it and so are we. Silver will kill a werewolf or any other Creature if the wound is bad enough, but I've taken some pretty nasty wounds from silver and survived. We're stronger and faster than werewolves, but not as strong or as fast as vampires."

He glanced around again, the feeling of being watched making his skin crawl. "I keep saying *we*, but I mean *me*. You might have other gifts or... drawbacks."

She ignored that last part. "Can we fly like vampires? I want to fly. Tell me we can fly."

That caught him by surprise. "Vampires can't fly."

"Really? How lame. What else then?"

The scent of blood grew stronger. If he wasn't mistaken, they were walking toward it. He slowed, really concerned now, but he tried not to let Zannah see it. "Well, I get antsy over the full moon, and I can only change form at night, but that's common among all werewolves. You don't want to try changing during the day. It's possible, but it messes you up pretty bad. Throws your system out."

"No day wolf. Got it. What else?"

"Um, during the day I'm not much more powerful than a human as far as strength and speed go. It's the same with vampires and some other Creatures. Sunlight isn't our friend." They reached the car, the smell of werewolf blood everywhere now, but he couldn't see any. It gave him a very disconcerting feeling. It couldn't be a coincidence.

"When am I going to get all of these superpowers? I'm feeling as human as I used to. Mostly."

He did a slow turn. "You'll probably transform during the next full moon. Everything should fully kick in then."

Zannah stiffened, staring over Kyle's shoulder. He spun and saw the vampire who'd attacked Zannah standing across the car park by a Mercedes, watching.

"Crap," Kyle said. "Get in the car."

"Um, there's more of them," she said, pointing toward the shops.

He glanced that way to see three people emerge from the shopping centre, another two from the opposite corners of the building, and three more from a nearby van that had just pulled up.

"Get in the car, Zannah. Now!"

She dropped her shopping bags and pulled the keys from her purse, hands trembling. He dumped his shopping too.

The werewolves charged. She barely had the key in the door before the first arrived.

Kyle punched him in the face, throwing him off his feet, but copped a blow in return from another. He got another hit in before someone clubbed him from behind and three of them dragged him to the ground. They slammed the back of his head against the asphalt and then really started laying into him.

"Zannah, run!" he hissed through pain, hoping she'd at least got away.

He curled up, unable to do more to protect himself, and resisted even as they forced him face down and bound his hands behind his back. Hogtied, his fears multiplied a thousand-fold when they dumped Zannah beside him on the asphalt, blood seeping from a cut lip, her nose broken, and a black eye that was swelling already. Her hands and feet were similarly bound.

"Rake, you better look at this," one of the werewolves said.

Kyle managed to twist enough to see. They had the rear door of Zannah's car open. There was silence for a long moment, and then one of them swore.

"Bitch," another said, and booted Zannah in the side. Hogtied like Kyle, she couldn't do much more than grunt as her face screwed up in pain.

"Hey!" Kyle said. "Leave her alone."

He strained against the ropes, but they only cut deeper. Someone put a knee between his shoulder blades, forcing his face against the ground in a sticky patch from a spilled drink.

"Shut up or I'll slit your throat with a silver blade."

"Do it," he said. "I can't imagine you've got better plans for us."

He couldn't see what had happened at the car, but heard Rake. "Find the bodies. We'll take them back to the warehouse along with these two ferals."

"Bodies?" Kyle asked, but the knee in his back only ground in harder. He grunted.

They hauled Kyle and then Zannah off the ground and threw them into the back of the van, the metal corrugations on the floor cool against Kyle's face.

"You okay?" he asked Zannah, though he couldn't see her face.

"Peachy," she hissed softly, pain in her voice. "This happen often?"

How the hell had she managed to keep a sense of humour? "Most weeks," he replied.

The vehicle started up and drove off, but only for about fifty yards or so. The driver backed into another spot and killed the engine.

A few minutes later the rear doors opened and they dumped a dozen plastic bags in with them, all reeking of werewolf blood and death. He recognised the shape of fingertips pressing against the plastic from the inside. Shit. They'd been set up.

With her car safely hidden behind the nearby service station well to the west of the car park, Taenorah crouched on a roof and watched Rake's werewolves take down Kyle and the girl.

Despite the fact she'd thought he was dead these last few centuries, she still watched on with more concern than she cared to admit to herself, and a good portion of guilt. The idiot should have taken her warning and cleared town already. She almost wanted to kill him herself for his stupidity. He was probably as good as dead now, anyway. She might regret it, but it wouldn't weigh on her. He'd been dead to her for centuries, anyway.

After they'd hauled Kyle and his pup into the van, she watched as they collected the body parts she'd ordered strewn across the nearby reserve. Some of them might recognise Lucky's scent, but hopefully they didn't know him.

When they were done, the van took off while the other werewolves dispersed. Rake stood where he was by his car, searching until he finally saw her.

She smiled. At least he knew it wasn't Kyle.

Rake stood there, watching, no doubt trying to figure out her game plan. She stood, waved with her middle finger, and returned to the rear of the building. She jumped off, landing near a skip and scaring the life out of a stray cat. "One down, eight left," she muttered to the fleeing cat. She half expected to see Rake before she got to her car and Ferguson, but he didn't show. Smart move. She was considerably older and stronger than him.

"All good?" Ferguson asked as she got into the car.

"Perfect."

CHAPTER 18

KIMBRIEL WORE a peasant dress as she and Kyle walked northward along the dirt track toward Liverpool, her hair bound at the nape of her neck. Both her hair and clothes seemed to change at her whim. Yesterday she'd looked like a wealthy merchant woman. Tomorrow it might be something more regal - or she could appear as common as a servant or farmer's wife.

She'd given him fresh clothes and the sort of long coat a merchant might wear, as well as a handful of coins he could use to start a new life.

"Three decades," he said, still struggling to believe it. "I was buried for that long?" Mostly, he only remembered starving and the earth suffocating him. An eternity of suffering, it seemed.

He'd found his smithy burned to the ground and rebuilt anew when he'd returned. Nobody had recognised him, and the faces he remembered from the village were no longer the familiar faces of friends. They stared back at him as if he were a stranger. An outsider.

He kept his eyes on the spring trees around them, his head and shoulders sun-warmed despite the cool breeze. "What am I to do alone in a big city?" he asked, determined not to think about Taenorah's fate. Better to assume she'd died quickly.

"Work as a smith, perhaps? Your skills won't be wasted in a city, no matter your path."

The day was growing warmer, tempting him to take off his jacket despite the cool breeze tousling his hair. "And on the full moon? Are you sure garlic will be enough?"

"It will be if you want it to be. Most werewolves can't control themselves no matter what. Only the lucky few can. You have an advantage with garlic."

"I should go after the Creature who did this to me. Running away seems like cowardice."

"You're not running away, you're seeking a new life. Look for people you want to be around and spend time with them. Find someone new to love, and love her as much as you did Taenorah."

He gave her a bitter smile. "I'll do everything you asked but love again. I'm not sure I'll survive it a second time. The prospect of watching a woman grow old while I stay young..."

Water splashed his face.

Kyle caught his breath as another bucket of water emptied over him. His left shoulder burned abominably from a silver spike driven through it to prevent him changing form. He gritted his teeth as pain came on like a blowtorch burning a hole through his flesh. He moaned.

"He's awake."

He blinked water from his eyes, resisting a natural instinct to shake.

The place smelled of dry mold, the smell not unlike an old library, though libraries were more intimate. They were in a warehouse. The place reeked of werewolves, the scents of more than a dozen individuals. Underlying it was the subtle coldness of vampire. Vampires must visit on occasion, but it wasn't where they gathered.

Kyle looked up and found himself chained to a crossbeam beside a post, his hands above his head.

Across the aisle, Zannah crouched against a shelving post with her hands behind her back, cuffed around the post, no doubt. Blood marked her shoulder where another spike had been driven through, the same as they'd done to Kyle, and her face was pale and sweaty from pain.

For an instant, he resented her for getting him into this situation, but none of it was her fault, really. She hadn't caused it. It was his own fault for getting involved. If he'd left her for dead when he'd seen her being hunted, or they'd gotten out of town instead of shopping, everything would be different.

He looked around. The warehouse was filled with heavy-duty shelves two storeys high, all stacked with pallets holding archival boxes, except for the row he was chained to. His shelves were against the wall. Beyond Zannah there must have been dozens of rows, the view obscured by cardboard boxes.

Two big werewolves watched them, the one with red hair almost double Kyle's build. Kyle let his head slump, the silver spike exhausting him, but the movement put Zannah back in his line of sight.

She must have sensed his stare as she slowly raised her head, a nasty bruise on her face and her bottom lip fat from a cut, her left eye swollen nearly shut and her nose crooked from the break. She looked far too young and vulnerable to be here, just as she had in the service alley.

Although crouched, Zannah shifted her weight on her feet, causing fresh blood to seep fresh from her shoulder around the embedded spike. She grimaced but didn't make any noise. After a couple of seconds she gave him an amazingly bright smile. "Well, ain't this a shit of a situation?"

Surprised, he couldn't help but return a smile. In some ways she reminded him of Taenorah, at least in her looks. Dark hair, beautiful eyes and smile, and a way of disarming him he could never see coming, but Taenorah had always seen problems. Zannah's thoughts seemed to move in the opposite direction.

Her smile broadened at his smile. Yeah, he'd save her again if he had the choice.

"I don't suppose you've got the key to my handcuffs?" she asked as she tested them, metal chain clinking against the post behind her. "I was thinking of using this nasty spike in my shoulder, but it's a little too thick."

The two werewolves watched Kyle, not Zannah, clearly recognising he was the real threat. They weren't wrong, but there wasn't much he could do now. "Why did you wake me?"

The ginger guy was huge. The other, perhaps of mixed Italian descent, was half a head shorter, but still considerably bigger than most men.

"Oy," Zannah said when they didn't answer, drawing their attention. "Any chance of a beer?"

They ignored her.

"Ass-wipes," she muttered, giving Kyle a cheeky grin as if the situation were a game. He gave her a subtle shake of his head. He didn't want to see her get hit again, or worse. This was a very dangerous game, and she didn't know how to play it.

Kyle tried to move his own arms but could barely flex them. The cuffs were painfully tight, locked over a strut above him where it met an upright support beam. It kept him painfully upright. If he slouched, it hurt. It hurt regardless, his body reacting to the silver like a human reacted to a bee sting. A thousand bee stings. He was a little surprised he hadn't gone into convulsions. Zannah, too.

He took his weight on his toes and the pain in his shoulder eased a little. It gave him the chance to give the cuffs an experimental tug. Steel links clunked against steel struts. Even an old vampire like Morrell would struggle to break them.

"What's the matter, feral? Caught in a rabbit snare?" asked the huge ginger fellow with muscles that had probably taken a decade to sculpt. His white t-shirt was tight against his chest and showed off his abs. Kyle doubted he'd have any trouble throwing him across a room.

Kyle met the werewolf's eyes. "I was planning on kissing your vampire master's ass in the hope of getting free, but that seemed too pathetic. It would make me look like you."

The ginger guy's expression changed from taunting to pissed off, but it was the smaller guy who stepped close and punched Kyle. He was still more than a head taller, and his punch had power.

Kyle's head slammed against the post behind him - a double hit. For a second he saw little but bright light and tasted his own blood in his mouth. When the pain eased, he focused on the smaller guy. "You ladies hit well. You might even get lucky and knock me out if you try hard enough."

He copped another blow to the jaw for that, his knees giving out. The smaller guy drove a fist into his stomach. Kyle would have doubled over if he'd been able. He gasped for breath, hanging like a cow carcass ready for butchering.

He struggled to raise his head and glare. "See. Pathetic." His whispered words sounded pathetic.

The Italian made a fist and drew back, but the ginger werewolf caught his shoulder. "Stop it, Sammy. He's asking for it. He wants you to knock him out so he doesn't have to face Samira. Don't make it easy on him."

Sammy pulled his shoulder free. "Yeah, well, fuck Samira." He swung and caught Kyle's jaw again, snapping his head to the right, and then hit him with the opposite fist. The back of Kyle's head clunked against the post both times, making him woozy. He couldn't find any strength in his legs to support his weight, making the spike grate in his shoulder.

Kyle vaguely heard Zannah yell something, but couldn't tell what as he was lost in a haze of red pain. He wasn't sure if he passed out or how much time had passed, but he woke to another bucket of cold water.

He felt his nose bleeding over his lips and chin, while a couple of teeth felt loose. His head hurt.

"What?" he slurred. "That it? Come on, give it a real go, you pathetic shit."

Another bucket of water splashed over him. Unprepared, he coughed and snorted some of it, making him cough more. It hurt to cough, and he tasted more blood in his mouth than he cared to admit.

He finally noticed someone new standing before him, a skinny guy about six foot tall with droopy eyes and a mouth to match. Lank brown hair fell across his eyes.

"Shit," Kyle said. "Did you fall face-first out of the ugly tree or did I wake up beside a puddle of my own vomit?"

His nose was so swollen he couldn't smell enough to tell if he was a werewolf or vampire. The man considered him for a few seconds and then caught Kyle by the neck. "Look into my eyes," he said. Vampire then. He disguised it well, but Kyle thought he might have had a French accent.

What would Zannah say? "So you can propose? Doing it on one knee usually gets the best results."

A backhanded blow almost sent Kyle into dreamland again, but another bucket of cold water brought him back. Where was the water coming from? They must have had hundreds of them lined up. He guessed they did this a lot.

"Do you mind?" Kyle slurred. "I was having a really nice dream." The ginger werewolf jogged off with empty buckets, no doubt to refill them.

Pressure constricted Kyle's throat again and he couldn't help but look up, staring into the mesmerising eyes of the vampire.

"My name is Marcel Legionella. Tell me why you killed two of our dogs."

Kyle tried to remember if he'd heard the name as he spat, but only succeeded in dribbling down his own chin. One of the advantages of his vampire taint was that he couldn't be mesmerised like a regular werewolf. "I didn't kill your wolves," he said after a few seconds of staring into the vampire's eyes, dropping all emotion from his voice to let the vampire think his coercion had worked.

The pressure on his throat disappeared.

Kyle took a few shallow breaths as the other werewolf... what was his name? Sam? No, Sammy, as Sammy pulled something about the size of a soccer ball from a hessian sack and tossed it at Kyle. Kyle saw dark hair and a bloodied, unrecognisable face. It hit his left leg, skull against flesh, and dropped to the concrete at his feet with a sound he didn't like to hear.

Zannah, across the aisle, turned her head away, her Polynesian skin going even paler than it had been. Another head hit his thighs and dropped beside the first. He didn't recognise either face and couldn't smell enough to catch a scent.

"Nice evasion, but not an answer. Why'd you kill them?" Marcel asked.

Kyle sighed, knowing where this was likely to go. "I didn't."

"Bullshit," said the werewolf who'd hit him. "Their heads were in your car!"

Kyle slowly turned his bloody face toward Sammy, and even moving that much hurt. "Sherlock Holmes, aren't you? I was set up to take the fall, you moron."

Kyle braced himself as the werewolf came at him again, but Marcel caught him and hauled him back. Sammy made a frustrated sound but backed off.

Kyle kept his eyes on Sammy. "Did you consider someone could be using us? We were clearing out of town to get away from this shit. We're not your enemies."

"He's lying, Marcel," Sammy said. "Let me beat the stupid out of him."

Kyle ignored the werewolf and focused on Marcel. "Your pet has a nose, doesn't he? Tell him to use it. Have him sniff us. You won't find their scents on us." He glanced down at his legs. "Okay, you'll find it on my legs now, but nowhere else." He glanced at Zannah. "Definitely not on her."

It might solve a question, but it wouldn't fix their problem. He had no doubt Marcel would kill them both regardless, and depending on how he did it, there was a good chance they wouldn't regenerate. Possibilities raced through Kyle's head. He was hard to kill, sure, but that didn't make him unkillable. Zannah, too, and she certainly deserved better.

Marcel considered that for a moment, and then nodded to the

ginger werewolf returning with four full buckets. "Sniff her."

Ginger placed the buckets on the wet concrete and knelt next to Zannah. She cringed away as he took a deep sniff. The big werewolf looked up and shook his head. "Bit hard to tell with the silver, but I'm fairly sure she's clean." He crossed the isle and sniffed Kyle's chest before shaking his head in the negative.

Marcel pursed his lips as if he'd just been forced to declare war and found it distasteful. "Morrell did this then?" he asked, his eyes distant but his expression livid. He turned to Sammy. "Go find Rake and Sanders to call the rest of the coven together and round up your pack."

Zannah sniggered. "Rake and Colonel Sanders? Don't any of you have real names?"

Marcel glared at her, clearly a vampire with a short temper. "You should be more polite. Samira doesn't have the same issues with ferals that Morrell seems to have developed, but that doesn't mean you're leaving here in anything but pieces if you piss me off. The only reason you're not already dead is because I still want to know why Morrell used you like this. There are easier ways to cause a war."

Kyle shifted his shoulder and winced at the pain from the silver spike. "The best way to get back at him would be to let us join your pack," he said, hoping it would at least buy them a little time.

Marcel raised an eyebrow. "Call me cynical, but I have suspicions about your loyalty."

Three people walked into the aisle from the far end of the warehouse, maybe thirty yards away.

"I'll deal with you two later," Marcel said as the three joined them - a woman and two men. They all seemed to defer to the woman. Samira, then. She appeared to be of Middle Eastern descent and was shorter than Kyle, though for all her power her clothes could have come from the local thrift shop. Clearly not one for vanity.

The woman glanced at Kyle, and there was a threat of murder there. If Kyle said anything now, she'd probably crush his throat before he could get out a second word.

She turned to the ginger werewolf. "Collar them both."

CHAPTER 19

KYLE WATCHED, useless to help, as they secured a heavy steel collar around Zannah's neck, connecting it to a chain via a large padlock. One of the werewolves climbed the shelves and looped the chain over a steel bar two cross beams above Zannah's head, the chain running over the metal to hit the ground with a clatter.

Zannah hissed in pain as they removed her cuffs and hauled her upright by the collar, gasping as they roughly secured her hands above her head the way they'd done with Kyle. The silver spike made it a thousand times worse than a regular wound, but a gasp was the only noise she made. She gritted her teeth as if refusing them further satisfaction.

Kyle had seen plenty of Creatures who'd be begging for mercy from less. A bright spill of fresh blood blossomed on her t-shirt around the spike.

The ginger werewolf pulled on the chain to force her to her tiptoes and secured the end to another support beam to Zannah's right, well out of her reach. He looped around and d-bolted it together.

They collared Kyle too, but didn't haul him up to his tiptoes. He probably looked hurt enough.

"Nothing to say?" Sammy asked Kyle.

"To a teacher's pet?" he said with as much sarcasm as he had left.

The werewolf smirked. "Even if you can get the spike out and change form, you'll choke. I'm a little tempted to pull the spike out just to see you try."

Zannah, despite her stoicism, was breathing too fast, the collar too tight or pulled too high. Both, probably.

Kyle indicated her with a nod, drawing the werewolf's attention to Zannah. "If she chokes to death with that spike in her shoulder, she won't regenerate. Your master might not be too happy with that."

Sammy looked her over. "You're right." Rather than loosen the chain, he ripped the spike from her shoulder.

She made a whimpering sound and almost passed out as the tips of her toes slipped on the concrete, but she still didn't beg. He'd known she was tough from the moment he'd seen Rake playing cat and mouse with her, but this was a whole new level.

Sammy dropped the spike. It hit the concrete with a high-pitched clatter. "There. All's well again."

"You're an ass," Kyle said

That made him smile. "Be nice or I'll bring in the whole pack and let them play with your bitch in front of you. I suspect a couple of them will like it a tad more than her."

Kyle clenched his jaw. He doubted it was an idle threat.

"Good doggy. Perhaps you can be trained. I'll bring a tennis ball when I come back."

"You're a hypocrite."

The werewolf ignored Kyle and walked back to Marcel and Samira, giving Kyle nothing to do but stare at Zannah. She had a look in her eye that suggested she was close to panic. "Calm down," he said, using his influence on her. Fortunately, it worked.

Marcel was speaking when Samira's phone rang. She answered and stepped away. "What?"

Kyle watched, wishing he could hear as well as a regular werewolf, but she was too far away for him to catch both sides of the conversation.

She hung up. "Marcel," she said. "Rake says he saw someone being taken into Morrell's nest like a hero. He thinks it was the dog who killed Spence and Bessy."

"Did he say who?" Marcel glanced down the aisle at Kyle.

"A newbie trying to make a name for himself. It seems to have worked. Rake heard the name *David*."

Kyle met Zannah's eyes. She returned his gaze with fear. He knew who was causing all this then. Rake had attacked Zannah, probably ripped Jaque's heart out, and set them up in the shopping mall car park. He'd probably dumped David at Morrell's door and called it in to Samira on purpose. Shit. Rake was playing both sides.

Zannah shook her head slightly to tell him not to interfere, though she was struggling for air.

"What are you two up to?" asked Samira as she caught the look between them.

Zannah gave Kyle another 'don't say anything' look.

Sammy watched, understanding blooming. "They know what's going on, Samira," he called.

The group of vampires and werewolves walked up to the two captives. "Speak," Samira said.

"I don't know anything," Kyle said. "We were passing through when we were set up."

This close, Kyle could smell the fresh blood on Samira's breath. Human blood. It was sickening in a morbidly enticing way.

"Really?" Samira asked. "If someone else had set up shop in this city, I'd know, or Morrell would, and he doesn't like the competition he already has. He'd have done something."

He hinted at the only bargaining chip he had left. "Then you have a traitor."

"Not likely." Samira unsheathed a knife, the blade made of silver. With a knowing glance at Kyle, she approached Zannah, gripped her jaw and forced the blade between her lips. Zannah cried out and opened her mouth to avoid the burning touch of silver.

"I could cut her tongue out," the woman said, though it was an awkward threat considering Zannah's mouth was above the vampire's head. "With a silver blade it could take years to grow back, if it does at all. But I'm sure you've got more to say." She purposely nicked Zannah's tongue.

"Ahh!" Zannah cried, the silver probably hurting more than the cut itself. "Bitch!"

Samira pressed the silver against Zannah's split and she let out a brief muffled cry, cringing back.

"Okay!" Kyle said, though he was determined to keep his bargaining chip for now. "David's her ex, but he's not a werewolf. Even if they'd bitten him today, he wouldn't be out making a name for himself, if ever. He's a bloody coward for a start."

Samira released Zannah's jaw and used the same hand to flick her long dark hair over her shoulder, the blade still poised. "You believe him?" she asked Marcel.

Marcel shrugged. "I think Morrell's up to something. Maybe this David's a pawn, someone new to pin the murders on in case we didn't buy it being these two."

Samira grimaced as if she'd been thinking the same thing, but she lowered the blade. "Then let's go teach Vincent Morrell and his dogs a lesson. Gather the pack and get ready. We'll hit them an hour before dawn and level Morrell's place with him in it."

"It's going to be a massacre," Kyle said as they left. "And Rake's done his best to orchestrate it."

"David," Zannah choked out. "He's... an ass... but he doesn't... deserve... to be caught up... in this... because of me."

He met her eyes, wishing he could free her and make it so she'd never have to deal with Creatures again. "None of us do, but I'm beginning to think I've got a score to settle."

He pulled on his cuffs, but even if the spike in his shoulder didn't feel like a constant blowtorch, he was too hurt to even come close to breaking anything but his wrist.

It wasn't long before Sammy returned. He swung at Zannah before she even saw it coming, catching her jaw. She slumped unconscious, her body held up by the collar and cuffs.

"You sadistic bas-"

He punched Kyle, and this time he didn't hold back at all. Another blow sent him into darkness, and he felt himself sliding anyway. Bastards weren't taking any risks at all.

CHAPTER 20

The streets of Malaysia were a world away from what Kyle knew, but after the horrors of the Second World War they were a welcome break, not that he'd done any fighting as a cook.

Malaysia was a place of change, ancient fishing boats next to modern ships, petrol-powered vehicles sharing the roads with hand-drawn carts, and new buildings replacing the old. The place felt energetic.

It wasn't the modern he sought, it was the old. Japanese, not Malaysian. Knowledge and skills, taught by a man who'd left Japan after the war, a master of self-defence.

Kyle kept the old samurai sword he'd only just purchased close to his body, the blade carefully wrapped in red cloth and bound with a strong cord. He'd spent everything he had to buy it, working hard for nearly a year.

As a former blacksmith, it was a weapon he could appreciate. If he'd known how to make blades like the one he now carried, he'd have been a rich man in his youth. Very rich.

Dodging pedestrians and push bikes, he stopped outside a decrepit-looking old building, the words above the door hand painted in Japanese. He couldn't read the words, but he knew what they said. Master Tanaka's Dojo, or something similar. It was a loose translation he'd received while asking for directions.

Nervous and unsure if he would even be welcomed, he took a calming breath and walked in.

Like most rooms devoted to physical exercise, the place carried a smell of sweat, even in the foyer.

He took a set of rickety stairs up to a gallery and watched Master Tanaka as he instructed his students in the art of unarmed fighting. They lined up on the hard-looking mats and bowed, listened to instructions Kyle couldn't understand, paired off, and threw each other around the room with surprising grace and agility. They practiced falling, attacking, and counter strikes, each one involving a throw of some kind.

As he watched, Kyle noticed Master Tanaka regularly pulling an individual aside to teach or correct something, and then supervising while they practiced what he taught. When he was satisfied, he moved to another group. The man had seen Kyle walk in, but ignored him.

After the class finished, a new class began, and they followed the same routine. Some students were Malaysian or Chinese, but many were westerners. Australian soldiers judging by the uniforms they changed out of and in to.

Watching them throw each other around like circus performers was an experience in itself, and something he desperately wanted to learn.

When the final class for the day was done, he entered the gym and approached Master Tanaka, standing well aside and waiting patiently until the barrel-chested man finished explaining something to several students.

"Excuse me, sir," Kyle said as the students left, all big westerners with Australian accents.

The short Japanese man, Kyle's height and maybe in his late thirties, acknowledged Kyle. "I know you," he said in a thick accent.

"Yes," Kyle said. "A year ago, I was disrespectful to you after I'd spent a lot of time in a bar. I was very drunk, and you taught me I should have more manners. I did not take the lesson well, but afterward I came to appreciate it. Watching today, I appreciate what you could have done to me, but didn't." He gave the man a slight bow. "Thank you."

The beating had been brutal, but the man hadn't broken anything or done any serious damage. Kyle's werewolf strength had been completely useless as Master Tanaka had humiliated him so badly, he'd never forgotten the lesson. Despite Kyle's superior strength and speed, he wasn't even close to being a match for the man.

"Please," Kyle held out the sword and watched as Master Tanaka unwrapped the cloth protecting it.

The master stared at it for a long time, the black sheath polished to perfection.

"Very rare blade. Very difficult to come by." He glanced warily at Kyle. "Why show me?"

"A gift," Kyle said. "In the hope you might forgive me my disrespect and offer me the chance to study your art. I promise to be a devoted and respectful student, and to use what you teach me with the restraint you showed to me."

The man drew the blade halfway out before sheathing it again. "And if I say no?"

Kyle met the man's eyes, glad to find someone his own height. "Then I'll find someone less worthy. The blade, though, is yours."

The man stared at the weapon a while longer, and to Kyle's relief gave a slight nod. "Return at dawn tomorrow. The katana, and your respect, are payment enough."

CHAPTER 21

KYLE JERKED AWAKE, struggling with pain as he remembered where he was. Calming down, he focused on the woman across from him, the toes of her boots barely touching the ground as she dangled unconscious from the collar and chain, her hands bound above her head, just as his were. His shoulder still burned from the silver spike, the fiery ache more than enough to block out the pain of his other injuries.

"Zannah," he whispered.

She remained unconscious, but breathing. The treatment wasn't likely to kill either of them, but there were worse things that could be done, and the unseen scars could last for generations. If they survived.

He checked the aisle for anyone who might be watching and tried to see between the shelves, listening at the same time. No sound. No movement. He didn't have an escape plan, but no guards were a good sign.

"Zannah," he said a little more loudly.

She stirred, moaned, and slumped into unconsciousness again.

He pulled at his cuffs, but only succeeded in making the chain slip loudly against steel. Fearing he might have roused attention, he held still for a full minute, but no one came.

He rested the back of his head against the steel post, closing his eyes and trying to fight down the fears preventing him from thinking clearly. He wasn't sure how long they had before Samira got back, but if things went to the vampire's plan, it wouldn't be long after dawn. At that point, he and Zannah could find themselves crammed into barrels filled with concrete and dropped to the bottom of the ocean. The local lake, at least.

The chain attached to his collar was still firmly looped over a strut well above his head and d-shackled to the next post, metres out of his reach.

He tried to reach the spike in his shoulder with his teeth, but it had been driven so far in that it was beyond him. Breathing hard and sweating from the pain, he rested his head back against the post.

He had to change form. The silver wouldn't prevent him from doing it, like it would a normal werewolf, but the collar would still choke him and the silver spike would prevent regeneration. It might even kill him if it didn't work properly.

Zannah moaned, coughed, choked and began to panic, struggling against the cuffs and collar.

"Calm down!" he hissed.

She saw him, but there was a wild look in her eyes.

And then he saw something that shouldn't have been possible. Her eyes went from dark brown to albino red in a heartbeat. She stiffened and screamed in agony.

Her body bucked, joints popping loud and painful, her teeth grew and her jaw and mouth reformed into a muzzle, all in the space of a heartbeat.

"Oh shit!" Kyle said. If she got free now, she'd kill everyone and everything she came across, and tear him apart too.

He pulled against his handcuffs with everything he had, but couldn't break them.

Zannah screamed again, her agonised cry changing to a wolf's howl of pain. Fur erupted from her skin like a sped-up film of mold growing on fruit. Her wrists narrowed as her hands changed to paws and slipped free of the cuffs.

Dangling due to her shortening wolf's legs, she struggled as her body contorted and she kicked her pants and boots to the ground. Covered in fur, her hips and legs had already shifted form, revealing the brand new body of a werewolf swinging from the collar and chain.

She kicked and yipped and howled, her legs trying to get purchase, but every time they touched the post, they just pushed her away.

Sammy and Ginger came running down the aisle but were wise enough to keep their distance as they looked on in surprise. Like this, she was far more deadly than them, perhaps even deadlier than a vampire. She was still collared, though.

If her paws had been able to get any purchase on the post or shelf, she'd have had a good chance of busting the chain. Fortunately, or perhaps unfortunately, she couldn't.

Her struggles had twisted the collar around, the chain now at her front and forcing her head back. It took the pressure off her throat, at least.

The ginger guy and his friend Sammy kept their distance, watching to make sure she didn't get free. After a minute, Zannah stopped struggling and just hung there, limp and trapped.

"What the heck?" the ginger guy finally said as he cautiously moved between Kyle and Zannah. "I thought she was brand new?"

"It's not friggin' possible," the other answered. He turned to Kyle. "I thought you only bit her last night?"

Kyle nodded, shocked himself. "I did. It must have been the fear and panic of choking. Some survival instinct."

The ginger werewolf moved toward Zannah, but her red eyes went wild and she snarled, huge teeth showing she wasn't completely helpless. He backed away. "She can stay there until morning. I don't need my arm ripped off. Let's go."

Kyle would have done the same thing if it were any other werewolf but Zannah. Even her paws were capable of disemboweling a man. At least the two captors weren't sadistic enough to taunt her, or maybe they were just smart enough to realise that Zannah might be able to break the chain with enough provocation. That, or she'd break her own neck.

He watched the werewolves walk around the end of the isle, silently cursing them for not doing something to help. He had no way to tell if she'd even keep her sanity after this. Werewolves who couldn't were usually killed by their Creature masters or hunted down by their own kind.

"I'm so sorry," he whispered to her. "We should have cleared town when we had the chance."

She gave him a baleful stare, no understanding in her eyes.

Survival instincts would be dominating her human thoughts right now, even if she remained sane. Most werewolves didn't remember changing the following morning, at least not until they were much older.

"You okay?" he asked the dark-haired wolf, mostly just to hear his own voice. Her red eyes stared back at him as she swung softly back and forth. At least she wasn't kicking in a panic anymore.

Think. Think. Think.

He had to deal with the spike in his shoulder. His body kept trying to regenerate around the wound, making it burn constantly as the repairing nerves seared against the silver, regenerated, and seared again. The spike, driven all the way through and then some, occasionally touched the steel behind him, sending a new wave of pain through his body.

Gritting his teeth, he carefully positioned the tip against the post, and cried out as he pushed back, forcing the silver an inch through his shoulder.

He almost blacked out as he dangled there, his feet unable to take his weight and the collar half choking him. It took him a full minute to recover.

Carefully, he tried to get a hold of the spike's tip with his teeth now he had more leverage. It burned the corner of his mouth and his lip, but he managed to get a grip and rip it out.

He cried out again and almost passed out as he dropped it with a clatter to the ground. Even his tongue felt blistered. He couldn't imagine how difficult that would have been for a normal werewolf. He slumped again, the cuffs and collar keeping him upright until the pain eased.

Zannah watched him with what he could only describe as a hungry glare, one paw twitching every now and again but not moving otherwise. The first shelf was over her head, the blue-coated steel pole the only thing she could get a paw to.

"And I'm still stuck," he said to her.

She gave no sign she understood him. He doubted she did. He didn't understand speech as a wolf either.

"Yeah, you just hang around while I do all the hard work," he muttered.

On the ground, a few inches beyond his boot, he noticed half of a woman's thin clip, the kind that clicked together. He could use that.

Straining against the chain, he reached out with his left foot, but it was just beyond his reach no matter how he pulled. He needed to grow a few more inches.

"I don't suppose you've got any ideas," he asked the wolf.

Zannah watched him, red eyes full of malevolence, or at least that was his interpretation.

His shoulder hurt far less now, but it would take a while to heal properly. A day or two, maybe a few weeks considering the wound had been made with silver. Zannah was still watching him, her top and bra caught around her chest and forelegs. It made her look like a toy dog half dressed up by her owner for a social media post. A bloody big toy dog.

He glanced at the clothes on the ground, her shoes... and noticed his own shoes. If he took off a shoe, he might be able to use it to drag the broken hair clip closer.

CHAPTER 22

Kyle grimaced as he worked his left shoe off by standing on the heel and pulling his other foot out of it. It was tight, but it finally came free. Using the side of his shoe to pin the end of his sock down, he managed to wiggle his foot free of that too, though it took a few curse words and a bit of effort to make it happen.

Picking up the shoe between toes, he was just able to lift it and get it over the hair clip. Lowering it carefully, he tried to drag the flat metal closer. Nothing. The clip remained where it was. "A pox upon this facility," he muttered, going old school with his curse.

If they were still here when Samira returned, he had no doubt they'd be killed. The only thing preventing that at the moment was the possibility he and Zannah might be useful, but once the fight was done, that tenuous value would vanish. He could rat on Rake, but he doubted even that would save them.

He tried using his shoe again, and then a third time, relief washing through him when he heard a tiny scrape of metal on concrete. He carefully lifted the shoe up with his toe and found it closer, but not quite close enough. Two more attempts and it was close enough to touch with his big toe. He carefully placed the shoe aside and positioned the clip, but it was far too flat to pick up between his toes. He couldn't grasp it between them.

What now? He had no way to pick it up without leverage and was out of inspiration. He tried a pincer movement using his other foot, but the shoe was more of a hindrance than a help.

Hoping the two werewolves didn't return, he got rid of his other shoe and worked his sock off, using his big toe to put pressure on one end of the hair clip to lever the opposite up. Almost sweating with the effort, he caught it between his toes.

"Oh, thank the heavens," he whispered.

Grasping the post above him with his hands, he hauled his body in a flip upward, his shoulder protesting as he went upside down.

Careful not to drop the broken hair clip, he wrapped his legs around the post to take some of the weight off his arms and shoulders, and carefully lowered the foot with the clip until it was as close to his hands as he could get it.

Breathing hard, blood rushing to his head and sweat in his eyes, he took a deep breath and released the clip.

It struck his palm. He clutched... and only just caught it.

Breathing a huge sigh of relief, he pushed himself feet-first further up the pole so he could see better, and then used his thighs to grip the metal as tightly as he could before relaxing his arms.

He slid a couple of inches, but that was okay. Breaking the clip so he had just one of the two slivers of metal to work with, he worked it into the little gap where the two halves closed, jiggling it in deeper until they disengaged and released.

Wriggling his wrist, the cuff came free from his hand.

"Thank the stars," he muttered, his face going red from the effort of maintaining his position facing toward the concrete. Grabbing the bar with his arms he did a slow motion forward roll down the post until his feet touched the cold concrete again, and after a little more work with the broken hair clip, he managed to get the other cuff free.

Now all he had to deal with was the collar. Quietly lowering the cuffs to the ground with his toes, he climbed the shelving, careful not to let the chain clink on the metal, and cautiously slipped over the strut the chain had been thrown over. As carefully as he could, he made his way back down, looping the loose lengths of the chain as he went. Once down, he undid the D-shackle. The collar was still locked around his neck and the chain still attached, but he could get rid of them later.

He eyed Zannah warily.

"You going to attack me if I release you?" he asked.

She stared at him, her red eyes showing no sign she understood. One of her ears twitched. At least her ears weren't back like an attack dog. He hoped that was a good sign.

He approached, moving slowly. Her upper lip instinctively drew back to expose large white teeth, but she didn't growl.

Cautiously, he reached out, his hand just above her nose so she could get a good whiff of his scent. She sniffed, but her red eyes never left him. You never could tell with werewolves.

"Are you sane? You look sane," he whispered with false confidence, hoping it was true more than believing it. At least she hadn't reacted with violence.

Cautiously, he touched a palm to the back of her neck, just below the collar. She eyed him warily, but didn't snarl.

"Okay," he said. "I'm going to take a risk and trust that you're not going to rip me apart." He went to the end of the chain, pulled on the links to take Zannah's weight, and unscrewed the D-shackle until the bolt slipped free.

He carefully lowered her to the ground, doing his best to keep it quiet, though the chain links clanked one at a time over the crossbeam and post.

With all four paws on the ground, she turned and watched him, but didn't attack or try to run. Relieved, he climbed the crossbeams and quietly lifted the chain over the beam rather than pull it free, and then carried it back to the ground so it didn't make noise.

Zannah watched him the whole time, ears up and listening.

There was no acknowledgement or obvious understanding in her eyes, but she didn't attack. He put his shoes back on, collected her clothes, but hesitated at attempting to remove the top and bra she still awkwardly wore.

He moved close to her and carefully reached out, touching her t-shirt.

She rolled her eyes in a completely human gesture and lifted a front paw, giving him permission to undress her.

"This is a first," he muttered to himself as he removed her clothes for her, running the shirt down the length of the chain until it was free. Collecting them together as well as the two bloody spikes they'd been impaled with, he picked up the chain attached to his collar and looped it several times across one shoulder so it was easier to carry.

"Now I'm not suggesting I'm taking you for a walk or anything, but I'm going to need to carry that chain so it doesn't scrape along the ground or catch on anything."

Uncertain she'd allow it, he quietly gathered up her chain, and when she didn't offer any resistance, he led her to the end of the aisle. At the far corner of the warehouse there was an office at the top of a flight of stairs, a light on inside.

That was where the keys to their collars were likely to be. It was also where the two werewolves would be. With or without the collars, they had to go past the office to reach the door leading outside. "I vote we leave and get the collars off later," he whispered. "Raise a paw if you disagree?"

She stared ahead, watching, her ears up and listening.

"Agreed, then."

They were almost at the stairs to the office when the door opened and the big ginger werewolf came out. Kyle froze, hoping to blend into the shadows, but the werewolf only got about halfway down the stairs when he saw them.

Kyle swore, tensing, but Zannah didn't hesitate. She ripped the chain from his hands as she charged. Leaping, she bounded off a stair halfway up and crashed into the man before he'd staggered back three steps. Kyle couldn't imagine the innocent girl he'd first met ripping anyone's throat out, but she did, blood spraying everywhere. It must have been instinctive.

She didn't stop there. She charged up the remaining stairs with a clatter of chain and crashed through the door, smashing it off its hinges.

Kyle started to run after her, but a scream of pain cut short and he froze. She might turn on him next. Silence.

Inside, her chain abruptly dragged over wood as she trotted out the door and back down the stairs as if completely unconcerned about anything, her red eyes locking onto his and her muzzle and chest bloody.

He watched her warily for any sign she might attack him too, but she just stood there, tail low and flat, her ears up.

"Not exactly the quiet escape I was hoping for," he said. "You do realise they're not actually dead, don't you?"

She stared at him without any comprehension in her eyes.

"You bit them. I'm going to have to finish the job now. Understand? They might regenerate and become like us."

One ear went back and then up again, but otherwise he couldn't read her expression. She certainly gave no indication she understood him.

Gripping the silver spikes in her shirt so they didn't burn him, he climbed the stairs to the first werewolf, laying halfway up. Blood dripped to the ground underneath. The man's eyes stared at the roof, but two or three days from now he'd wake up, fully regenerated.

Without a mortal wound from silver or some other catastrophic injury such as beheading, Kyle couldn't be sure what would happen. Still using the shirt to hold one of the spikes so it wouldn't burn his skin, he positioned the tip over the werewolf's heart and drove it in.

No reaction. He hoped that was a good thing. He pulled the spike free, turned the werewolf over, and drove the same spike between the vertebrae in his neck, leaving it there.

In the office he found the other werewolf in three pieces - an arm and a leg ripped clean off. A chair had been knocked over and the water cooler had spilled, but otherwise the room was remarkably intact except for the spray of blood and body parts.

It turned his stomach, but he couldn't let it get to him.

Sammy lay in his own blood, still breathing shallowly, the sound wet and uneven. Plenty more blood covered strewn papers and stationery, not to mention the lone laptop computer. More than a fair share streaked the werewolf's face too, making it difficult to see where the injuries stopped and the damage began.

The Creature's eyes watched Kyle in fear as the former blacksmith knelt. "I'm sorry," Kyle said softly as he positioned the second spike over his heart and drove it home. If he'd hesitated, he wasn't sure he'd have been able to do it, but that would be the equivalent of murdering Zannah. He pulled the spike free, rolled the werewolf over, and used it to sever his spinal column as well, just to be sure.

He got back to his feet and searched the body for the key to his collar, but it wasn't there. After more distasteful searching through blood and around torn limbs, he found it on top of the filing cabinet near the door. With relief, he unlocked himself and dropped his chain and collar to the ground.

Zannah waited at the bottom of the stairs, and despite his trepidation in approaching her, she didn't react when he unlocked her collar.

"I know you don't feel any guilt now, but you will tomorrow." She met his eyes without any clear comprehension. Tomorrow, he was going to have his hands full consoling her. He'd probably have to find her professional help. At least for now she didn't care.

They found Zannah's car outside, the keys in the ignition and the blood wiped up enough to pass a causal inspection. Kyle could still smell the reek of werewolf blood and see a couple of darker patches on the tired old cloth seats. There were some clothes on the floor, but they didn't seem to be dirty. Samira's crew probably intended to dump and burn it somewhere, so cleaning the blood was just a sensible precaution in case the driver got pulled over.

It still stank. He opened the door and Zannah beat him in, trying to turn her huge werewolf's body in the driver's seat for a good couple of seconds before realising she wasn't going to be able to drive. With almost disdainful movements, she raised her head like she'd always intended to move aside, and daintily stepped across the manual gears to the other seat, sitting. It was a little hard to read her expression, but embarrassment probably covered it.

"Bit crammed?" he asked.

Baleful red eyes narrowed at him.

He held his hands up. "Just a joke about your size, not your weight."

As a human, she'd be pretty close to six foot tall. Five ten or eleven. As a werewolf, she was probably twice as heavy and all muscle, but not quite as tall. Where the extra weight came from Kyle had no idea, but it happened to him too. He probably doubled his weight as a werewolf.

With a glance over his shoulder he considered leaving the building as it was, but there was too much evidence that could be linked to him and Zannah, including fingerprints and blood. It was mostly Zannah he was concerned for, though. He could flee the country and call it even. She had friends and family here.

"Wait here," he said, raising a hand flat toward her. He left the door open in case she decided to follow him. He didn't want her smashing free. Surprisingly, she stayed put.

After a few minutes of looking around, he found a box of matches in the office and several jerry cans full of diesel in a storeroom under the stairs, as well as a small can of regular fuel. He used the smaller can to douse the area where he and Zannah had been chained. Standing well clear, he flicked a match at the area.

Flame burst through the air, making him stumble back with singed brows and stinging eyes. Fortunately, the shelves where they'd been kept were entirely empty. The flames burned out quickly.

He dragged the ginger werewolf on the stairs into the office and did the same thing with the diesel, leaving a trail of fuel down the stairs. Within seconds the office was roaring. Alarms sounded and fire extinguishers in the roof rained down a hail of noxious gasses.

He backed out of the warehouse, choking and coughing. The fire still roared, but not for long.

"Okay," he said as he got back into the car. "We have to clear out of town before they figure out what's happened." Kyle suspected, with more than a little unease, that they'd made an enemy who could harass them for centuries. As the fire sprinkler system tried and failed to deal with the fire he'd set, at least for now, he drove away as quickly as he could without attracting unnecessary attention.

CHAPTER 23

"ONCE THEY FIND out what you, no we, did, they'll come after us. We might be better off getting out of the country too, at least for a few years." It wasn't worth the effort to go and get his gear from the motel. It was mostly just spare clothes and toiletries anyway, though his passport was in the safe there. If he contacted them, they could forward it.

She stared at him, ears up as if trying to work out what he'd said. He was mostly thinking aloud, anyway.

Within ten minutes he'd managed to find signs leading onto one of the roads heading out of town, his mind struggling to defy logic and drive on the wrong side of the road.

Zannah growled.

"What?"

She stared at him, canines showing.

"I'm only guessing here, but... you're hungry?"

She growled again.

He tightened his grip on the steering wheel, determined not to provoke her. "Can you save it for dawn? I'm not familiar with this city or even driving on the left side of the road. I can't interpret your growls at the same time."

She snarled again, showing pristine white canines.

"Seriously, Zannah? Can we please save this until we're safe?"

She glanced out the rear window and whimpered, and then leaned forward and licked his face.

"Ew!" He wiped his cheek as he checked the rear-view mirror, but there wasn't a car or anything else behind them. "What is it, Lassie? Is the kid in trouble and the bad guys are after him?"

She yipped at him and glanced at the rear window again.

Frustrated, Kyle pulled over before she caused an accident. "What? Did you leave something behind that's worth risking your life for?"

She just cocked her head slightly, like a dog listening uncertainly.

"I really don't know what you want other than to go back. Drop some hints."

As if she finally understood him, she jumped into the back seat, picked a shirt up off the floor and jumped back, dropping it between them.

He sniffed it. "This is David's."

She stared at him.

"Are you trying to tell me you want to go back and rescue David?"

She cocked her head, but she gave no indication she understood what he said.

He put his head against the backrest. "We don't even know where he is."

She nudged the shirt with her nose.

"It's a stupid idea. There's a turf war about to erupt and you want to run through the middle of it?"

She just stared at him with those baleful red eyes.

"Shit," he whispered, scratching his head. "Okay, what if we check things out? I'm not making any commitment to this stupidity though." He had a better idea. "How about we go and see Kimbriel?" He dry-wiped his face, wishing Kimbriel wasn't across town. "I still think this is a bad idea." He stared at the road leading out of town with regret. Why was he even listening to Zannah? What did he care if they hurt her ex? What did she care?

With a sigh, he turned the car around at the next roundabout and headed back toward Kimbriel's home, getting lost three times on the way. Only Zannah's yipped directions, which weren't all that easy to interpret, got them there.

Mal answered the door again, and didn't seem at all surprised to see them. "Come in," he said.

Kimbriel waited for them in the kitchen, a mug of tea clasped between her hands as she leant against the counter. Her eyes went from Kyle to Zannah and back, and if anything, he saw amusement there.

"Go on," Kyle said. "Say it."

Kimbriel shrugged. "I was thinking how impressive she is. Very few werewolves can transform at will, and she's brand new."

"It wasn't exactly at will," he said softly. He stared at Kimbriel, certain she knew his intent already. "I think Zannah wants to save her ex-boyfriend. David."

Kimbriel smiled, and there was warmth there he'd rarely seen. "She's also got a big heart. Do you think I'd let you keep just anyone you bit?"

He held her gaze for a long while, not wishing to talk about it. "Do you know where David is?"

"Yes."

He waited, but as usual she volunteered nothing. "Would you mind telling me?" he asked acerbically.

She nodded. "Yes. I would."

What? She'd never denied information before, though she'd always made him work for it. "Kimbriel, please. I'm not in the mood. Can you stop being cryptic just for tonight?"

She took a sip of her tea, but didn't respond.

"Please tell me where David is."

Kimbriel glanced at Zannah. "Does she mean that much to you already?"

"What? Of course not... okay, maybe. I like her. She's... like you said, got a lot of heart. Look, she killed a couple of people tonight and she's going to regret it tomorrow. If I can help her save her ex, it might be enough to help her through the anguish."

Kimbriel gave him a measuring look before writing an address down on a sticky note and handing it to him. "You're a good man, Kyle."

"No advice? No cautionary comment?" he asked. It sounded harsher than he'd intended.

"You know I don't get involved in these things. Where would I stop if I started?"

So that was it? And all this time he simply thought she liked to annoy people, but he knew what she meant. "You're powerful enough you could rule the world if you wanted to. You could make it a much better place."

She shrugged. "I could rule the universe if I wanted to, but who says my vision for it is better than anyone else's? I'd certainly make changes most people wouldn't like. The world can sort itself out. I'm neither its saviour nor its ruler."

He tried one last time, not expecting any real answers though. "I could use your advice."

She picked up her tea again but paused. She didn't sip it, merely cupped it between both hands. "If you want to put yourself in the middle of a war, Kyle, that's your choice. My advice is to stay out of it. The local clans will sort themselves out and eventually forget about chasing you."

"And the kid Zannah wants to save?" He still couldn't figure out a good reason why, but if she was in, he was in.

"David's fate is neither a consequence of your actions nor your responsibility. If it weren't for you, he'd already be dead. You owe him nothing, and neither does Zannah."

Kyle glanced at Zannah, who merely stared at Kimbriel, head slightly cocked. "I doubt she'll see it that way. Besides, it's not me who's asking."

Kimbriel gave a slight smile. "You could do a lot worse than Zannah, you know that Kyle?"

He laughed bitterly. "She's as tall as a catwalk model and drop-dead gorgeous. I'm the size of a garden gnome and hardly good looking. She can do better."

Kimbriel smiled at the description. "You're taller than me."

"Mice are taller than you."

She laughed at that. "I'd just like to see you happy."

"You made me happy a long time ago." He held up the sticky note. "Care to share anything else?"

She watched him for a long moment, considering, and then sighed. "You know you've been used, don't you, Kyle? You were the catalyst for this turf war."

"And David is collateral damage?"

"Don't use David as an excuse. You're not trying to save him because you feel any responsibility. You're doing it for her."

He glanced away.

"She rules your heart already, doesn't she?"

Anger rose up in him. "Screw you, Kimbriel. How long have you been nudging me toward this?" Kyle said, the flash of insight tearing through him. "Look at the poor girl," he said, pointing to the large wolf beside him. "Do you think she wanted any of this?"

Kimbriel held his eyes for a drawn out moment, showing no signs of intimidation. "Do you think she wanted to be dead?" Kimbriel replied with a raised eyebrow.

He clenched his fists, impotent anger rising. "But..."

She put her tea down. "I can't see the future Kyle, I never could. Just possibilities, and whenever I interfere those possibilities vanish. I didn't call you here for me. Not even Zannah. I did it for Jimmy, her brother."

He stared. "Why, Jimmy?" he finally asked.

She shrugged. "I like him."

It was a straight-out lie, but he didn't think he'd be getting any other answer. "I don't suppose you could magic David here so we don't have to go after him?"

"I have no power over him unless he gives it to me. Same as you and Zannah."

Kyle flicked the piece of paper she'd given him to draw attention to it. "Do you have a spare map I could borrow?"

"Use the app on Zannah's phone. It's in the console of her car. I wrote the code below the address you're holding."

CHAPTER 24

Samira got out of her Ferrari a few blocks away from Morrell's compound, not far from a strip joint that remained open until dawn. She suspected Morrell owned the venue, though rumour suggested a local biker gang owned it. Either way, she'd made sure they'd arrived over a couple of hours to avoid drawing attention.

Nobody knew she owned a Ferrari, as she'd only taken delivery of it a few days ago. Although it stood out, it wouldn't be recognised.

Most of her dogs were in the strip bar while they waited, getting an eyeful. If her dogs were noticed there'd be trouble, but if that happened she'd use them to draw resources away from Morrell's compound.

Morrell's car yard and compound was on the other side of Mitchell's industrial area, but still only a mile or so away. Hopefully Morrell's dogs weren't patrolling this far out. Now she was sure that they weren't casing the strip joint, she wanted the attack to be a complete surprise.

She nodded to a couple of her vampires, Sorrento and Haythe, giving them the signal it was time to begin. Sorrento walked toward the strip joint to round up the troops. Marcel was on reconnaissance, but no news was good news at this point. He'd been checking in regularly for hours now.

"You think we'll surprise them?" Haythe asked as Sorrento came back, moving up close to listen in. He had a wicked silver blade in his hand, disguised as a walking cane. He didn't look old, but affected a limp when he needed to.

Samira shook her head. "No one's reported seeing any of Morrell's dogs or vampires in the area. We might get in totally clean." She doubted it though, but remained hopeful.

She watched the streets for movement, but saw nothing. Either a trap was set, in which case she had more plans of her own, or she'd take Morrell by surprise.

Her dogs began to file out of the bar, some still with drinks in their hands. Despite rumours in the Creature world, werewolves actually could get drunk, but it took a lot of alcohol to do it. A few beers wouldn't make a difference.

Nobody tried to force her dogs to leave their drinks behind on the way out or even finish them before they left. Humans seemed to have that much instinct, at least. When her dogs noticed her watching them, some downed their drinks, while others abandoned them on the ground.

Miguel walked up and handed Samira a katana from under a coat too hot and heavy not to attract notice on a hot night like this. Her vampires were already armed, while the dogs didn't need to be for the most part. She'd only bought those who could force their change. The rest were still in cages.

She checked her matching pair of hand guns one last time, making sure the clips were full of silver bullets. A cliché, but it was going to be deadly in there and she had no intention of using the sword unless she had to. She slipped the guns back into their holsters under her jacket and checked the spare clips.

Despite the fact that guns were hard to get a hold of in Australia, all her vampire crew had firearms; shotguns mostly, but a few kept handguns and one had a rifle. It was going to be a massacre, and afterward, she'd rule the city unchallenged.

As her crew gathered around her, she smiled in anticipation. Over thirty werewolves and ten vampires. She should have done this decades ago.

"Everyone ready?" she called to a round of cheers. "Where's Rake?"

"He's watching Morrell's compound," Haythe replied. He pulled a phone from his pocket and dialled. After a moment, he put it away. "Didn't answer. Probably on silent to make sure he doesn't give himself away."

She'd rather have had Rake by her side, but she couldn't wait. "We're going in. If they've caught Rake, they probably know we're coming, but we've got the numbers and you all know the backup plan - retreat to draw them out and have the flanks cut them down when they give chase. Morrell won't have had enough time to call his crew together so we can expect to surprise them."

"We kill them all!" Haythe yelled, and the entire crew cheered. "No prisoners. After tonight, we'll rule the entire city!"

The werewolves took off at a dead sprint while Samira and her vampires followed at a jog. Werewolves were expendable. The older, more experienced werewolves changed form before they got there and leapt the chain wire fence, while the younger ones used bolt cutters to bust the gate and allow for easier access for Samira and the vampires, or an easier retreat for them all.

The large roller door at the bottom of the car ramp was closed, so his dogs smashed their way through glass windows upstairs and into the showroom.

Samira pulled her pistols out as she jogged through the gates behind her crew, the first screams of pain erupting from the building. She smiled, thumbing off the safeties. She intended to kill Morrell herself, and almost wished swords were a better weapon than guns, as the first shot rang out from inside.

"Go," she said to Haythe and the rest of his vampire crew. "Split up and call for me if you spot Morrell."

Kyle pulled up outside a closed gym on the opposite side of the block from Morrell's car repair and second-hand dealership, the gym's floor to ceiling windows dark.

Most werewolves heard exceptionally well, even when human, and they could smell even better. It was both a blessing and a curse in a city. Too many strong smells tended to mess with their senses, though it didn't affect Kyle nearly as much as he'd only inherited part of their sensitivity. It meant that he and Zannah had to be cautious or the werewolves would smell them coming.

Still, they were downwind and he could smell dozens of werewolves in the dealership's direction. "There can't be that many," he murmured. A single vampire could control a pack of ten or fifteen, but that many could turn on a vampire. Morrell had probably given control of some of them to his crew of vampires. If that was the case, there could be several dozen.

"We're in trouble," he said to Zannah. She raised her ears and looked at him, her tail wagging once. "That wasn't encouragement," he said. "It was fear. You should be able to smell it on me."

They got out of the car and followed the street around the block, stopping at the next corner. Glass shattered somewhere ahead, quickly followed by a scream of pain. A gun blast shattered another window a moment later, and more glass shattered before he heard a cry of agony. A short intervening silence was broken with yelling and another gunshot, and then everything happened all at once. Gunfire. Screams. Barks and shouting.

His heart thumped in genuine fear. "We really shouldn't be here," he said softly, though there was no need to speak. Zannah couldn't understand language anyway. Zannah padded a few paces ahead of him and then looked back, clearly expecting him to follow. "Who's taking who for a walk now?" he asked.

He couldn't see anything from where they were, but he could hear enough to know the turf war would be decided tonight.

"Okay," he said as Zannah stared impatiently at him. "But you better keep yourself under control. You haven't experienced bloodlust yet and I'm telling you, it's terrible, and worse the next day when you realise what you've done."

Tense, he recognised his own desire to delay in the hope it'd all be resolved before they could get near. He didn't want to risk facing Taenorah, or any of them for that matter.

Zannah padded a few steps forward, but he hissed. "Zannah!" He pointed at her so she would at least understand the body language. "Watch," he pointed at his eyes, hers, and then his own back. "My back." To make sure she understood, he half turned and pointed at his back. He mimed it all over again. "Understand? You watch my back. Don't get ahead of me. If we're going to do this, we need to stay together and I need you to protect me. I can't get David out if I change form."

She watched him for a moment longer and then padded back so she was slightly behind him. At least she understood that part. He took a deep breath and jogged ahead as guns fired and people fought. He wished he had a weapon. Even a metal bar would be better than nothing.

A friendly werewolf at his back would have to do.

A shadow stepped out from the corner of a building and he froze, Zannah snarling in response. Kyle tensed as a second shadow joined the first, but he recognised her. "Sellendria?" he asked.

The strange young woman walked forward, a grin on her face and a sword in her hand. Her companion, no, her protector, moved up beside her, holding a longbow with a quiver at his hip.

Sellendria nodded. "Kimbriel dropped a few hints that you might need some help tonight and gave me an address."

Not sure whether to be relieved or annoyed that the two of them might be putting themselves in danger, he looked around for Zannah's brother, just in case he'd decided to be an idiot too. Zannah would kill Kyle if her brother got hurt. He was sure of it.

"Jimmy's safe. I can promise he won't get involved in any fighting," Sellendria said, as if reading his mind. "It is Jimmy you're looking around for, right?"

"Maybe," Kyle said. "Where is he?"

She flicked her hair from her eyes with a toss of her head. "Safe. Get in and out as quickly as you can. Gordon will cover you. I'll cover Gordon."

Kyle gave the surrounds another quick glance but couldn't catch a trace of Jimmy's scent. Good. He'd better be safe. He began to move, but hesitated. "Thanks," he said. "And tell Kimbriel the same when you see her."

Zannah was beginning to get the feel of being a wolf, surprising herself at how much she liked it. She'd thought she was going to die when she transformed, it was that painful, like being dipped in molten metal. But now? Awesome!

She wanted to bounce on all fours with enthusiasm. She could smell everything, hear everything, and she felt stronger than ever, like she could do anything. Kyle certainly seemed to have a lot of respect for her in this form, his scent changing from fear to concern to nervousness and back almost constantly, not that she understood a word he said. It was like he spoke a different language now.

Still, they'd found other ways to communicate.

His scent suggested he was surprisingly protective of her, his fear for her greater than his fear she might go rabid and attack some innocent bystander. Or him. It was amazing how she could tell such subtle differences in his scent.

The world of Creatures, of being one at least, was definitely something she liked. She could get used to it, and to being able to read people through their scent. It was almost as if Kyle was the first person she'd ever been able to trust.

For now, though, he wanted her to watch his back, and she intended to do so. The sounds of guns, shouting and fighting in the building were good enough reasons to be cautious, particularly from people who knew what werewolves and vampires were capable of and were fully prepared to kill them.

Sneak in. Sneak out with David. That was Kyle's plan, she

guessed. No fighting if possible. She could do that. Keep Kyle safe, rescue the shithead David, and get out before the werewolves and vampires knew they'd been there.

Anger rose at the thought of David, but the anger was more inward than directed at him. He honestly didn't matter to her anymore, and it was only her sense of responsibility that pushed her toward helping him. He would have been safe if she hadn't insisted Kyle take her to him on the way home from the hospital. Now he was worse off than her. She needed to make up for that.

After talking with Jimmy's girlfriend, Kyle moved frustratingly slowly. At least she hadn't been able to scent Jimmy anywhere nearby, though his scent was fresh on Sellendria. They'd probably kissed before she'd left. How could anyone kiss her brother? Ew.

She wanted to run ahead, find David and get this over with, but put a poorly fitting lid on her impatience. She had to have Kyle's back or they'd both end up dead. Or worse. She assumed there was a worse. She'd seen plenty of vampire movies and could imagine similar stuff being done to her. That silver spike through her shoulder had been a taste of agony she didn't want to repeat.

Kyle froze as someone crashed through an upper-story window and slammed onto a car bonnet out front before bouncing to the ground. Whoever it was staggered to their feet, and without bothering to look around, they ran back into the building for more.

Kyle turned to her, put a finger to his lips to indicate quiet, and continued to the edge of the property. There was nothing but a chain wire fence between them and the car yard now.

Inside, fighting continued, the sounds of gunshots and things getting broken so loud she was surprised it couldn't be heard across the city. A car alarm went off, quickly silenced by a rending sound. What could smash through metal? That's how it sounded, at least. Metal tearing.

Despite the danger, some primal instinct began to ignite inside Zannah, and it excited her. It shouldn't, so maybe it was the form she was in, but she wanted to get in among the fighting. Was this the beginnings of some kind of destructive streak she'd have to deal with for the rest of her life? She liked it and feared it.

She could smell blood too. Lots of blood. The werewolf blood was rich but off-putting, but the vampire blood was entirely different. It infuriated her in a way that triggered murderous instincts, making her want to kill them. Any vampires. All vampires. It must have been a werewolf survival trait. Kill them or become a pet, she guessed.

She was inclined to heed the instinctive warning that vampires were more deadly and dangerous than werewolves, so the more of them that died tonight, the safer she and Kyle would be. Kyle certainly seemed to have a lot of respect for them, in a fearful kind of way.

He edged further forward and then sprinted to a car, ducking behind it. She followed close behind, the smell of blood growing stronger. Her stomach growled at the scent, all of it tied to her emotions in a terribly beautiful way.

It made her think of the two werewolves she'd killed, and she couldn't suppress her excitement at wanting to kill again. Somewhere within her human self, she realised she should feel guilty or at least a little upset, but it was the thrill she remembered, more than anything. She'd have to keep herself under control if she didn't want to hurt people unintentionally.

An arrow flew past them and struck a vampire with his back to a broken window. He dropped to his knees, futilely reaching for the shaft but unable to grasp it. After a moment, he fell face-first to the ground.

Zannah glanced back and saw Sellendria's friend drawing another arrow, the glint of silver reflecting from the tip. He'd better not aim that weapon at her or she'd tear him apart... shit. What was she thinking?

Kyle abruptly ran for the business's broken doors, one completely off its hinges and the other partly smashed in. She followed him into the building, staying close as he ducked into the main display area.

About a dozen display cars were already trashed or worse, most with bullet holes or shotgun blasts, and one had its bonnet ripped off. Several bodies were strewn about the showroom as well, two vampires with their hearts torn out and someone with a broken neck, her head facing the wrong way. A werewolf flew backwards through the air, smashing through a windscreen not far from Zannah and into the car's front seats.

She ducked as another car's window shattered from a shotgun blast fired too close. It made her ears ring as glass turned to shrapnel. The smell of silver ammunition mixed with gun-powder sickened her.

Another shotgun blast blew a hole in the wall a scant inch above her back and she nearly panicked, the pellets reeking of silver. She knew the touch of silver on flesh and didn't want to experience it again.

The short vampire who'd shot at her turned and fended off a werewolf in wolf form. Zannah skittered aside, determined to be a moving target rather than an easy one.

She avoided the werewolf and vampire as they struggled, and within seconds she heard the werewolf's neck snap under pressure. The short vampire threw the body aside, and before he could regather the shotgun and aim it at Kyle or herself, Zannah gathered her courage and sprang at him with all the strength she had.

She body-slammed him with surprising power, carrying him off his feet and onto the roof of a convertible, tearing through the roof's fabric with her claws. He tried to grab her and bring his gun around, but she caught his arm in her teeth and bit as hard as she could.

The vampire screamed in agony and tried to kick her away, but she twisted, tearing his arm free at the elbow.

He stared in shock, and then screamed again, trying to grab her neck with his good arm, the stump spraying blood through the torn roof of the convertible. Vampire blood. Rage and desire filled her and she snarled, the vampire's face contorting in pure fear.

Zannah caught his other wrist and bit until she felt bones break. He cried out again and tried to get away, kicking futilely, but she pounced and caught him by the neck, tearing out his jugular. Blood sprayed across her face and it tasted even better than it smelled. Full bloodlust overcame her and she ripped into him, tearing his head completely off, dropping it into the back seat of the convertible.

Two Creatures came at her, werewolves or vampires she couldn't tell, but the fact they weren't in wolf form suggested the latter. One held a sword low while the other gripped a silver knife, the metal giving off a reek like caustic fumes.

Bloodlust high, she didn't bother to consider strategy and attacked them, leaping above the sword and carrying the vampire to the ground. She broke his arm and crushed his spine before turning on the other. His knife opened her shoulder in a sharp slice of pain as she leapt and carried him to the ground. He took another stab at her shoulder before she crushed his skull in her jaws. He tasted like a werewolf, not a vampire.

The pain from the wound drove her bloodlust.

Another Creature, most likely an injured vampire by the way she tried to drag herself away from Zannah, whimpered when she saw her take notice. Zannah tore her throat out before she could call for help.

Something inside her forced her to turn back and rip through her spine with her jaws. Her neck hadn't been severed. Kimbriel's work. The promise she'd made. At least it was working for her.

A bullet punched through her hind leg and she yelped, ducking behind a car to avoid another shot, the pain excruciating. Silver. It had to be.

Another shot ricocheted off the car, but it gave her a good idea of where the shooter was. Limping slightly, she sprinted around several cars, rounded another and came at the vampire woman from the side.

The woman spun at the last moment and tried to bring her gun up, but Zannah hit her full-on and went for the throat. The vampire was dead by the time Zannah crashed to the ground, her neck torn so badly only skin kept the head in place. The spine was definitely severed. Good.

She noticed a scent she recognised, one of the vampires from the warehouse. She snarled in pure pleasure.

CHAPTER 25

"I THINK she brought her entire crew," Taenorah said with more disquiet than she'd expected to hear in her own voice. She kept her eyes on the stairs leading up from the basement, expecting the battle above to spill down here at any moment.

"Settle," Morrell said.

She riled against his control of her. She didn't want to be caught in open warfare between the two factions.

"Closer to me," Morrell said, and Taenorah obediently complied, though she fought the control.

His control over her was still bloody strong despite the centuries. The half dozen werewolves and both vampires, Simone and Kent, glanced her way and she could almost sense their envy of her position. They could have it.

Kent and Simone should be able to hold their own against werewolves one-on-one, but against more experienced vampires like herself, they'd be cut down. Regardless, they should be upstairs, defending their turf with the rest of the crew. This was a numbers game and Morrell was holding back.

"We need to send everyone," she said, not bothering to hide her fear.

He raised a fist and she cringed back, but he held the blow. "I didn't ask for your opinion." He was powerful enough he could break her jaw with a punch.

The muted sounds of guns and fighting echoed down to them, punctuated by the occasional shake as if someone had been thrown through a brick wall or a car dropped on them. Throwing a car would take a couple of vampires working together, but she didn't doubt it might happen.

She glanced at Morrell, his face impassive, though she could see the tension around his eyes.

"We need to get out there," she repeated, risking more than a broken jaw. "Hear me out," she said as he turned his glare on her. When he didn't tell her to shut up, she continued. "If we don't swing the odds soon, this will go against us."

What she really wanted was Morrell out there, preferably getting his head cut off. Despite the fact she loved fucking him, more than anything she wanted her freedom. That, and power, but she'd start with freedom.

In the chaos above, with Taenorah at his back, she might get a chance to punch a knife through the back of his skull.

The werewolves stood around the pool table looking just as nervous as she felt. Some even risked looking up to gauge Morrell's reaction. Simone and Kent waited at either side of the door, ready to surprise anyone stupid enough to come down.

Several of the dogs glanced her way, agreement in their expressions. They wanted to get into the fight too. She could almost see their bloodlust rising. They certainly weren't any good in human form.

"It's a good thing you saw Rake hanging around," Morrell said, as if he hadn't heard her protests. "Gave us time to rally the crew." He shifted a long sword to his right hand, drawing a handgun in the other as he faced the door in clear view of anyone who came down. He was using himself as bait, with Simone and Kent as his offensive weapons. The werewolves were backup, as was Taenorah.

Taenorah took a deep breath, risking more than a rebuke. "I know our dogs and crew are dug in up there and it's easier to defend than attack, but the odds are against us while we're divided and outnumbered. We should be out there fighting, not laying traps."

"I'm sure our boys and girls are holding their own well enough." Morrell didn't sound worried. He was probably more concerned about protecting his own back, which was why Taenorah, Kent, Simone and half a dozen werewolves had been kept out of the fighting.

Idiot. They were outnumbered, and this strategy was going to get them killed. Even on their own turf it was a big risk to hide down here. There was only one way in or out. Trapped. Samira could kill them at her leisure once she'd cleared out the showroom and workshop.

Taenorah met Morrell's eyes, hoping he didn't try to order her to do anything that would get her killed. He was a cunning bastard, but he wasn't a strategist. Money was his game, not war.

"We weren't prepared for this," she tried again, wincing at the distant sound of glass breaking. She was surprised there was any left. She couldn't hear anything but the fight escalating. "Where are the cops? You'd have thought someone would have reported gunshots by now." Her own phone was useless in the basement and there was no landline. Morrell should have planned better, the overconfident asshole.

Kent cleared his throat. "I heard Samira has connections high in the police force. She probably tipped them off and suggested they stay out of the way."

Morrell glared at Kent, the younger vampire wilting under the stare. "And you know this because?"

Kent tried to stand slightly taller, as if drawing confidence from his stance. "My grandson's a cop. I still talk to my son on the phone. He doesn't know what you did to me."

What Morrell did? Asshole. He'd forced Taenorah to do it to limit her power. Morrell certainly wasn't going to risk his own strength by creating a new Creature, not until he had to in order to shore up his power, as he'd done with Taenorah. Technically, that made Kent Taenorah's vampire, but not while Morrell still controlled her.

Breaking a master's control was about maturity, not physical power. The loss of her strength wouldn't prevent her from breaking his hold eventually, and when she did, she'd take Kent with her. Ferguson too, if he was still alive.

Taenorah met Morrell's eyes. "It makes no difference. In a few minutes we'll be fighting for our lives down here, whether the cops bail us out or not. We need to get up there now. She's got us cornered."

"Cops wouldn't hurt our cause," Morrell finally muttered. "Okay Kent, take Simone and the rest of the werewolves and see if you can surprise some of Samira's crew. Go now."

Kent smiled. "Finally!"

"What about us?" Taenorah asked as the two vampires and the rest of the werewolves piled up the stairs. She needed Morrell upstairs in the chaos if she was going to have any chance of getting her freedom early. Hell, this was the best chance she'd had in three centuries.

"Stay with me. I'm not risking you."

"How sweet," she muttered. "I'm the oldest, strongest vampire in your crew. You and I should be out there." Strongest, yes, but not quite as strong as she should have been. It took decades to rebuild strength after making a new vampire, and she was only just now starting to get back to regaining her strength after siring Kent. For the first ten years after making Kent she could barely do more than sleep. Some vampires couldn't manage making a new Creature more than once a century. More than any other factor, it was what kept their numbers down.

"You're my last line of defence."

She pursed her lips, a shiver of disgust passing through her. Not if she could help it. Instead of showing her feelings, she smiled seductively. She'd gotten really good at it over the centuries. "Want to fuck while we're waiting?"

———

Kyle grabbed a werewolf still in human form and slammed her into a brick wall, the woman dropping to the ground with a sickening crack as her shoulder busted. She didn't get up, and blood ran from her temple.

He picked up her silver knife and ducked into an office under a shotgun blast. The opposite wall already had a huge hole in it, the supports busted through so he could see into the next office. He dived through the hole and stood, slamming his knife into a surprised vampire's throat before he slipped through the broken door to the showroom, determined not to be trapped in the small room.

A car tyre smashed into the wall beside him before a huge werewolf ran at him.

Kyle barely sidestepped as he slashed at the Creature's side, opening a huge gash just above its hip. The wolf yelped in rage and pain, but fell as a bullet meant for Kyle punched into his back. Kyle threw his knife, taking the shooter in the throat. It wasn't likely to be a mortal wound unless he'd severed the Creature's spine, but it would be enough to take him out of the fight.

He ducked behind a car, jumped across another's bonnet, and dropped to the ground near the building's rear wall, a huge unbroken window before him. There were dozens more cars out the back of the place, and the fighting had spilled out there as well.

He saw Zannah spring over three cars with a single leap and take a vampire out as she landed, violently shaking the Creature by the shoulder until he went limp. She finished him off by tearing out his heart with her paw, half gutting him at the same time before crushing the Creature's heart between her teeth.

Several bullets pelted into the ground at her feet and she leapt among a group of three Creatures, two holding guns which they were using to hold back another group. She tore the leg off the first one and leapt at the next before they even realised what had happened, carrying him over the boot of a car and to the ground with a savage snarl.

"Holy shit," he muttered, both a little shocked and surprised at how violent and deadly she was. He hoped she wouldn't remember too much tomorrow, assuming they survived. At least she seemed to be a match for any vampire or werewolf out there. More than a match. Unless they ganged up on her, she stood a decent chance of surviving.

"So much for having my back," he said softly, though he was more concerned for her than himself. If he thought it'd do any good, he'd back her up, but considering the bloodlust she displayed, he'd probably be her next target, his compulsion useless in the face of her rage.

A werewolf in wolf form crashed through the upper-story window directly above him, slamming to the ground amid a rain of glass shards, his chest blown open by a shotgun blast. He didn't move and didn't look like he ever would again. No doubt the pellets were silver and the werewolf was dead.

He and Zannah needed to leave. It was stupid to think that they might have snuck in to get David out while everything else was chaos. Zannah was clearly lost in bloodlust and wasn't likely to be any help at all, even if he could get her attention.

He'd have left already if he didn't feel a need to protect her.

Kyle looked around for a weapon. By the time he found a knife, Zannah was struggling with another werewolf between a couple of pale blue cars, this wolf almost twice her weight in animal form. Kyle almost made a break for her, but she was holding her own as the two of them thrashed and rolled, trying to get an advantage over the other.

Zannah, despite her size, was clearly much faster and stronger. She finally caught the pale werewolf by the hind leg and hauled him backwards with a whipping motion, shaking to try to tear the leg away.

The werewolf cried in pain and fought to get to his paws, but she released his leg and got on top of him. They gnashed at each other, the pair in a standoff until Zannah caught her opponent's throat and crushed it, cutting his cry off with a high-pitched yelp.

"Fuck," Kyle swore. The bigger werewolf should have had her covered, easily, yet she tore his throat out and bit again until he heard the spine break. She looked up, clearly seeking another opponent.

She saw Kyle, her hackles raising.

"Oh crap," he said as she snarled, too lost in bloodlust to recognise him. Fighting down panic, he sprang over the car to land beside a vampire reloading a pistol.

The window behind them exploded from a gunshot and glass showered over the pair of them. Kyle covered his head to protect himself from falling glass as Zannah sailed over him and the vampire. She crashed into the car opposite them, caving the door in and shoving the car back nearly a foot. The vampire next to Kyle stood and aimed, but Kyle knocked the gun from his hand.

Rather than fight, he ran for the heavy door down to the workshop as Zannah pounced on the vampire like a lion looking for vengeance.

A bullet grazed his thigh, sending him sprawling across the ground and shattered glass from another broken window. He grunted as someone landed on him, a knife in the Creature's hand. It was a vampire with a throat wound. Kyle had hit him with the same knife a minute earlier.

He stabbed at Kyle's chest, but Kyle blocked with both hands, trying to twist the blade from the vampire's hands. Where'd his own knife go? He couldn't remember dropping it.

The blade inched closer to his chest. The vampire abruptly flew backwards as if hauled by a spring-loaded cable, his knife clattering to the floor.

Kyle scrambled back to find Zannah had the Creature by the coat as she slammed him into the ground with a bone-cracking sound before breaking his arm above the elbow.

"No, no, no, please!"

She crushed his throat, blood spraying as she tore, and then went back to make sure she finished him off.

Kyle skittered back as she turned on him next, her muzzle red with dripping blood and insanity in her red eyes.

Her ears pricked up as a noise caught her attention and she

sprang straight over Kyle as if he weren't enough of a challenge. He stood and turned in time to see her slam into a Creature coming through a doorway from a staircase.

They crashed downward together, taking several more people behind them in the tangle.

Others rushed out through the doorway. Kyle rolled under a red four-wheel drive as silver bullets sent up concrete shrapnel where he'd been laying a moment before.

He came out the other side up in time to stand and slam stiffened fingers into the throat of a female vampire swinging a crowbar at him. She dropped, hands to her crushed throat. It wouldn't kill her, but it might put her out for the night.

Bullets sprayed through the area and a werewolf dropped while the others took cover.

Kyle used the distraction to body-slam one of the vampires nearest him, carrying him back through the door and down the same stairs Zannah had disappeared through.

They crashed, rolled and slammed hard into the concrete, stopping atop the bloody body of a dead vampire, his head missing.

Kyle fought to get on top of his opponent, seeing a fallen sword nearby, but the vampire got a punch in. Kyle fell back and tried to stand, but the vampire's boot caught him in the chest like he was kicking a soccer ball, lifting Kyle off his feet and throwing him hard into a car hoist.

His breath already gone, Kyle slumped to the oily concrete, struggling to breathe. It felt like his chest had been crushed in.

The vampire came for him.

He fought to get to his hands and knees, but the strength had been knocked out of him. He barely saw the boot coming at his head in time to twist, taking it on the shoulder instead.

He groaned. His shoulder hurt as much as his chest. He glared as the vampire casually strode up to him, the longsword in his hand, the Creature's long dark curly hair bouncing around like he'd just had a perm.

"I don't suppose you want to call it a draw?" Kyle grunted with a grimace, his voice barely above a whisper.

The vampire smiled wickedly and raised his sword as something dark crashed into him from the side. Kyle rolled to protect himself, but the vampire had disappeared from sight. It had to have been Zannah.

Kyle looked around as he struggled to sit up, while screams sounded halfway across the workshop. They cut off amid a crash of falling tools and the horrible sound of flesh tearing. He saw the vampire's head roll up against a toolbox.

Zannah padded up to him, head lowered and bloodlust fresh in her eyes.

"Oh, come on," Kyle whispered, kicking his feet on the greasy concrete to try to get away. He wished he at least had enough strength to stand and try to fend her off.

His only chance was to transform, but he doubted even that would be enough now. He was hurt too badly. Zannah padded toward him like a lion stalking prey, teeth showing in a snarl. He could smell the blood on her without needing to see it.

Her muzzle came within an inch from his face and he could feel her hot breath on his cheek. At least it was better than being killed by a vampire.

She surprised the hell out of him by licking his face, and then she made a choking sound. He leaned away, staring. She was laughing? Relief and anger washed over him like a bucket of ice water to the face. "Oh, you're going to pay for that!" he said. "You scared the crap out of me."

She padded around behind him and he noticed a long gash across her ribs, the skin partly peeled back at the deepest point of the wound. A paw scratched his back, and then she came around before him again.

"You got my back, huh? Thanks."

Struggling through what was probably a cracked sternum, he got to his feet, finally noticing three other bodies in the workshop. "They're going to be cleaning up for days.

CHAPTER 26

Samira sliced her katana through the guts of one of Morrell's werewolves, spun, and threw her empty handgun at the face of a distant vampire.

The dog she'd gutted gasped in pain as its legs gave way. Samira swung at the one she'd thrown her gun at, opening his throat, surprised at how much resistance they'd faced. Morrell shouldn't have had enough time to organise his entire crew so soon. The vampire fell back, hands to his throat, choking on his own blood.

Either Rake had been caught or she had a traitor. Perhaps both.

A boot crunched glass behind her and she spun, sword raised, but held the killing blow as Rake raised his arms in alarm and backed away. Rake's sword was bloody too, werewolf blood dripping from it. There was more blood on his forearm and spattered across his face and chest.

Samira narrowed her eyes. "Where have you been?"

Fear crossed his face and he backed a step. "Killing the bastards, same as you." He glanced at the workshop door across the showroom as two werewolves slammed each other into a car and then tried for each other's throats, both bloody. One managed to throw the other across the car's roof and then leapt after it.

Samira accepted the excuse, though the fool should have been with the initial attack. "We need to get to Morrell soon or this plan's going to leave us both weakened and ready for someone else to move in," she said. She should have had control of the entire city by now, but she'd already lost more of her crew than she'd anticipated. It was supposed to have been an easy victory.

Still not sure Rake hadn't betrayed her, she looked around to assess the situation. If it wasn't over soon, she would have to fall back. "Let's go."

They dodged bullets as they ran across the room, bodies and body parts as abundant as damaged cars, and got to the staircase down to the workshop without having to fight anyone off.

She jumped to the bottom and held her ground there.

There was another fight going on in the car workshop. She couldn't help cursing in surprise as she recognised the male werewolf she thought was chained up at her warehouse. He and another werewolf were fighting some of Morrell's own crew. Good. At least they weren't fighting her own.

Samira pushed Rake toward the basement door across the large workshop. "Let them fight it out. The moment Morrell dies, this all ends and I can rebuild." It needed to happen soon, though.

She used a crowbar to bust the basement door's deadbolt and rip the door handle free. Samira kept her sword ready as Rake kicked in the damaged door. It slammed against the concrete wall with a hollow thud, the sound echoing down into the basement.

Rake went down first, Samira close behind.

Bullets sprayed the wall at the stairwell's corner and Samira pressed herself close to the opposite wall. She could smell silver, enough to put her down or even kill her.

"Morrell, we just want to talk!" she called, trying not to grin at the words. Without a gun she was at a serious disadvantage. She needed dogs to charge in ahead, but wasn't even sure how many survived. More bullets sent out chips of concrete shrapnel.

"How about we settle this without involving anyone else?" Samira called. "Just you and me?"

"Sure. Come down. I'll settle a bullet in your brain."

Wait here, Samira mouthed to Rake.

There'd been a body near the door, a werewolf who'd been part of Morrell's crew. The dead werewolf would be useful at least one more time.

The fight in the workshop seemed to have ended. The feral werewolves she'd captured earlier had won, but they paid her no attention. The male was clearly injured, and Samira could take any werewolf, even in animal form.

Samira grabbed the dead werewolf as more gunfire sounded from down below, the shots echoing loud in the stairwell, and carried the body back down, handing it to Rake.

Rake knew what to do. He got close to the bottom and used it to draw fire, sticking it out just slightly and pulling it back. The second time bullets cut through the body's shoulder, Rake gave a fake cry of pain.

The third time, the gun ran out of bullets.

"Now!"

They ran out, Samira behind Rake who still used the body as a shield, and slid to a stop.

A pool table had been shoved against a wall and Taenorah stood in front of Morrell, a longsword in her hand. That conniving vampire had been a pain for decades. She'd make her kneel as soon as she killed Morrell. She had plans for Taenorah. Painful plans, but she had to kill Morrell first.

Rake drew his own sword, keeping it low and levelled at Taenorah.

"You could walk away," Rake said to Taenorah. "You're probably old enough to break his hold on you."

Catlike, she moved into the centre of the room, blade low and Morrell at her back. "Oh, I don't think so. Morrell and I have a closer relationship than that."

Rake moved forward until the tips of their blades were almost touching. "You know I'm far better with a sword than you," he said.

She smiled. "Oh, but I've been practicing, darling. A lot."

Kyle coughed blood, but at least he could feel his supernatural healing beginning to work. Zannah's wet nose pressed into his neck and then she licked him.

"Hey, just because you're a wolf right now doesn't mean you have to act like one. I know you can think rationally. That's just being cheeky."

She licked his ear.

He ground his teeth. "Fine, I'm getting up. Stop hassling me."

He got to his feet, but it hurt to breathe. He needed blood, and lots of it. He had broken ribs for sure, and they'd take hours if not days to heal properly unless he drank blood. Vampire blood. He took a deeper breath, expanding his chest, and almost collapsed to his knees. His fingers went white where he gripped the hoist for support.

"Wow. Been a while since I've felt this bad." Carefully, he stretched his arms outward. At least he had a full range of movement, even if it hurt.

Wincing as he lowered his arms, Zannah glanced at the doorway where he'd seen Samira and Rake go. It would be stupid to follow them, although it was the most likely place to find David. He went to the vampire she'd killed, bit into his arm and sucked blood. There wasn't nearly enough considering the damage she'd caused, but it got him moving again.

The fighting upstairs was still going on, though it sounded like a standoff compared to the free-for-all it had been. There was less gunfire and bodies crashing around, at least. Perhaps he should send Zannah up there to stir things up again, and silently chastised himself for the thought.

The best thing they could do now would be to open the workshop's roller door and clear out while they still could. Sooner or later, Samira or Morrell would get the upper hand and the remaining vampires and werewolves would either fall into line or flee. Those who bent a knee would come straight for him and Zannah, with beheadings high on their agenda.

Zannah suddenly took off toward a car, sniffed around it, and then padded toward the broken door leading into the basement.

"No chance," Kyle said. "We need to go. It's far too dangerous. David's not worth our own lives." He was sure of that.

She did the Lassie thing again, looking between him and the door and back again with a soft whine, and then went for the stairs.

"Oh, for the love of anything sane!" he yelled. "Stop being stupid! He doesn't love you, he doesn't want you, and you don't owe him anything."

He was speaking to an empty workshop.

"Fuck!"

Zannah couldn't believe the world of smells that had opened up to her, and now that the bloodlust had subsided she could concentrate on it. It was as if the part of her brain that controlled speech and language had switched to smell.

She could think clearly, too. Since they'd entered the building, all she'd wanted to do was kill. She still did, but it wasn't as overwhelming as it was before, so she guessed the fighting she'd already done had quenched the desire.

Something about Kyle, his presence, kept her calmer too, which she appreciated. He was the only person she didn't feel any desire to attack. It was a good thing too, considering the amount of blood on him and everywhere else.

David's scent went directly down the stairs. She'd made a promise to herself that something good was going to come out of all this, and David drew the lucky straw. Asshole.

The trail of his scent was overlaid with dozens of werewolf and vampire smells as well, some of which she recognised because she'd already killed them. Samira and Rake had gone down there, and she had a grudge to settle with Rake. If it weren't for him, she'd be a normal human right now, studying for her degree. Shit, what was going to happen to her studies now?

She padded down the stairs, freezing as swords clashed four times. It went quiet again except for the sound of breathing and shifting feet, as if the strikes had been a quick test of their opponent's abilities. She listened as well as she could to fabric rubbing against fabric, vampires moving preternaturally fast and quiet, their tread light.

She heard Kyle behind her and turned as he appeared at the top of the stairs, his own blood on his lips. She could smell the healing process though, and it was an odd scent, sharp and hot and tangy all at the same time. She wanted to tell him to back off, but... She really missed speech. She returned her attention to the sounds of people squaring off.

Her own cuts and bruises barely hurt now, but she felt an occasional sharp pain when she moved the wrong way and there was a subtle ache all over. Bruising.

Kyle gestured to her, again pointing to the way out. She really should do as he demanded and leave with him. He'd given her so much already, but running away felt wrong. She had to finish what she'd started. It was a good thing she couldn't understand his words, as she had no doubt he was trying to compel her.

Prepared to pay for it later, she padded all the way down to where the stairs turned to the right, cautiously listening to the sound of voices in heated debate, or perhaps anger. Guardedly looking around the corner, she found four vampires, including Samira, her back to Zannah.

The opportunity was almost too much. She could attack her right then and perhaps kill her outright.

Something told her Samira was aware of Zannah, though. Her posture, or perhaps her scent. Maybe it was simply the vampire taint she carried herself.

She shifted her arm and stance, moving her sword in a position to swing backwards in a single motion.

Zannah snarled and scratched a claw on the ground as if springing to attack, and as she'd expected Samira shifted her weight and spun, sword swinging in an arc that would have taken Zannah's head off if she'd actually attacked.

Meeting no resistance almost threw her off balance. Zannah wanted to snicker.

The other three vampires stopped and stared, the two groups moving apart. Zannah glared at Rake, the vampire who'd been facing the female. He was the one who'd broken her neck in the alley. She couldn't help another snarl as her hackles rose. She was going to kill the bastard.

CHAPTER 27

Despite his misgivings about the likelihood of having his life cut short, Kyle crept to the bottom of the stairs. The brick walls had once been painted white, but over the years they'd been marked and scuffed. Paint had even been scraped off in places, revealing dull grey bricks underneath. Further down, the bricks had been shattered from gunfire.

Kyle paused just behind Zannah, the scent of werewolf and vampire blood thick on her fur, and streaked along the wall where she'd rubbed against it. Her ears were flat, hackles raised, and body tense.

There was nothing but silence beyond the open door, the quiet of enemies squaring off. Kyle cautiously moved into view, hands up, hoping to avoid a spray of bullets.

Samira, Rake, Taenorah and Morrell pointed swords at him, though neither party turned their back to the other. They'd spread out, Morrell and Taenorah to his left close to a pool table shoved against the wall, the other two on his right.

"I'm unarmed," Kyle said, unless they counted Zannah. By their expressions, they did, and were wise to do so.

"The ferals," Samira said disdainfully as she shifted her katana's balance. With a potential three-way fight, the first to move could easily be the first to die.

Taenorah caught Kyle's eyes, and the look she gave him suggested he should get away while he still had the chance. He agreed with her. He wanted to grab Zannah by the scruff of the neck and haul her back up the stairs.

"Um," Kyle said, breaking the silence as he tried to think of a way to get David out and leave without being attacked. "We-"

"I recognise you," Morrell whispered, his expression so shocked it was a surprise Samira didn't take advantage of it and attack him. "I killed you centuries ago. You should be long dead." Morrell turned to Taenorah. "You knew?" The words were half accusation, half question.

Taenorah clearly missed her calling. She shook her head, her expression mystified. "No," she whispered, surprise and shock in her voice too. "Is... Kyle?" she asked as if they hadn't recently met. Kyle would have bought the act himself if he hadn't known.

Rake and Samira backed a half step each. "You know each other?" Samira asked with genuine curiosity, no doubt trying to figure out a way to take advantage of it.

Zannah, half a step behind Kyle, focused her attention on Rake, teeth drawing back in a snarl. Kyle swore the vampire blanched.

Still unsure of Taenorah's game, Kyle decided to stick to her lie. He kept his eyes on Morrell. "You forced me to drink your tainted blood, you bastard. It kept me alive and young."

Morrell's fingers turned white as he gripped his sword's hilt. "I cut your heart out and burned it too. That would kill any vampire."

"Not a werewolf, though."

"What do you want, Kyle? We're busy," Taenorah said with such understatement, Kyle almost laughed.

With his hands still up to show he wasn't a threat, he focused on Morrell and tried to hide the disgust and hate he felt. If he could get out of here with David, he'd consider it all the win he needed. "The kid you brought down here recently. David. Let him go and we'll leave."

He spared a quick glance at Samira to ensure she wasn't preparing to take advantage of his distraction.

"What's he to you?" Morrell asked.

Kyle pointed to Zannah, the huge werewolf's posture stiff as if she were prepared to attack right there. "Guilt, I guess. It's her fault he got dragged into this."

Morrell laughed, though he didn't let his attention slip from his other opponents. "If you leave town now, I'll forget the pair of you were here." He paused, reconsidering. "Better yet, help me kill these two and you can have the kid and leave with my blessing."

Kyle didn't have a clue how Zannah might react to the offer. No doubt she'd be happy to rip Rake's head off, judging by the way she'd focused on him. If he had a way to explain it to her, she'd probably go for the deal though.

"And I'd trust you... why?" From the corner of his eye he caught Taenorah give him the slightest nod of agreement. She thought it was a bad deal too.

"Because I said so," Morrell said, his tone suggesting he'd been insulted.

Taenorah swung at Rake, but he hadn't been stupid enough to drop his guard.

"I've got a better plan," she said, attacking again. Their blades clashed a dozen times before they found themselves face-to-face, swords crossed between them and bodies inches apart as their supernatural muscles strained against each other. Rake was bigger, but Taenorah was older and stronger.

Kyle put a calming hand on Zannah's hip in case she decided to give Taenorah the advantage. Morrell and Samira watched but kept their focus on each other.

Rake broke the deadlock and shoved Taenorah back. Kyle saw something pass between them as Taenorah shifted her feet to move with his shove, the pair of them pushing away from each other like trained dancers performing a choreographed move.

In perfect union, they spun and drove their blades through their sires' hearts. Both ancient vampires gasped and fell to their knees before their protégés, helpless.

Kyle moved back half a step, shocked at the casual cruelty on Taenorah's victorious face.

"You intended this," Kyle said to Taenorah. "Both of you." It made sense. They must have been planning it for years. Decades perhaps.

How many vampires and werewolves had died tonight so the two of them could be free of their makers' influence?

"Leave now, Kyle," Taenorah said, her back to him though she looked over her shoulder. "Don't come back."

"You used me," he said, surprised at the hurt he felt.

Rake picked up his mistress's katana as Samira remained on her knees, mouth still open in shock, body paralysed with pain as her bloody hands tried to pull Rake's blade from her heart. If left in place it would eventually kill her, the effect similar to cutting out her heart. Morrell faced a similar fate.

"We've been trying to set this up for decades, Kyle," Taenorah said. "But the two of them kept dancing around each other instead of fighting. And then you showed up. I should thank you." There was nothing recognisable of the woman he'd married. She revelled in her victory, hatred and viciousness showing through.

Kyle tried to see past the killer who stood in place of his former wife, now a master manipulator, liar and accomplished actor.

"You did all this for revenge?" he asked. "You're old enough to have broken his control. You could have walked away."

Taenorah faced Kyle, her expression hard. "You think this was about revenge? I *love* Morrell, but he's been standing in my way for far too long. This was always going to be *my* city."

"Our city," Rake amended.

She hesitated, but nodded. "As we agreed. Samira and Morrell were stupid to think no one would challenge them, divided as they were."

Rake pointed Samira's katana toward Morrell. "We need to finish this."

Taenorah drew a gun from under her jacket and aimed it at Kyle. "In three seconds, I shoot," she said. "Leave Kyle."

Kyle raised his hands a little higher as he sensed Zannah tense beside him. "Wait," he said.

Her expression went flat, and he stared into the eyes of a cold-blooded killer. "You had your chance." He felt the impact in his chest before he heard the blast. He crashed backwards to the stairs, barely registering the pain or the sound of more shots, but it wasn't until he saw Zannah fall that he realised they weren't for him.

He coughed as blood filled his lungs and soaked into his shirt, both front and back. The bullet had gone through, not lodged in his lungs, but it was more than enough to keep him down. Pain kept him still as blood bubbled into his mouth.

Taenorah lowered the gun. "I'm sorry, Kyle. If I'd tried to walk away, Morrell would have killed me, and I can't risk you returning either."

Rake touched the tip of Samira's katana to the ground, almost as if he was going to lean on it. "Finish the dogs off."

"Our masters first," Taenorah said. "They're both far more dangerous than any werewolf, particularly an incapacitated one."

She put several bullets into Morrell's chest and he collapsed, surprise still on his face.

Kyle coughed blood, the movement sending shooting pain through his chest.

He was helpless to intervene as Taenorah moved to Zannah's body, pointing the weapon at the wolf's chest. Zannah struggled to breathe, blood soaking her side where the silver bullets had punched into her chest. Only some had gone through, the rest keeping her helpless. She probably had shattered ribs, and the silver buried inside her would be agonising.

"I really don't know if silver bullets will kill either of you, though I have to say you're not looking too sprightly, Kyle. Remind me to cut off your heads and burn your bodies, just to be sure."

She emptied the clip into Zannah's chest and then slapped a fresh clip in. Zannah's body spasmed and went still.

Kyle looked away, shocked at the brutality. "Why?" he whispered. "She just wanted to save the kid. She wasn't any threat to you or your power."

Rake laughed. "I say good riddance. The bitch caused far too much trouble," he said with a grin.

Taenorah's smile matched Rake's, and it was a smile that held no regrets. "You should have taken your new bitch and left town when I gave you the chance." She crouched before him and touched a finger to the blood seeping from his chest just above his heart. "An inch or two lower would have been better. I'll have to work on my aim."

"Taen-"

"No, Kyle." She put the barrel against his forehead. "If you hadn't made yourself a new bitch to fuck, I might have been inclined to let you live. But then, I've always been the jealous type. You should know that."

Kyle caught movement behind her. Taenorah twisted in reaction, too slow. A katana blade punched through her neck and out. She gasped, choking, the blade still in place.

The sword was a slashing weapon, not made for thrusting, but it pierced well enough. Taenorah was still making choking sounds as she shot Rake twice in the stomach. As he staggered back she put three more bullets into his chest. He staggered backwards.

With a sickly sucking sound, Taenorah pulled the blade free from her neck and pressed her hand against the wound. She collapsed beside Kyle, blood running through her fingers.

Rake dropped and clutched at his bloody stomach and chest. "Fuck," he whispered, blood flecking his lips. He turned to face his mistress. "You bitch," he whispered to Samira. "You made me do that."

He collapsed.

Samira smiled, although she remained on her knees, the sword that had been through her chest now resting on the ground.

Taenorah, still choking on her own blood, raised the gun and shot Rake in the head.

His body jerked once and lay still as Taenorah turned the weapon on Samira. "Fuck you," she hissed, the sound wet. She shot Samira in the head too, the ancient vampire's body falling backwards. She put another bullet into the unmoving vampire, just to be sure.

"Taenorah?" Kyle whispered.

Taenorah turned her weapon on Kyle, her hand still squeezing her neck as blood pumped through her fingers. She appeared ready to pass out.

"Taen?" Kyle asked. "It's over."

CHAPTER 28

Taenorah lowered the gun and coughed blood. "At least your bitch is dead," she whispered vindictively, her voice harsh from the damage to her neck. Blood formed bubbles on her lips, more blood bubbles dribbling down her chin.

"Zannah didn't deserve it," Kyle said, wishing he'd ignored Zannah's desire to help David. The happy-go-lucky girl would still be alive if they'd left town.

"I didn't deserve what happened to me either," Taenorah whispered, her anger-filled grimace revealing bloody teeth. "You know I couldn't risk her coming back and causing trouble for me, and you're attached to her. Problem solved."

"You'd have killed me too," he said, the truth of it hurting as much as the bullet hole through his chest. He coughed blood.

Morrell abruptly took in a huge breath across the room before pushing himself to his knees, his body trembling with the effort. He glared murder at Taenorah as blood ran down his chest from the bullet wounds and sword thrust. The sword was on the ground beside him.

"Hello, lover," Taenorah whispered with a wicked grin. She licked her own blood from her lips as she raised her gun, but there was nothing but a click. "Oh shit," she said, her expression turning to fear.

As Morrell stood, Taenorah released the clip and fumbled for a new one, but before she could get it into the gun Morrell threw a knife. As it punched into her shoulder, she cried out and dropped the gun, the spare clip falling with a clatter beside it.

Agony ripped through his chest as Kyle went for the gun, another throwing knife narrowly missing his neck. He grunted as he gripped the weapon's hilt in one hand and slammed the fresh clip home with the other. He turned the weapon on Morrell.

"Stay down, dog," Morrell said, clearly trying to use compulsion.

Kyle smiled and filled the vampire's chest with bullets. Morrell staggered back, his expression shocked.

"Compulsion doesn't work on me," Kyle said.

Morrell touched the wounds with bloody fingertips before raising his hand to his face in disbelief. He winced and staggered back another step.

Kyle aimed at the vampire's head and pulled the trigger. Nothing.

Looking around for another clip, he staggered to his feet and grabbed Samira's katana. Morrell, slow to recover but glaring defiance, carefully bent and picked up Taenorah's longsword.

Wiping blood from his chin, Morrell glared at Kyle. "I'm over a thousand years old, dog. It'll take more than a feral shit like you to stop me." He spat blood and staggered to Zannah's body, sword point touching her fur.

"She's dead," Kyle said, his voice breaking with unexpected sorrow. He'd barely known her for a day, but her death hurt a lot more than he'd expected.

"Then I'll kill her again," Morrell said with a bloody grin. "Just to watch your face as I do it."

If Kyle fought Morrell now, he might survive, but he probably wouldn't. "How about we call it even? I'll take her body and go and you can do what you want with the others."

Morrell laughed, but then clenched his jaw in pain. Kyle half expected to see him cough up a bullet or two. The silver would be burning like molten lead inside him, but for a vampire as old as Morrell, it wouldn't be enough to kill.

"I'll make you a deal, pup. Cut Samira's head off and you can walk away. No reprisals."

Kyle glanced at Samira's unmoving body, clear fluid mixed with blood leaking from the hole in the vampire's head.

She wasn't going to be getting up for days, if ever, and with a wound like that it would probably take her months to regenerate, if she did. Even so, someone would have to dig the silver out of her head to make it happen. Morrell wouldn't be in much better shape, but he was still up and lethal enough. Pity Taenorah hadn't shot him in the head too.

Pretending to comply, Kyle staggered to Samira's body. This close, he could smell her blood. It was oddly similar to Morrell's. He suddenly realised why they hadn't sorted their feud out years ago. Samira had sired Morrell.

"Do it yourself," Kyle said.

Morrell glared in disbelief. "Samira would kill you and forget about it before your body was cold," he said.

"I'm not Samira."

Morrell coughed and spat more blood, pain pulling at his features. "Even injured, I'm still stronger and faster than you. Don't defy me, dog. You won't like the consequences."

"Let me get Zannah's body and her friend, and we'll leave."

"Kill Samira properly or I'll find and murder everyone you know, and make you watch."

Kyle clenched his jaw at the threat, even if it was a hollow one. He could only imagine the world of trouble Morrell would be picking if he threatened Kimbriel. Kyle lowered the tip of his katana in a traditional two-handed grip.

"I walk out of here with David, Taenorah, and Zannah, and let you do what you like with your enemies." Considering what Taenorah had done to Zannah, he was inclined to let Morrell keep her, but she'd been his wife once. He couldn't leave her to him again.

Morrell kept his blade near Zannah's neck. "I think you failed to notice your bitch's chest is moving slightly. We're not negotiating. You're going to be a good little dog and do as you're told." He pressed the point of his blade into Zannah's fur. "Or you're going to watch me sever her spine."

Kyle swallowed as he shifted his feet, glancing at Zannah's body. Relief and a new wave of fear coursed through him, as he realised Morrell wasn't lying.

"You think I care about a girl I barely know?" he asked, bluffing.

Morrell raised an eyebrow, pressing the tip of his blade hard enough into Zannah's fur that he may have pierced her skin. "Yes."

Shit. "And if you do kill her, do you think you can get your blade free of her body before I cut you down?" Kyle asked. It was a bluff. He'd never risk Zannah's life, but he doubted Morrell would know that.

Morrell smiled, though it was more of a grimace, yet he conceded the point with a nod. "Nice play."

Kyle couldn't help the relief he felt. "Just let us go. We won't be back."

Morrell gave a pain-filled smirk. "Okay, but Taenorah and the kid stay. I'm short on soldiers, and she's going to be repaying some debts over the next few years. There's a lot of interest due."

Kyle watched Morrell's stance. Morrell's longsword was designed for thrusting and hacking, best used in one hand with a shield. He held it like an expert though, daring Kyle to make a move.

Kyle, at least, held his own weapon of choice.

"Taenorah's my wife," Kyle said. Despite her betrayal, he couldn't leave her to Morrell.

"*Was* your wife. I've been fucking her for centuries." Morrell winced. The blood had stopped seeping from his chest, but he clearly didn't want to fight. "I doubt she's thought of you at all in centuries."

"You mean you've been raping her for centuries?"

Morrell narrowed his eyes. "You don't know her as well as you think you do. She'd slit your throat to get what she wants. Mine too."

"She did what she had to do to survive."

Morrell laughed, the sound weak. "What she wants is power. I thought I had her under control, but I won't make that mistake again.

Take Samira's head and you've got yourself a bargain. You, your bitch and the kid, but Taenorah stays."

Kyle watched Morrell's face, pale with blood loss. There was probably more blood outside him than in, but he'd recover soon enough if he got the silver out.

"Okay. Deal," Kyle said, still assuming betrayal and trying to come up with an excuse to stall. "But then we're even. Forever."

"Deal," Morrell said, the word coming too fast to imply sincerity. "Take Samira's head and we're done."

"Take it yourself after we're gone," Kyle said. The only reason Morrell could want Kyle to do it would be to take advantage of Kyle's distraction.

"You want the kid and your bitch alive? Do it." He leaned on his blade, pressing it into Zannah's neck.

Fear spiked through him. "Okay!"

Cautiously, eyes still on Morrell, Kyle lowered his blade to Samira's neck to line up the strike. Morrell kept the tip of his blade against Zannah's neck.

Inwardly cursing, Kyle raised his sword. It was a slashing weapon, not a hacking implement like a broadsword. Bringing it down on someone's neck as they lay against the ground was one of the best ways he could think of to damage it. He'd have to sweep through, but the moment he did, he'd be vulnerable.

"Do it!" Morrell said.

Watching Morrell from the corner of his eye, Kyle tensed to swing.

Like a viper, Morrell moved, leaping forward with his blade already swinging to take off Kyle's head.

Kyle ducked and pivoted, and as Morrell came through he drew his katana across Morrell's stomach and continued the stroke until the blade came free. In the same movement, he bought the weapon back up, preparing for a counter-strike, but Morrell fell to the ground, sliced clean in half at the waist. A huge pool of blood spread outward.

Fresh blood began to flow from Kyle's own chest as his bullet wound opened from the exertion, a warm, pain-filled trickle. He staggered, ready to collapse himself.

"Regenerate that," Kyle muttered to Morrell's dead body. "If you're going to use a longsword, use a shield with it."

"Cut his head off," Taenorah whispered.

Kyle spun, raising his blade. She was deathly pale, her own blood all over her clothes, but she was conscious.

"He's dead," Kyle said.

She shook her head. "Remove the head or the heart. They're the only ways to be sure."

She was right. Trying not to think about it, Kyle swung the katana one last time while Taenorah propped herself up against a wall, the tip of the blade sparking against the concrete just before it met Morrell's neck. The vampire's head rolled free as the blade rose.

Kyle bent over and grasped Samira's arm, dragging the vampire's limp body to Zannah. "Zannah?" Kyle asked, staring at the wolf's still unmoving form.

"What are you doing?" Taenorah asked.

"Reviving her. She's part vampire. She'll heal much faster with vampire blood."

Ignoring his own pain, he lifted Samira's body and cut the vampire's jugular. Blood gushed out over Zannah's muzzle and began pooling under her head. Despite the shallow breathing, she didn't move. Didn't even flinch.

"Drink," he said as she lay motionless. "Please, Zannah. Drink."

Nothing.

Taenorah finally managed to pull the throwing knife from her shoulder, dropping. "Stay with me, Kyle. Rule this city with me."

"Really?" he asked. "After what you did. You'd cut my head off the first chance you got."

"Never," she whispered, and if he didn't know better, he might have believed her.

Zannah's body abruptly jerked and she convulsively licked at the blood on her muzzle, instinctively lapping up the vampire blood.

"I don't want to rule anything," Kyle muttered.

Kyle needed to heal as well. He hauled Samira's body up, drinking the spilling blood directly from her neck. As much gushed over his face as chest as he drank, but vitality flowed back into him and he felt his wounds healing.

After a minute, he dropped Samira's body and used the katana to behead her, ensuring she was dead too.

He glanced at Taenorah. "You can have the city all by your lonesome."

CHAPTER 29

ZANNAH'S WORLD was red with pain, yet her heart pounded like someone had shoved a syringe of adrenaline into her. Vampire blood. Distilled lifeforce.

She licked it from the concrete until the ground was clean, willing the rest of the spread out blood to come to her. When it didn't, she struggled to her paws and went to it, not caring that the floor was filthy or she had plenty more blood all over herself.

She'd tasted blood like this from the vampires in the fight upstairs, but never this strong. Young vampires. Weak in comparison. This blood came from one of the oldest vampires around, and she couldn't consume it fast enough as she licked it from the concrete. She heard footsteps approach and snarled without looking up. The footsteps backed away.

The clicks of metal hitting concrete sounded next to her, and she was shocked to find mushroomed silver bullets dropping around her paws, stained with her own blood. She crinkled her nose at the reek of silver and her whole body shuddered. Blood and silver, not a good combination.

When she'd finished cleaning up the blood, she found Kyle standing beside a headless body, covered in his own blood and more. She could smell the difference between the werewolf and vampire blood on him, even from a couple of metres away. He watched her warily.

She looked around, finding three more vampires in the room, one still alive. The injured female vampire sat in the corner but didn't look threatening, while Rake lay on the floor and didn't look like he'd be moving soon, if ever. Good.

The wisdom of deciding to save David haunted her a little. It was not her best choice, and forcing Kyle to help her had nearly seen them both killed, though it had felt like the right thing to do at the time. Perhaps her priorities needed adjusting.

The vampire woman moved, propping herself up a little more. She'd been bleeding pretty badly from the neck, but it seemed to have slowed down.

Kyle said something. It frustrated her how she couldn't understand any of it. He looked concerned, at least, yet fierce as he held a slightly curved Asian-style sword in one hand. He said something else and pointed toward a door across the room. David's smell was much stronger that way.

Kyle turned his back on the injured woman and moved in the direction David's scent went. Zannah followed, and halfway down a short corridor they found a room filled with reinforced steel cages, all but one empty.

David was locked in the first one with a simple bolt that couldn't be reached from within. Kyle slid the bolt free and hauled David out. Her former boyfriend smelled so scared she was surprised he hadn't messed himself.

David saw Zannah and cringed behind Kyle like the coward she recognised him for. He and Kyle spoke, and again Zannah wished she could understand them. Rather than wait, she left the room and checked the other rooms, finding a female werewolf pinned against a wall by heavy steel rods bent over to prevent her pulling free. What kind of cruel bastard would do that to a person?

She yipped, went to the door and barked, the sound not at all like a dog's bark, though that was what she was aiming for. After a moment Kyle came out of the cage room with David and she led them to the girl.

She was pretty sure Kyle swore.

Kyle stared at the poor werewolf girl pinned to the concrete wall. Gaunt and pale with dried blood staining two runs down her shirt from the spikes driven under her collarbones, she could barely raise her head when he touched her face.

Kyle put the sword down. "I'm going to help you," he said, but she only stared back uncomprehendingly. "What's your name?"

She took a moment to respond, as if she'd needed to first figure out what he'd said. "Shannon," she whispered. "Who are you?"

"Kyle. I'm a friend. I'm going to get you out of here."

"No," she said, her voice barely louder than the first whisper. "Mister Morrell will kill you. Kill me, too."

"Morrell's dead," he replied.

He took a hold of the first steel bar and hauled on it with all his strength, bending it until it was reasonably straight again.

She whimpered as it moved, but didn't cry out. He did the same with the bar going through her other shoulder, bringing perspiration to her face from the pain.

Breathing a little hard himself, he took her cheeks in his hands until she met his eyes again. "I'm going to have to pull you free. Understand? It's going to hurt. A lot."

She stared for a moment longer, but finally nodded. Even that seemed to take more effort than she seemed to have.

"David, she's probably going to faint as I pull her free. Catch her."

David looked like he was going to vomit. "Yeah, sure."

David positioned himself beside the girl while Kyle took a hold of her shoulders.

"On three. One. Two. Now!"

He pulled, and Shannon cried out as the rough bars ran through her body. She didn't quite faint, but her legs gave way and she fell. David only just caught her.

"Can you carry her out?" Kyle asked as he picked up the katana. "We might have trouble leaving. There's probably fighting still going on above us."

"I think so. She's pretty thin."

David swore as they got to the main room with the decapitated bodies still strewn about. Only instead of two there were now three, and Taenorah was back on her feet, rejuvenated from drinking Rake's blood. She held the sword Morrell had used.

"You killed Rake," Kyle said.

She grinned, her teeth red with his blood. "What do you care?" she asked, standing casually between Kyle and the exit.

Kyle hesitated. "You planning on staying between me and the door?" He'd loved her once and honestly didn't think he could kill her.

"I'm going to need a good man by my side to restore order to the region. Thought you might be interested."

"Then you probably shouldn't have killed Rake."

"Rake had ambitions of his own. It was just a matter of time before he betrayed me."

"So you betrayed him first? I'll pass. Enjoy playing queen of the heap."

She seemed disappointed, hurt even, but she stepped aside. "Whatever. If that's your final decision, don't come back Kyle."

"Taen-"

"Don't, Kyle. Just leave and stay gone. I don't want to see you again."

Kyle tried to find a way to end this on good terms, but admitted to himself that the woman he had loved so long ago was gone. Perhaps she never really existed. "Let's go," he said to Zannah and David.

As he walked past Taenorah, he sensed her shifting her stance, and from the corner of his eye saw her blade move for a backhanded swing at his head.

He spun, sword up, and just caught Taenorah's swing before her blade could behead him. Before he could protest, Zannah leapt and caught his former wife by the shoulder and dragged her from her feet. Taenorah screamed in pain and tried to bring her sword up, but Zannah shook the vampire until she dropped the weapon with a loud clatter.

Kyle stared in shock as Taenorah reached out, mouth agape as she tried to get a hand to her sword and couldn't. "I'll kill you and your bitch! This is my city! Tainted dogs like you should never have been allowed to breathe!"

She'd never intended to let them go, he realised. She'd manipulated everyone, including Morrell, Rake and himself to get what she wanted. Zannah released Taenorah, and without even questioning it, he knew what she was asking. She'd bitten the woman, which meant she had to kill her. They no longer had a choice.

"I'm sorry, Taen." Kyle raised his sword, not wanting to, but there was no other choice now. He tensed, preparing to swing despite the shock in Taenorah's eyes. "I can't," he whispered. "I just can't." Instead of taking that one final swing, he lowered the sword.

Relief crossed Taenorah's face. "More fool you," she whispered, drawing the gun, a fresh clip loaded.

Zannah growled and leapt, her jaws closing around Taenorah's wrist and crushing, drawing a scream of agony from Taenorah.

He swung, choosing Zannah over Taenorah.

Taenorah's agonised cry cut off as her head fell from her neck and her body went limp. Zannah dropped the woman's wrist, the gun never firing.

Kyle closed his eyes. Not wanting to see, he turned and walked away, determined to avoid the sight of his wife's remains.

"Holy fuck," David whispered, staying close behind him and reeking of fear.

CHAPTER 30

STRANGELY NUMB to all the slaughter she'd caused, Zannah couldn't help but drink as much of Taenorah's blood as she could before she padded up the stairs after Kyle and David, ready to kill again if necessary. She should have been concerned she liked the taste of vampire blood so much, but... whatever.

Pausing at the top of the stairs, she glanced around the workshop to make sure it was safe. Silence. Unless there were werewolves and vampires ready to spring an elaborate trap on them, the fight had finished. Kyle, still holding the sword, was already across the workshop, David carrying the werewolf girl over one shoulder, her back streaked with blood.

No sound came from the showroom up the stairs, though she could smell lots of blood. Vampire blood. Werewolf blood. And flesh too, some of it she'd torn herself. Her stomach growled with fresh hunger, but she ignored it. She had to protect Kyle, the injured werewolf girl, and even David, though if she had to pick and choose who to save, David would be last. Bloody lot of effort gone to waste if that happened, though.

Moving silently, her ears turning at any hint of danger, she kept watch as Kyle got the roller door to open. It made a lot of noise. If anyone was around and looking for trouble she was going to have to get bloody again, but at least her body had expelled the silver and her wounds had healed. Vampire blood was like magic.

Guarding Kyle's back, she followed him out.

When they reached the road, she could see significant damage to the windows and doors. Where were the cops? Even though it was close to dawn in an industrial district, surely someone must have heard and reported something.

Several bodies were strewn on the concrete before the showroom, unmoving, some with their throats and hearts torn out. The fight had been brutal. She'd been brutal.

Considering she'd never picked a fight in her life, she was surprised and more than a little scared by how much she'd loved it. She really had loved it.

Maybe she'd freak out when she changed back into human form, but right now she could happily do it all again, and almost wished some idiot would rush out and try to kill her. If there were any survivors though, and there had to be some, they'd left.

So had Jimmy's girlfriend. Her scent remained, but that was all. Hopefully, she was okay and vampires or werewolves hadn't got her.

To the east, the sky was getting brighter with the approaching dawn, the sun still below the horizon as they reached her car. There was a soft glow across the sky. She could almost feel the rapidly approaching daylight like a welcoming ache in her muscles, as if she'd done a heavy workout but felt energised by it rather than sore.

With all the vampire blood rushing through her, she felt amazingly good, super strong and vital. Stronger and healthier than when she'd first been healed by Kyle's blood and Kimbriel's magic. Kyle opened her car's front door for her and then helped David get the werewolf girl into the back seat. Zannah shook her bloody fur out and then sprang in, watching as David put the seatbelt around the girl and got in on the other side.

As Kyle sat behind the wheel and put the key in the ignition, Zannah felt the transition between night and day wash over her like a bout of fever. She stiffened with the inevitable shift of celestial bodies and transitioned back into human form like a stretched rubber band finally returning to shape. It felt good.

When she'd changed into a wolf, all she'd felt was pain. Returning to her human form was the opposite. Ecstasy. She moaned with pleasure, taking a deep breath and sighing as she slumped on the seat.

"Oh God, that feels good," she said, slouching. "Wow, I'm tired. Is anyone else tired?"

"You're naked," Kyle said, his face flushing red as he tried not to look. "Please pass me her clothes," he said to David, who couldn't comply fast enough.

"Geez, I'm filthy," Zannah said, glancing down at her bloody skin as she accepted the clothes. She had more blood on her than she'd realised. She raised an arm and sniffed. "And my sense of smell has turned to crap. I swear I stank more just a minute ago. Ditto my hearing. I mean, they're way better than they ever were, but nothing compared to last night."

"Please get dressed," Kyle said as he prodded the clothes at her.

She grinned, enjoying his embarrassment enough that she could ignore her own. "Aww, you've gone all red. That's so sweet!" Most men she knew would be ogling her right now.

"He's not the only one that's embarrassed," David said tersely from the back seat.

She turned, making sure he saw. "Take a good look, dipshit. You won't ever be playing with these puppies again."

He looked away. Good. Asshole.

"Please get dressed," Kyle said. "Please."

She sighed. "Whatever." She put her clothes on in the cramped front seat, a bit of a contortionist's act, but manageable. They were Sellendria's clothes really, but Zannah doubted Jimmy's girlfriend would want them back. Once Zannah was dressed, Kyle turned the engine over and they drove off, leaving Mitchell behind.

"What's going to happen now?" David asked. "I mean, there're bodies on the street."

"Someone else's problem," Kyle said a little too quickly. "I hope. Creatures tend to cover these things up themselves."

"You know, I could really go for a hamburger right now," Zannah said. "A big greasy one with egg and bacon and cheese. Beetroot and pineapple, too. You know, a real hamburger, not one of those pint-sized chain-restaurant things full of pickled crap."

Kyle gave her a look, disbelief on his face. "A hamburger. Now?"

"Don't you like beetroot and pineapple on a burger?" she asked.

"How could you not feel guilty?" Kyle asked as he drove Zannah's car around a corner and into the street where Kimbriel lived. The question had been bugging him for the last fifteen minutes, and she'd failed to give him an adequate response.

"It's not like I killed anyone who wouldn't have done the same to me, given the chance."

"But... they're people! Some of them didn't have a choice about what they were doing."

She shrugged. "Whatever. Would you have done anything different?"

"Yeah. Lots of things, probably." Her cavalier attitude was really bothering him.

"Well, you can't, so get over it. I watched your back, didn't I?"

He gave her a long look. "Yeah, you watched my back, and then some. Thank you."

"Thank you for helping me save David. How you doing back there, dipshit?"

David refused to respond.

Kyle pulled into Kimbriel's driveway and killed the engine. As he went to open his door, Zannah caught his hand. He stiffened at the touch, the warmth and softness of her skin unfamiliar. The last person who'd touched him with such familiarity was Taenorah, and despite everything she'd done, he regretted that he'd never feel her touch again.

"Kyle," she said gently as David got out, her eyes completely serious now. "I know saving David wasn't worth the effort-"

"Hey!" David said, pausing with one leg out of the car.

Kyle hadn't paid much attention before, but she had really beautiful eyes. Big and brown and full of life.

"But not doing something would have haunted me much more than helping him."

David leaned back through the door. "What do you mean by that?" Irritation tainted his words.

Zannah glared at him. "I wasn't talking to you," she said.

There was a ferocious undercurrent to her tone that Kyle recognised through long experience, and he wasn't stupid enough to get involved in it.

"But it's okay to talk about me right in front of my face?" David asked.

She narrowed her eyes, and Kyle suspected David might be in for more than he'd bargained for. Zannah wasn't the same girl he'd been dating a week ago. Not anymore. "You ran and left me for dead, and then you dumped me at the hospital when I was more vulnerable than I've ever been in my life. If you ever whine at me again about how hard done by you are, I'll rip your pathetic head off, and you know I can do it."

David pursed his lips, clearly too stupid to sense the danger he was in, but lucky for him he didn't seem to have an adequate response. "Whatever."

Kyle watched Zannah's face, marvelling at her. She'd recently been a happy-go-lucky young woman who wanted nothing more than a bit of adventure. When that adventure had found her, she'd grabbed it with both arms and held on.

Kyle squeezed her hand back. "You're an amazing woman, Zannah. I'm glad..." he hesitated, not sure what he wanted to say. "I'm glad Kimbriel didn't hold me to my promise."

"Pfft. The world would shrivel up and die of despair without me. Moving on. I need a shower. Let's go in."

He couldn't help but laugh. "Yes. You definitely need a shower. We all do."

Mal opened the door to Zannah's knock while Kyle helped David get Shannon out of the car.

"Zannah," Mal said. "You look like you've been dragged through an abattoir. It's not the best look for you."

"But I still look sexy, right?" she said with a big grin.

He returned it. "Of course. Come in. Please. All of you."

"Thanks for the invite," Zannah said after they were inside. "Do I actually need an invitation?"

"It's the vampire taint. That doesn't depend on whether you're human or a wolf, so yeah, but you're welcome here anytime."

David carried Shannon to the couch as Kyle stopped at Zannah's side. "What happens if I don't get an invitation?" she asked Kyle.

"I don't know. I've never tried to force my way into anyone's residence." Kyle couldn't help a smile as Zannah rolled her eyes.

"Who made up that stupid rule, anyway?"

Mal seemed to take the question seriously. "Whatever God shapes our universe, I guess. They keep a low profile though, so it's a little hard to ask such questions. I'm sure there's a good reason for it."

"Whatever God?" Zannah asked. "Seriously? I know I'm new to all this supernatural stuff, but are you telling me there's more than one God?"

Mal nodded. "Kimbriel thinks there are lots of Gods, all vying for control of universes. She doesn't know which God owns this universe though."

Zannah stared at Mal, her expression doubting. "You're nuts, you know that?"

Kyle hesitantly placed a hand on the small of Zannah's back. "It's time you went for a shower, if that's all right with you, Mal?"

If anything, Mal looked amused. "Zannah and I can continue this conversation another day. The bathroom's down the hall, Zannah. Your clothes will be clean by the time you get out."

"Hey, thanks," she said. "I like Mal," she whispered theatrically to Kyle with a wink, clearly intending for Mal to hear.

When she left, Mal chuckled in his deep voice and slapped Kyle on the back. The big guy's blow was staggering. "I think you've got your hands full with that one, mate," Mal said.

"I don't suppose you can hide me until she goes home?"

"*I heard that!*" Zannah yelled from the bathroom a moment before the shower turned on.

Mal just kept grinning. Kimbriel was already in the lounge room tending to the unconscious Shannon. She looked up with a smile when Kyle approached. "Zannah's good for you, Kyle."

He gave her a look. "Vitamins are good for me. She's more like a cyclone."

"*I heard that too!*"

Kyle sighed. The girl definitely had keener senses than he did. "Remind me to keep my voice down from now on." He pointed at Shannon. "How is she?"

"She'll be fine. She can stay here for a couple of days until she recovers."

"Thanks, Kimbriel. I owe you."

"You owe me lots already, but we'll call this one even."

"What about me?" David asked.

Kimbriel stared at him, one eyebrow raised. "What about you?"

"They bit me."

Kimbriel continued staring. The silence grew uncomfortable until David finally got the message. "I mean, I don't want to be a werewolf."

"I'm sure you don't want to be a mermaid either," Kimbriel said. "Are you going to get to the point?"

David stared as if it were obvious. "Can you fix me?"

"I could turn you into a pumpkin. That would fix a lot of things. Is that what you're asking?"

Kyle hid a smile, but David didn't seem to get the joke. "I want to be normal again. Just human. Can you do that?"

"Of course."

David stared, waiting. "Well? Can you do it now?"

"That's a little more specific, but let me clarify. Are you asking me to make you human again, or are you asking me if I can *do it now*?"

"Both!"

"Male or female?"

"What?"

"You weren't specific. Male or female?"

"Male! I want to be me still."

"With or without arms?"

He stared at her as if she were crazy. Kyle was sure Kimbriel could keep this up forever.

"The same as I am now!"

"So you want to stay a werewolf?"

David was going red. "No! Me, without the werewolf curse. Like I was before I got bitten."

"A baby, then?"

David closed his mouth, lips tight as he realised what was going on. Almost grudgingly, he said, "Please."

Kimbriel stood and reached up to hold his face in her hands. "See. That wasn't so hard, now was it?"

"You mean you fixed me already?"

"Of course not. Nobody can fix someone like you without causing major head trauma."

Kyle couldn't help a laugh.

David gave him a look. "Please Kimbriel, can you just remove the... werewolf curse from me? Make me a normal human again, the same as I was a few days ago?"

"Of course."

David shuddered and collapsed to the floor, writhing in pain for nearly a full minute before passing out.

"Remind me not to ask for that," Kyle said.

She raised an eyebrow. "The pain was a freebie."

"Oh."

"We need to talk, Kyle, but it involves Zannah. Coffee?"

"Coffee would be great. It's been a very long night."

CHAPTER 31

ZANNAH LEFT the bathroom feeling cleaner than she had in days, her long damp hair wrapped in a pink towel. Even her borrowed clothes were fresh, though she had no idea how. Magic, she guessed, and found herself surprisingly okay with it. Hell, she was an immortal werewolf with superhuman everything. Self-cleaning magical clothes were simply a cool part of her new existence, and one she wanted to keep.

She looked around, wondering how the place had been magically dressed up to look like a wreck. There was some serious magic going on, but she'd seen enough weird stuff lately to accept it without needing to figure it out. If Kimbriel wanted to keep it looking like a wreck, she probably had her reasons.

Drying her hair as she walked, she found Kyle and Kimbriel drinking coffee at the table in the family room, a small television on the opposite wall showing a game of cricket, the sound muted.

Kyle pushed a steaming mug of black coffee toward her. "How was the shower?" he asked.

She smiled. "Like a religious experience."

She dropped the towel over the back of a chair and sat, shaking out her long hair, the dampness keeping it in tight ringlets.

She picked the mug up in both hands and took a sip of the coffee.

"Wow. This is really good, and I know coffee." She closed her eyes, leaning over it while inhaling. She preferred her coffee with milk, but any coffee right now was good. "You know, I never thought I'd get the chance to do... anything again. Ever. Thank you. Both of you."

When no one spoke, she opened her eyes to find Kimbriel and Kyle watching her. She half smiled. "What?"

Kimbriel returned her smile. "Nothing. It's just nice to see you enjoying life."

"Life? I'm part vampire now, aren't I? Doesn't that mean I'm undead and have to sleep in a coffin?"

"No. It makes you a Creature," Kyle said.

"But undead sounds so much cooler."

He cracked a smile at that. "I suppose it does. Kimbriel wants to talk about something."

"Reneging on our deal?" Zannah asked. That drew a frown from Kyle, but no response from Kimbriel. It was supposed to have been a joke. "What?"

"She wants to alter the terms of our agreement," Kyle said.

Zannah thought she knew what he meant. "The no-bite-em policy?"

Kimbriel responded with a nod. "I gave you what you asked for, but I was hoping we could reduce the risks to you and Kyle. Sooner or later one of you will pass on your affliction and you won't be able to... fix it. I would like to avoid the problem entirely, if possible."

"You wanna explain this epic proposal in a bit more detail? How can we avoid this wretched fate you foretell?" she asked dramatically. "You want to turn us into gummy bears?"

"Something like gummy bears," Kyle said.

Judging by his expression, Kyle wanted her approval. No, not approval. Her support. There was a subtle difference. She glanced at Kimbriel. "So what do you propose, your magicalness?"

"Magicalness?" Kimbriel asked.

"Yeah. Seems to fit. What do you want from us?"

"You're very direct."

She grinned. "Refreshing, isn't it?"

Kimbriel smiled at Kyle. "Did I mention I like her?"

"She's certainly one of a kind," Kyle said.

"One of two," Zannah replied with a pointed glance at Kyle. "Can we hear the deal before I go grey and my werevamp teeth get loose and rattle out of my head from disuse?"

"Zannah, please show at least a little respect," Kyle said.

"It's okay, Kyle. Like she said, it's refreshing. Here's the rules, Zannah. I can't change anything without being granted permission. It's simply how I'm forced to do things. On the flip side of being granted permission, I can't normally give you anything unless you ask for it or I offer and you accept. I rarely offer because it messes up my foresight. And no. I didn't make the rules."

"Is this part of the 'no-come-in without an invitation thing'?"

"No."

That wasn't what she expected to hear. "So... you're saying you want to offer us a deal, but we have to ask for it, probably, and you're not going to tell us the specific details because...?" she tried to think back to the previous conversation they'd had on the topic. "It messes up your magic?"

"More or less. I've already told you the problem. Your bite could spread like a virus and I'd hate to see you and Kyle suffering for it. Let's just say I don't like the potential consequences any more than you do."

Zannah shrugged. She'd deal with it when it happened, if it happened. "So what's the solution?" She glanced at Kyle for the explanation.

Kyle reached out, but hesitated in gripping her hand as if he feared rejection. She wasn't sure how that made her feel. She wanted him to hold her hand. A lot. "Kimbriel wants to prevent us from passing on our condition at all."

"And I'm willing to offer... gifts, in return," Kimbriel added.

Gifts? Zannah shrugged. "Sure. I trust your judgement. It's not like I intend to create werevamps on my weekends off."

"Zannah," Kyle began, this time squeezing her hand to make sure he had her attention. "There's much more to it than that. We all feel the need to procreate, and biting is how werewolves do it. It's the *only* way you and I can do it, thanks to the vampire taint."

She stared for a long moment. "You mean I can't have children of my own?" It surprised her how much that hurt.

"That's right," Kimbriel said. "You can pass on your Creature traits through your bite, but I want to remove that option. If I do, you'll have nothing in that regard."

Zannah couldn't help the unexpected pit she felt building up inside her chest, though she'd never really imagined herself having kids, anyway. Well, she did, but not anytime soon. "After Rake broke my neck, the option of kids kind of fell out of the tarot deck, anyway. I can't exactly complain."

"So you want children then?" Kimbriel asked.

Zannah bit her lip. "I never considered not having children, but I'm only nineteen. It just wasn't high on my list of things to do before I finish studying, travelling and getting a job."

Kyle let go of her hand. "Are you suggesting you could help us have children, Kimbriel? Human children?"

Kimbriel hesitated for a long moment. "If Zannah were still human her body would be capable of producing children for the next few decades or so. I could offer you both that much."

"Both?" Zannah asked. "You mean we could each have our own regular edition children?"

"Yes."

Zannah gave the former blacksmith another look over. Broad shoulders. Strong. Way too short for the modern age, but she'd never really considered that a bad thing. Not too bad on the eyes, though. More importantly, he was the sweetest guy she'd ever met. "I think you'd look better with a beard," she said. "Just a short one, mind you, not a wild-man beard."

"You looked pretty good with a beard yourself last night," he responded, quicker than she'd expected from him.

She grinned. "Touché!" She held her fist out for a bump, but he just stared. "You're supposed to bump my fist with yours."

"Oh." He did so awkwardly, and then tried to cover up his awkwardness by taking a sip of his coffee.

"So, you wanna get married?" she asked him. "It's not like I've got another guy lined up waiting to get me pregnant."

Kyle choked, coughed, and almost sprayed coffee across the room.

"Besides, if I'm going to be immortal with someone, we should at least have a family to hold us together."

His mouth worked, but nothing seemed to come out as he stared at her.

"Come on. If you're going to be the only constant in my life, we should squeeze out some rug rats and go legit."

His face flushed scarlet, though it could have been the coffee. "I... Um-"

"You're not going to go all old school on me now, are you? Girls are allowed to ask these days. Apparently we can even own property *after* we get married."

He gave her a long look, a fair bit of worry in it, judging by his expression. "Err..."

Zannah caught Kimbriel's amused look. "Do you think he'll come around? I know I just forced him to cut his wife's head off, but I hope he'll forgive me."

Kimbriel smirked and shook her head. "I think you'll be perfect together. It's all about balance."

"Okay, time's up," she said to Kyle. "We getting hitched or am I going to have to put on a short skirt and fishnet stockings to dredge the local pubs to get me some kids?"

"You're serious? About getting married, I mean?" He appeared to be at a loss as he stared worriedly at Kimbriel.

The woman met his eyes. "Don't look to me for guidance."

He pursed his lips, slowly returning his stare to Zannah. "Um... I-"

"Brilliant! That's clearly a yes." She reached out and took his hand, kissing his knuckles like he was the lady. "I promise not to be one of those nagging wives, and to respect you in the morning." Zannah turned to Kimbriel. "Okay, that's sorted. Magic us up. I've only got a couple of fertile decades left. We need to start on the sprogging thing as soon as possible."

Kyle tried to speak but sounded like he was choking, no coffee needed. He was so easy to tease.

"I do have one condition," Kimbriel said.

Zannah sighed. "I should have guessed."

Kimbriel waited for Kyle to recover a little before speaking. "There is a void in the leadership among the local werewolves and vampires. Without someone to fill it, things could get out of control very quickly."

"No," Kyle said immediately. "I've spent three hundred years avoiding Creature politics. I'm not getting involved now."

"No way," Zannah agreed. "I want to travel and see the world. Besides, most of the Creatures you're talking about tried to kill me last night, remember?"

"I remember too," Kyle said.

"They're all young," Kimbriel replied. "Kyle, you'd be the strongest among them, and Zannah has inherited much of that strength thanks in part to the blood she drank from the ancient vampires last night. You both did. It's why they don't share their blood very often. Creating offspring weakens them as it dilutes their distilled lifeforce."

"That's all well and good until another old vampire comes to town and kicks our butts. We're not a match for a Creature like that, even together," Kyle said.

"I tell you what, you make us as strong as the strongest vampire out there, and you've got a deal," Zannah said.

"No."

"Ouch," Zannah said, feeling hurt. "Maybe you want to think about it?"

"Isn't that what you want, Kimbriel?" Kyle asked. "Us, strong enough to hold the fort?"

"If we're going to have human children, we need to be able to protect them," Zannah added. "You want us mixing it with werewolves and vamps, that's the price. We have to be able to protect our children."

Kimbriel closed her eyes. "I'm merely trying to fix the immediate problem of your infectiousness. Making you strong will have other long-term effects, none of which I can predict. I can't even predict the ones I'm offering, and I'm only offering because I think the risks are worth it."

Zannah shrugged. "If we can't be as strong, how about making our senses as keen as theirs?"

"Again, no."

Kyle met Kimbriel's eyes. "I owe you everything already, Kimbriel. There's no need to strike a bargain with me. You know that. I'll do whatever you ask."

Kimbriel glanced pointedly at Zannah. "This is a deal you need to agree on with each other. It's both or nothing."

Zannah gave Kyle a look. "It'd be really cool to be able to fly, like vampires in movies."

Kyle shook his head, but he couldn't contain a half smile. "You're irrepressible."

"This is my second life, Kyle. What have I got to lose by asking?"

"Nothing, I guess."

"So," Zannah asked Kimbriel. "Can we fly? That's pretty harmless, and might just save our butts one day."

Kimbriel stared at Zannah as if she really hadn't seen her coming, though she seemed to see everything else. She sighed. "Fine, but only at night when you're less likely to be seen."

"Deal. We're both in," she said.

Kyle gave Zannah a look before shaking his head. "Deal," he finally said.

"Give me your hands," Kimbriel said. "This signifies acceptance."

Zannah reached out first, Kyle a little more slowly. She felt a jolt and stiffened, but then it was gone. "Is that it? Can we go rule the city now?" Travel plans would have to wait, but she was okay with that. She was already set for a new adventure right here.

"Almost," Kimbriel said, releasing their hands. "I mentioned gifts, didn't I?"

"Didn't that just happen?"

She removed two envelopes from a black handbag beside her chair and handed them one each.

"Apparently Samira and Morrell left their fortunes to you. Both had extensive property portfolios in the region, and substantial cash, businesses and share assets as well. I doubt you'll be needing money any time soon."

"You sly dog!" Zannah said with a grin. "Waiting for us to agree first. When did you make these things up?"

Kimbriel smiled. "I'm not above generosity."

Zannah stood, walked around the table and hugged the small woman. "You are something, I'll give you that. Thank you."

Kimbriel smiled. "I believe your mother is waiting for you at home. Your brother has told her everything, though he was a little sketchy on the details. Don't forget to ask her if you can come in. Could be a little awkward if you forget."

"Can you hold on long enough for me to take a shower?" Kyle asked. "I'd like to meet your mother."

Zannah crinkled her nose. "The entire neighbourhood would appreciate it."

CHAPTER 32

"Zannah!" David called as Kyle preceded her out Kimbriel's front door. Zannah felt a momentary rush of anxiety at his voice, as if she were getting into the kind of fight she couldn't win. Kyle hesitated as Zannah stopped. She gave him a slight shake of her head to indicate everything was okay, though he could probably tell from her scent it wasn't.

David waited by Zannah's old car, looking Zannah over and staring as if he could decipher what might have happened following the talk with Kimbriel. He probably expected fangs or claws. She felt mildly offended and really didn't like the way he watched her. She'd seen that look before, many times, but had never noticed how possessive it was.

"So, is everything all right now?" he asked. "You okay again?"

Zannah put a hand on Kyle's shoulder and gave a slight squeeze before she left his side and approached David, forcing a spring into her step. "I'm fine. What are you doing here? Still?" It didn't hurt to be polite.

"Kimbriel fixed me. I'm not a werewolf anymore."

Kyle waited a few steps back, concern in his scent. It was funny how she could tell, but it was there. It was as clear as the fear in

David's scent, though she could only guess about the source of that fear.

"Good for you, David. Do you need a lift home or something?" She owed him nothing. Less than nothing. Maybe a punch in the nose, if anything, but she'd spring for a lift out of politeness.

David glanced at Kyle, frowning and clearly unhappy that Kyle was close enough to listen to the conversation. He lowered his voice, but if he thought that made a difference, he was an idiot. Kyle might not be able to hear as well as a regular werewolf, but he could hear much better than a human, just like Zannah.

"I wanted to make sure you were you again, you know? Just a regular girl like before. With things back to normal, we can pick up where we left off."

"Really?" Zannah asked softly, hoping he didn't pick up on the growl at the edge of her voice. "That's very sweet of you."

He shrugged modestly, as if he'd expected to hear nothing less and that she'd just accepted his offer. "Of course. So, we good?"

She leaned in close as if going for a kiss, but as his lips parted she moved aside so she could whisper into his ear. "How about I ask my fiancé to tear you a new one instead? I'll do it myself if you ever speak to me again."

David leaned away, sharp surprise in his expression. His eyes went from Zannah to Kyle and back again, the shock quickly turning to disdain as his top lip curled. "Fiancé? Him?"

Zannah forced a pleasant smile. "His name's Kyle, and he helped save your life, remember?"

Disdain crept into David's scent and it showed more strongly on his face. "Are you frigging insane? He's one of *them*!"

She barely held her temper. "*So am I.*"

"But... I thought you said you were back to normal!"

She sensed more than heard Kyle move up beside her, his presence comforting and calming. She really wasn't a violent person despite what she'd done as a werewolf, but she'd be happy to do some damage to David.

"Grow up," she said.

By his expression he couldn't let it go, his pride outweighing any common sense he might have had. "Didn't you ask Kimbriel to make you human again?"

He was taller than her, but he might as well have been a turd on her shoe for all she cared about his feelings. "I'd rather be a freak of an undead werewolf than live another moment with you at my side. Lucky me, I got my wish." Undead still sounded much cooler than *Creature*.

She walked around David and got in her car, the reek of blood magically gone from the vehicle. She needed to remind herself to thank Kimbriel for that, too.

"You did this," David accused Kyle. "You turned her against me. If it wasn't for you-"

"Shut up," Kyle said as he passed David. "You really are an idiot."

He got in the car and shut the door as Zannah kicked the engine over and reversed out the driveway.

"We're not undead, you know?" he said.

"Sounds far more awesome though, right?" she was going to win this argument if it took a century.

He shook his head. "No, it doesn't. Not at all."

She laughed. "You'll come around. Hey, maybe we should try flying to Mum's house? Oh wait, daytime. Never mind." She looked like she'd just been given a new toy and couldn't play with it. "I wonder how flying works?"

<hr>

It was a surprisingly short journey to Zannah's home, no more than a few blocks. She pulled into the driveway of the smallish-looking place, the front grass mown but otherwise dry and dying, and killed the engine.

Kyle was about to get out, but Zannah stayed where she was, staring at nothing.

"You okay?" he asked. "A minute ago, you wanted to fly everywhere, now you look rooted in place."

She blinked a couple of times before turning his way, all seriousness now.

"I don't think I can do this." She sounded worried. Looked worried. She even smelled of fear, like she was about to run away.

He wasn't sure how to comfort her. He hadn't thought of his own parents in a very long time. He could barely remember their faces. He took her hand and found himself oddly surprised and gratified when she didn't pull away.

He got the feeling it was what she wanted, regardless of the teasing marriage proposal and the fact they'd only known each other for about a day. He certainly wouldn't hold her to the proposal, but it was a strange sensation to offer such physical familiarity and to have it accepted. It felt nice. Very nice.

"She's your mother," he said gently. He wasn't sure what else to say. He couldn't fix the situation or wind back the clock, and he didn't know her mother, anyway. She had to face it.

She shook her head, clearly nervous. "Mothers aren't human. They're like superheroes, and now I'm a werewolf with vampire muck inside me. I'm the evil overlord, she's the good guy. Besides, I have a whole lot of immortality she doesn't have and never will. What if she doesn't accept what's happened to me? Or fears me? Or hates me? Maybe I should go back to Kimbriel and ask her to make me human. Do you think she would?"

"Would your mother prefer you lying in a hospital bed with a broken neck? Or dead? She'll love you, no matter what."

Zannah closed her eyes, and he could see tears building. When she looked at him again, her eyes were brimming and the fear remained. "What would she have thought when she got to the hospital and I wasn't there? She must have been devastated. Wait. Jimmy told her what happened. She wouldn't have gone back. Still..."

Kyle noticed movement at the front door. A woman with short dark hair and a similar cast to Zannah's features took a half a step out. She was barely a couple of decades older than her daughter, though with a pale complexion compared to Zannah's Polynesian looks. She probably wasn't much taller than Kyle.

"Maybe you could ask her," he said gently. "She's waiting, and she looks like she needs a hug."

Zannah went about three shades paler when she saw her mother.

"Go to her," Kyle said softly. "Go."

Almost reluctantly, Zannah opened the car door, her glistening eyes never leaving her mother. Just as cautiously, she got out as if afraid she'd scare her mother off if she moved any faster, and then merely stood there as if unable to move.

"Go," Kyle said.

He got out as Zannah stiffly walked toward her mother and climbed the three steps to the porch. Her mother stared as if seeing a miracle.

Uncertain whether Zannah needed him for support, Kyle followed, but not too close. Zannah stopped within touching distance of her mother.

"Suzy?" Helen didn't seem to believe she was actually seeing her daughter.

"Mum."

Helen looked Zannah over. "You look the same," she said, more than a little surprise in her voice.

"But with more awesomeness, right?"

Helen blinked tears, held out her arms and drew her daughter in close for a hug. "Oh God, it is you," she whispered, her body shaking with huge sobs as she squeezed. "I didn't believe it when Jimmy told me. I truly didn't."

"It's me, Mum. Nothing that matters has changed," Zannah said, hugging her back. "Just me."

Blinking back more tears, Helen stepped back. She reached up and wiped Zannah's tears away with her thumbs. "Who's your friend?" she asked, looking at Kyle. "Couldn't you find a guy over three feet tall?"

Kyle felt his jaw drop.

"This is Kyle, Mum. He saved my life, so I promised to marry him as a reward."

"What? I never agreed to that."

Helen, her eyes still brimming, but with a knowing smirk on her face, let go of Zannah, walked around her daughter and wrapped Kyle in a hug that was just as warm and caring. "You're welcome in my home any time, Kyle. Any time."

"We really are getting married," Zannah added. "He said yes."

"No, I didn't."

Helen stepped back, giving Kyle a more appraising look. "You're clearly braver than you look if you're planning on marrying my daughter."

"Mum!"

Helen held her fist up for Kyle to bump, trying to hold back a grin. He obliged.

ALSO BY CHRIS ANDREWS

Fiction

Divine Prey: Normagaell Saga #1 - A Veil of Gods Novel

Epicentre: Leviathan's Chronicles #1 - A Veil of Gods Novel

Urban Magic and Other Tales

Non-Fiction

Character and Structure: An Unholy Alliance

Use the QR code to go to Chris's website:

PLEASE LEAVE A REVIEW

Thank you for reading Moonlit Genesis. I hope you enjoyed the story as much as I loved writing it.

If you have the time, would you be kind enough to leave a review? I really can't express how much reviews mean to independent authors.

Thank you.

(Scan to review on Amazon)

ABOUT THE AUTHOR

Chris Andrews is an author of fantasy, science fiction, horror, and non-fiction.

Find him at - http://chrisandrews.me

Stay in Touch
Subscribe to Chris's Newsletter
Via his website or: https://mailchi.mp/b9f6f483c373/signup

facebook.com/chrisandrewsau
x.com/ChrisAndrewsAU
instagram.com/chrisandrews.me
amazon.com/author/chrisandrews